# The Piratization of Daniel Barnes

Alex McGlothlin

*The Piratization of Daniel Barnes*
Written by Alex McGlothlin
A Fictional Novel
U.S.A Copyright 2015
Originally Published June 14th, 2016
ISBN-13: 978-0-9890488-7-3
ISBN-10: 0-9890488-7-X
Second Edition
Published by MountainLion Press, LCC
www.mountainlionpress.com

# *One*

Somalia was already by far the most cumbersome, vexing, unwilling-to-submit story, and Daniel Barnes wasn't even there yet. His journalistic experience until now had consisted of a METRO ride across D.C. to the halls of Congress, to convention center conference rooms, and federal administrative agencies, where he arrived early, snapped a few photos, scribbled a few pages of notes and returned home to write the story.

He had been in Kenya for five days, Mombasa for three, and had yet to secure passage to Mogadishu. Common carriers had ceased transport to Somalia since the latest outbreak of civil war. He managed to engage the assistance of a local man, an aspiring reporter, but the only burden Keanjaho had managed to relieve Daniel of was the weight of his wallet.

They were on their way to the boat docks at Kilindini Harbour, in hopes of chartering a ferry to shuttle them up the coast. With every tepid word Keanjaho spoke, Daniel felt the futility towards which his once generous expense budget was being depleted.

"Have you given thought to interviewing refugees, here in Kenya, to get their stories?"

"I'm not being paid for second hand accounts."

"Some of the stories told, here in Mombasa, are among the most gripping I've heard."

Daniel could hear the cheesy music, stiff drinks, and sunbathing tourists back at the resort calling Keanjaho's name. He saw how mistaken he had been to acquire his Nairobi-native aid such comfortable accommodations. If comfort was what Daniel had come for, he would have chosen a more sophisticated destination, like the French Riviera, or even stayed in the District. But then, to get away was the reason he had accepted the assignment in the first instance.

The private dock Keanjaho led him to was a humble, seedy cousin in comparison to its industrial-sized neighbor. He was certain some of the boats had to be beached to remain above water. How much money would it cost, to travel safely, just up the coast?

"So why is a story from Mogadishu so much better than a story from Mombasa? They're both just stories. No one else is going there for them."

"I'm going precisely because no one else is."

"They aren't going because they value their lives."

I don't value mine, Daniel thought. Etched in his mind was a scene from just last week, of his childhood sweetheart Bally, standing on her porch wearing another man's engagement ring. Burton Woods wasn't just any man, either, but a longtime nemesis in the love triangle that had persisted so long it seemed an institution. The diamond solitaire set in white gold represented the final loss of a lifelong struggle. If he could smuggle a good story out of Somalia, then he had a shot at garnering some international attention. With the world's attention, perhaps he would recapture Bally's as well. And if he died trying in his pursuit, well, the pain of a life filled with loneliness would dissolve into the eternal ether and flicker out, forgotten.

"There's a nice boat," Keanjaho said.

A gleaming white fishing boat bobbed gently at the dock, attended to by a handsome young man in a navy polo tucked into navy pants. He wore no shoes as he sprayed his boat.

"Hello there. Are you available for charter?"

"I might be man," the young man said, undistracted from his hosing. "What are you thinking? Deep-sea fishing? Dinner cruise?"

"I need a lift to Mogadishu."

He laughed a hearty, houndish laugh. He continued hosing.

"So how about it? You could at least throw out a price."

"I'm not taking my last cruise today. Sorry, not interested. If you change your mind about fishing."

"Yea."

Daniel and Keanjaho kept walking. Their luck seemed to diminish with every inquiry. A seagull discovered discarded food on the dock, and soon its friends flocked the area, temporarily sealing the only avenue of return to land.

"Well isn't this fantastic," Keanjaho said.

Keanjaho was awfully impatient for a man with no desire to go to Somalia. But mostly he was just awful.

Daniel leaned against a gnarled dock beam that twisted unnecessarily in to the sky and was hewn with curves like a corkscrew. He let his gaze fall to the ground and massaged his temples. Seagulls squawked, fighting over what little carrion remained. He had discovered thirty-four different ways one could not travel from Kenya to Somalia, and why was Keanjaho still talking.

"What?" Daniel finally yelled, submitting to the interruption from his attempted meditation.

"There's a new boat coming to dock," Keanjaho said, pointing.

Daniel looked just in time to see the sails being lowered. It was a magnificent little craft. He regretted having not seen it interact more with the wind, before it cut on the motors.

"Should we wait and talk to him?" Keanjaho asked.

7

"That's what we came here for."

Daniel watched, anxiously, as the boat bubbled towards the dock.

"Hello there," Daniel called as the boat inched closer to its berth.

"What troubles you," the captain yelled out. He was a shirtless, sinewy older man with a determined look in his eye.

"Nothing troubles me."

"Then why waste time talking to strangers? Go drink with friends."

"I'm not troubled, I need to charter a boat."

"I don't do fishing excursions."

"What do you do then?"

"I don't ask other men about their business, and don't tell them about mine."

Keanjaho grabbed Daniel by the arm. "Come, this is pointless."

Daniel jerked his arm free of Keanjaho's clutch. "I need a ride up the coast to Mogadishu."

This grabbed the captain's attention.

"What business do you have there?"

"I thought you didn't ask other men about their business?"

The captain laughed. "I go to Mogadishu, occasionally, but given the war, asking your business is my business. To understand the risk, all that."

"I'm a journalist."

"Everyone is."

Keanjaho nodded. "He is, captain. He's got the name badge, equipment and money to prove it."

The captain's shoulders relaxed a degree.

"When you thinking of going?"

"As soon as possible."

"I'm booked up tomorrow and the next day."

"What are you doing now?"

The time was just after two in the afternoon. The captain peered north, out to sea. Keanjaho was moving a lot. His face contorted into a multitude of related expressions, as if trying them on to see which fit; he checked his pants zipper no less than twice.

"You alright?" Daniel asked.

Keanjaho took a deep, calming breath and buried his wild hands in his pockets. He nodded he was, but he had clearly just managed, no doubt with every last fiber of his will, to stave off a panic attack.

"We can take off later this afternoon. Let me do a few things in town, plot a course, and we'll go," the captain said.

"What time should we be back?" Daniel asked.

"5pm."

"We'll see you then, Captain--"

"Zakia."

"Nice to meet you Captain Zakia. I'm Daniel Barnes, this is Keanjaho."

"Okay. 5pm."

Daniel started down the dock in a haste.

"Don't you want to talk money?" Zakia called.

Daniel returned to the dock's edge.

"What is it?"

"I charge a thousand for the trip, another thousand for the risk."

"Half here, half on arrival."

Captain Zakia nodded assent, disappearing into the cabin without further ceremony. Daniel hurried away, to gather his belongings and check out of the resort.

Daniel found the car locked, and turned to see Keanjaho trailing him a hundred feet.

"Come on! We've got little time!"

Keanjaho came along, in a shuffling hurry. He gulped every five seconds. He had the hiccups; his eyes were wide with fright.

"Hurry up, I said."

Keanjaho unlocked the door, and soon they motored with traffic along Nkrumah Road, one of Mombasa's main thoroughfares. They hit traffic, Keanjaho turned on a side road, and Daniel lost track of where they were.

"We can stop at the bank, check out of the hotel, then I say we drop by the grocery for whatever odds and ends we'll want for the next couple of weeks. Damn, I guess we'll need to arrange for this guy to pick up us up when we're ready to come home. Could you imagine being stuck in Somalia with this civil war raging? What a nightmare."

"Yes, a nightmare," Keanjaho echoed.

Despite the vehicle being well air conditioned, Keanjaho was sweating rivers.

"Liven up man! Get excited. This is what we've been working towards."

"Yes, we've become very successful today."

"Look man, are you seriously considering backing out on me? Today? At go time?"

"It's just, the situation in Somalia, it's so much worse than I thought when we first met. People say you'd have to be crazy to go there. The refugees, the Al-Shabaab. I heard a story of a man sitting on his porch, minding his own business, when a stray bullet fell from the sky and cut him through his chest. Stray bullets are like mosquitoes there. Everyone's killing everyone."

"You're really going to back out? When I don't have the time to find anyone else?"

Keanjaho didn't reply.

"Fine."

"I'll help you with your errands, but I can't get on that boat with you. I have a family, a mother, sister, cousins."

"Yea, I get it."

10

Daniel sighed without attempting to conceal his agitation, turning his attention to the streets of Mombasa. The place was an African version of Miami's South Beach, with junky gift shops, dive bars, throngs of vacationers. Hard to get work done in a town built for leisure.

# *Two*

Daniel peered out at the beach houses, clubs, and docks as they snaked along the Kenyan coastline aboard Zakia's yacht. Keanjaho had pitched a fit when Daniel refused to pay him at the last moment, but that much had been predictable.

"We're going to go start out to sea now. I don't want to be visible from land when we enter Somalian waters," Zakia said.

"That's fine." Daniel didn't give a damn how they got there. If the old man didn't run fishing charters, then what was his business? He felt like it was a question that deserved answering, need answering, but as they plied the waters, he found his thoughts magnetizing towards the life he had left back in the States. Since it had happened, his thoughts had been frozen in the memory of arriving at Bally's party. The vision of watching her guests track leaves and mud into her living room and smudging her Parisian. He was with her when she bought it. She had thought the asking price was a steal, for a hand-woven Parisian rug. He told her it was probably factory made. She asked him why he always ruined good illusions. He didn't have an answer.

He had been so excited to arrive at that party, to tell her the big story he had just written that was being released on the wire that very moment, no doubt being picked up and redistributed by major newspapers across the nation. He'd gotten paid extra, and he wanted to use his new wealth to take her on a lavish date. Then he saw that damned ring. The next thing he knew he was being arrested because he had passed out drunk in a pile of nasty restaurant trash bags. Luckily, he was in such bad shape they took him to the hospital instead of jail. When he woke the next morning, handcuffed to the bed and under psych watch, he felt broken. An emotional nausea gripped him, a suffering as uncontrollable as the ground shaking underneath his feet, a building toppling down on him, brick after brick striking his chest, maintaining consciousness only to bear witness to his own suffering. He wasn't a great guy, he didn't volunteer or donate, but he was certain he hadn't done anything to deserve this life bending agony.

**"You like fish?"** Zakia asked.

Daniel looked over to see whether or not Zakia was being facetious. He appeared to be serious.

"As much as anyone else."

"This is a great place to see the fish. There is a deep-sea reef underneath us. Tautog, triggerfish, mackerel, sailfish, electric eel, tons of sharks."

"How come no one fishes here?" Daniel asked, surveying his surroundings to ascertain whether he was correct no one was fishing.

"It's polluted man. It's a shame. The Somali let other countries throw away their nuclear waste. They just threw it overboard. Why do it just off the coast? I don't know. They could have gone out deep just as easily. Some people say it was a conspiracy, that the power *wants* Somalia to be a mess."

"A situation like Somalia's isn't supposed to happen in the modern age."

"Not hardly, no no. You hear stories of spies, secrets, all sorts of intrigue around Somalia. Who knows whether any of it's true. Still, the stories started somewhere."

"All fiction has some basis in reality."

"Something like that—oh shit."

"What?" Daniel asked.

Zakia took off sprinting, pulling ropes underneath the mast. The main sail was already full, and soon two auxiliary sails blossomed, Daniel uncertain of their purpose.

"Come help me goddam it," Zakia cried.

"What is wrong with you?"

"Pirates!" Zakia yelled. The veins popped in the captain's fright troubled eyes.

Daniel frantically shot wild glances around the periphery. Then he saw a small, smoky boat emerging from the horizon, getting larger and larger.

"Oh my god, what do we do?"

"We can't out run them with the sails," Zakia said, seeming to realize only as he verbalized the thought.

When Daniel's depressed thoughts of having lost Bally were compounded with the realization they were about to be murdered by pirates, he panicked. His heart rate increased to an unsustainable pace. His vision blurred in and out. He partially fainted, his conscious flickering in and out. His life was in jeopardy, and he was submitting to fate.

The pirates pulled alongside the sailboat.

"Hel on sagxad ah ama aan idinku dili doonaa," the lead pirate yelled. The three mangy gunmen brandished AK-47's as they boarded the sailboat. "Hel on sagxad ah ama aan idinku dili doonaa!"

Zakia produced a handgun from some hidden compartment and started popping off rounds. The scene was far too frightening, far too surreal for Daniel to comprehend. Daniel collapsed on to the deck. Once he had settled, following the collision of his body with the ground, he directed his attention to Zakia, just in time to see bullets rip gaping red holes in the captain's body. Daniel bellowed a frightened scream. Please don't kill me. Bally. Bally. He thought back to when they were in Paris, skinny dipping in the Rhine, her body covered in chill bumps, her nipples hard, her jet black hair slowly submerging into the river as the spectacle of her nude body disappeared below the water's surface.

A pirate stood over top of him.

"Hello waxaa."

"Hello," Daniel said, his voice trembling.

The pirate turned his AK-47 around backwards, and thrust its butt down towards Daniel's face.

# *Three*

Locked in a five-by-five cell made of a heinous amalgamation of chicken and barbed wire, Daniel had only the freedom of thought. It was a rudimentary cage made to house captive livestock, like goat and pheasant. It didn't matter that his makeshift cage was too constricting for him to either stand or stretch out on his back, because he was hog-tied, wrists bound with duct tape to his ankles. Whether most of his body was covered in feces or mud, he couldn't be certain.

When big brother and Tiny got drunk and bored, they came for him. He was dragged out of the cage and totally defenseless due to the manner in which he was bound. After the first day, they bludgeoned him so badly he couldn't see through his blackened eyes for some unknowable amount of time. They had since refrained from kicking him in the face, so his vision had returned, but he wasn't exactly provided a holding pen with a view. He was kept in the slaughterhouse. The first form he was able to discern when his eyesight returned was a goat's carcass hanging from hooks, blood leaking like the oil that drips from an unserviced car. Occasionally, one of them would carry three or four chickens in by their necks and lock them in a similar cage rigged beside his own, until one of them would come back and decapitate the birds in the evening. They were probably just having chicken on those nights, but he also imagined they used them for some sort of primitive blood ritual, smearing the blood all over their naked bodies in preparation for the full moon orgy, half Wahhabism and half pagan. He didn't know which religious inclination he favored them to act on next.

Every other day an old lady came around, her worn black face harbored unmistakably compassionate eyes. She kept her distance at five feet or more, no doubt afraid the caged white devil would snatch a finger clean from her hand if she cheated too close, but she was charitable and sustaining his life, so he limited his ill opinion of her to a minimum. But, maybe he should wish her dead. If it weren't for her keeping him alive, then he'd finally be released from this nightmare.

He believed they were brothers. One was just a tad huskier than the other and balder, too. The younger one was flashier, but in a backwoods way, with his cheap gold necklace and ancient knockoff Air Jordan's. The younger one had a habit of coming in drunk, then kicking Daniel in the chest until a rib cracked. Then he would chuck Daniel back in to the cage. He always muttered some gibberish in Somali, a language Daniel foolishly hadn't troubled to learn before venturing in to the notorious Horn of Africa. Wherever he had found himself in this nameless rural pastoral land, no one spoke a word of English, save for the occasional product name such as Coca-cola, Camel, and so forth.

Even if one were to subtract the times he'd been unconscious, which were numerous and unquantifiable, he'd been held there in that degraded state for about six waking weeks. After every beating, every indignity visited on him by the brothers, he grew closer and closer to wishing they would just kill him. He thought about biting his own tongue, to drown himself in his own iron-deficient blood. But there was still some hope in him yet, and the same hope that perpetuated his physical existence was splashing water on the torch of his soul so all that was left to burn was but a candle's light of spiritual incandescence.

When he was able to control his waking and sleeping, he let himself close his eyes late in the night, when he was fairly certain no one would come for him. Then he slept until the break of the first light.

**He was startled awake this morning** by the rattle of a poorly serviced automobile. The smell of its diesel exhaust was the closest he'd come to civilization since being captured.

The brothers entered the shed with three unfamiliar men.

The presence of the strangers was unusual, but the morning visit was actually one of the daily activities he looked forward to most. The brothers usually came in rather sober and good-natured, picked him up and sat him on top of a bucket. After he relieved himself, they would hold him up and spray his ass clean. It may not have been a proper bidet, but luxuries were short when hogtied in Somalia and licking individual corn kernels out of muddy goat shit to survive.

The three strangers fanned out to scrutinize Daniel.

"Waa," the older brother said as Daniel lifted his head, examining the men through the interlinked metal cage.

"Fadlan u, walaal," the younger brother pled, grasping his brother's forearm.

"Waa intee?" Spoke one of the strange men, who stepped forward, hovering not more than a foot over the cage as he inspected Daniel.

"Laba kun ee marey kanka dollar," the older brother said. He pried his brother's fingers from his arm and dealt him a hard backhand across the face. The younger one fell to the ground, tearing up, moaning like a coward but otherwise complacent to remain on the sidelines of the transaction.

"Waa ka badan kun," the strange man said. The older brother and the stranger shook hands. The stranger opened the cage, cut loose Daniel's restraints, and stood him to his feet. Daniel was gently carried to a nearby Land Cruiser, where he was returned to handcuffs and delicately seat belted into the SUV.

The older brother and the stranger stood back while cash was exchanged and they finished whatever ungodly business it was which employed him as a commodity.

19

The younger brother snuck up to the Land Cruiser, and surprising Daniel, wrapped his arms around Daniel's neck and started crying. As far as Daniel considered himself, he was the living dead. If this animal was lamenting for Daniel because of the misfortune of his next employment, then Daniel had nothing to look forward to but the final liberation. Daniel knew he would only get one shot at it, so he opened his jaws wide to get the younger brother's whole ear in there, and after it was all the way inside he clenched down with the wrath of the Old Testament God. The skinny Somali cried out, punched Daniel helplessly, but Daniel didn't let go. He could taste the man's briny blood oozed over his tongue, and the man was really screaming like a little animal caught in a snare, flopping around, convulsing, squealing pathetically. Finally, one of those three strangers walked over and crushed his fist, just right, into Daniel's jaw, so that he released the little Somali. The little brother, short an ear, fell to the ground and wiggled about. Daniel spit the severed ear onto the desert floor. Big brother flipped open a pocketknife and started towards Daniel, but the strangers were quick to brandish guns in defense of their latest possession. The big brother backed down and one of the strangers closed Daniel's car door. The big brother started towards the car again, fury flaring in his soul, but there was nothing for him to do now that he had sold Daniel away. It was no longer his right to determine whether Daniel lived or died.

Soon the strange men were loaded in the SUV, tracking their route with a compass across a barren dessert to their next destination, no other habitats or abodes within eyeshot, a small rise of rocky hills to the left horizon, a land so barren that even cacti couldn't endure without irrigation. He had been on an island alone with those monsters.

The armed man sitting next to Daniel motioned for him to bow his head. A cotton sack was placed over his head, and he became surrounded by an imperceptible halo of light, each gasp filtered through the cotton bag.

# *Four*

Daniel fell semi-unconscious with his head covered in the SUV as they traversed an extended stretch of frictionless terrain, more comfortable than he had been since being taken captive. He vaguely imagined waking up at a UN satellite office or the American Consulate. He dreamt of Bally, wondering if his experience in Somalia ended with this car ride, whether an edited version of his story would be heroic enough to win her over. It wouldn't, but its possibility, though improbable, gave him some comfort. Nice thoughts had been rare. The SUV shuddered and he was jolted alert as it transitioned from the smooth desert terrain to rumbling over gravel. Then there was an abrupt halt, and Daniel's body swung forward. A car window whimpered down, and the driver initiated a conversation with someone outside the vehicle in accented Somali, just loud enough for Daniel to recognize an exchange. Daniel understood none of it. Camels barked, a dozen of them, perhaps more.

When the conversation ended, the SUV continued forward for hours. Much later they halted again, only this time all of the men exited the vehicle. Daniel's door opened, his seatbelt undone for him, and a tender hand led him out of the vehicle. Suddenly, the bag covering his head was removed and the hot Somali sunshine came rushing into his field of vision. He saw only white, felt dizzy and nearly collapsed for lack of strength, but two of the men supported him by the arms. A fourth man, bespectacled and wearing a well-worn and sweat dampened suit examined Daniel. The man circled him, and spoke to the other men. They lifted his shirt off his torso. Daniel started to resist, but one of them patted him gently on the back and said, "is ok" and Daniel let them take his shirt off. He was too weak to resist. The bespectacled man circled Daniel again, and the men holding him lifted his arms.

The bespectacled man squinted as he examined one of Daniel's armpits, and lightly prodded his ribs.

"Waxa uu daciif ah, laakiin waxaan ku bixin doonaa lacag ah oo joogto ah tan iyo markii uu gaalo ah," the bespectacled man said.

"Maya, maya. Waxaa kaliya uu u baahan yahay in uu wax cuno, jimicsi qaar ka mid ah oo naso. Waxa uu qiimihiisu nasiib ah," the driver of the SUV replied.

The man removed his spectacles and wiped the sweat from them. After he put them on, he peered through them at Daniel, then gave a slight nod of assent. The men holding Daniel carried him through a nearby door, where he was sat on a hewn bench in a windowless cinderblock room. A single light bulb dangled from the ceiling. The men closed the heavy metal door and sunlight seeped through gaps where the door was slightly too small for the frame. Daniel heard them outside talking in their alien tongue, then there was the sound of an engine starting and the SUV's tires crunched on the ground until it trailed away and became inaudible. Footsteps gradually approached the door until it swung open, and the bespectacled man entered the room.

"You're English?" He asked in a learned though unpolished English. There were two unfamiliar men flanking him, wearing surgical scrubs.

"I'm American."

"This is a fine distinction. Let my men help clean you. Then we talk later." The bespectacled man left the room.

Daniel didn't care for the presence of the scrubbed men or the eerily black-market medical vibe they exuded. Had the goat farmers sold him so the bespectacled man could harvest his organs? The men lifted him to his feet and gently assisted him in to the next

22

room, which was a large empty shower chamber with a dozen showerheads and a central drain.

"I'm a photojournalist. An American. People are looking for me," Daniel said.

One of them nodded affirmatively, but neither spoke a word. They stripped him naked, and one retrieved a water hose from the corner of the room while the other doused him with liquid body soap and massaged it across Daniel's body with his bare hands. Daniel squirmed and insisted the man quit touching him, but he ignored Daniel's request.

"Please quit this."

The scrubbed man nodded again.

"Can you understand me? Do you speak English?" Daniel asked.

"No anglish," the lathering one finally said.

Daniel started crying. The man who had lathered his body took a step back. The sting of the water hose bit across his skin, but it felt good to have the accumulated grim stripped from his body. Despite his misgivings toward these men touching and bathing him, he felt oddly humanized to be given a bath. With each layer of dirt washed from his skin, he began to feel less and less like chattel and feel more and more like his former self. By the time he'd been rinsed of the soap and given a towel to dry himself, he felt a degree of dignity bind to his mood. He even forgot he had been given no promise of a better situation than his last; a shower and gentle hands *were* a better situation.

His attendants eventually escorted him down a hall, unlocked a door, and showed him inside. There was a small spring cot, a plain wooden chair, and a porcelain water basin. There was what looked like a Roman toga lying across the bed, and a small ceramic coffee mug rested on top of a paper-thin pillow. One of the men took the cup, dipped it in the water basin and pretended to drink. Daniel nodded his head that he understood. One of them held up the toga and said "suit." Daniel nodded comprehension. The men left the room, and an ancient lock creaked.

23

Daniel folded his towel, placed it on the bed and put on the toga best he knew how. Clothed, he took the mug and filled himself a drink of water from the basin. When he leaned over, he saw his gaunt reflection in the mirror. He was beyond malnourished; he was a small malfunction away from death. He lied on the bed and sipped water from his cup. His heart began pounding when he had the idea they might use him as a human sacrifice. That would explain the robes, the bathing, the gentle treatment.

He began to have trouble breathing at the prospect of a blessed knife being raised above him from where he lay bound to an alter as holy words spoken in a foreign tongue were read over him, before an amassed crowd would grow silent and the blessed knife plunge down into his chest, pierce his heart and blood bubble like oil and a coldness envelop like the moment after diving into a cold spring, and he would be aware no longer.

When the lock creaked and the door pivoted open, the attendants returned not chanting sacred psalms of offering, but rather with food, a goat stew smothered over a fortune of basmati rice with a warm bottle of Coca-Cola.

After the nutrients had time to work their way through his body and replenish his organs and muscles, he found himself thinking more clearly, enjoying sharper vision and hearing. He smelled the heavy use of bleach in the cell. The scent reminded him of the only other time he was incarcerated. He had been with Bally, and they were arrested together for underage drinking. They were either too young to drink booze and thus too young for jail, or old enough to drink booze and had committed no crime for which to be punished. The police disregarded the transgressors' logic and left them in the holding cell. That was when Bally told him her secret. She didn't want to be a virgin anymore. Daniel was so blindsided by the revelation he didn't exercise the least bit of tact: He told her once she had done it she could never go back to being a virgin again. Only after he had spoken did he recognize the sinister, unmistakably sexual glow in her eyes. He watched it fade while he damn near unhinged his mind trying to figure how to recapture the squandered opportunity. The words never came to him. Once her desire had smoldered to naught, she drifted asleep, her head lying uncomfortably against the cold bleached cement. Since then, he comforted himself by rationalizing that a cold, filthy cement jail cell wasn't the proper place to defrock his virgin love.

Locked in jail with Bally was in all likelihood his only chance in eternity to bridge the gulf from friendship to love. He should have made love to her in that dungeon rather than rest and let some chod do it a few months later in more agreeable accommodations.

The lock creaked again, and the scrubbed-attendants returned with a small man carrying a medical bag. The attendants suggested Daniel sit on the bed while the small man opened his kit and removed a stethoscope. Daniel flew against the wall at first, but the man had caring eyes and a ready smile. Daniel relaxed and let the man sit next to him. He listened to Daniel's heart through his chest and his back. He examined Daniel's ribs, and suggested Daniel touch his toes. Daniel indulged the man. Seemingly satisfied, the man took an otoscope and examined Daniel's eyes, ears, nose and mouth. It shone brightly in his eyes, was cold in his ear. The small man returned the instrument to his kit and departed the room with the attendants.

Daniel laughed to himself. The visit was the most thorough medical exam he had had in years. He had even shrugged off his editor's suggestion he get a physical and the recommended shots before traveling to Africa.

He eventually lied down and fell asleep. He dreamt of being back at his apartment in Adams Morgan, walking just down the block to the pizza place for a couple of slices of fresh mozzarella or barbeque chicken with red onion. He walked back up the pedestrian-littered street, realizing that he lived in a near utopia and that his former qualms he had with D.C. were petty and lacking perspective. He could taste the hot cheese in his mouth, cozy on his couch, and it was this vision of comfort that made his sudden awakening that much more disruptive. The attendants were standing over him, beckoning him to rise and follow them. He stretched his arms out over his head, and like a sleepy child who had to summon a great amount of will just to stand on his feet, drug himself behind them along the hallway.

He was shown to an office where the bespectacled man sat fondling some mail at a side table behind the big desk.

"Sit down, please," the man said.

Daniel obliged while examining the overwhelming peculiarity of the office. There was a small collection of Qurans, perhaps six or seven distinct volumes and perched next to them on a bookshelf was, was that a porno magazine? Daniel wasn't certain, and he diverted his attention before he was caught staring. He winced when he spotted a bottle of hand lotion and a box of tissue paper situated near a recliner in the corner of the room. Was he imagining things?

"You are American?" The man said. He sat at the big desk.

Daniel was afraid to answer.

"You must talk if I help you."

Daniel reconsidered his position, but still felt reluctant to divulge any information.

"So you know, I Amir Sharif. I am an elder. I help the kidnapped when I learn about them. You were kidnapped, yes?"

Daniel nodded yes.

"I help you. I pay my own money to have you released. Unfortunately, we live in a land very hostile to gaalo. You tell me what country you are, and I will message your Consulate and get you home."

Daniel considered the man's words. His situation had improved since he was moved from the goat farm. He had been bathed, fed, sheltered, given medical attention. The thought of getting home to Washington caused his eyes to mist up, but he resisted the urge to shed tears. He weighed the risk of revealing his biographical information, but given his situation he couldn't imagine any hard benefits to maintaining his anonymity. If he wanted the bespectacled man to help him, he was going to have to talk.

"My name is Daniel Barnes. I am an American."

The bespectacled man whipped a pen across a notepad, phonetically mumbling the information.

"Profession?"

"Photojournalist."

"You have any travel credentials."

"No. They were taken from me."

The bespectacled man asked Daniel his date and place of birth, social security number, permanent address and employer. Then he tore the sheet from the pad, folded it, and slid it in to a plain white envelope.

"Thank you. I will contact your Consulate immediately. Please take notice that you are presently in a Somali hinterland. My tribe is a good people, but they have much bad information about gaalo. They must not see you else you risk your life and my ability to help others like you in the future. You will honor my request and remain in this compound, out of sight?"

That shouldn't be a problem.

"Yes, I can agree to that condition."

"Good. You will be permitted regular access to a courtyard and Western-style fitness room. Please take advantage of these facilities to regain your health. I apologize for insisting my attendants keep a close eye on you in your quarters, but you must understand that if your presence here is discovered my family's safety would be threatened. Therefore I must insist you honor this request."

Daniel laughed. "Emir, I have no problem laying low."

"Pardon?"

"Yes, I will accept your request."

"Thank you. Then that is all for now. I shall keep you updated with regards to the arrangements to deliver you to your consulate."

The Emir pushed a button on his phone, the attendants entered the room and escorted Daniel away. They showed him a modest gym, where a young African male was walking on an antiquated but functional treadmill. The room was also populated with a bench press and numerous mismatched dumbbells of various size and weight. "Later," one of the attendants said. Daniel was led back to the room. As always, the lock creaked and their feet pattered away.

So that was it! He was going to be sent home after all. It was amazing how suddenly his impression of the country changed, how dangerous and vile some men could be while others risked the lives of their families and squandered their fortunes to help absolute strangers. Whether or not he would ever write a story about this morbid experience was a decision remaining to be made. Perhaps months of therapy would be required to decide. He wondered whether there was someone he could sue, someone with money like his employer, for this happening to him.

# *Five*

Daniel fell into a routine during the days that followed: breakfast, sunshine, gym, shower, lunch, rest, dinner, then allowed to screen one of the few American language movies the place had, including Disney's *Cinderella*, *Beauty and the Beast*, and Ian Fleming's *Doctor No*. A random assortment of movies to say the least. After ten days he had seen each feature three times, and *Doctor No* four times. There were numerous Bollywood features, but he didn't speak Hindi. Besides, they were only to help pass the time. Soon, he would be back in Washington, D.C. and at liberty to watch whatever movie he wanted.

The physician returned for a follow-up examination. The physician spoke no English, but after he inspected Daniel, the man led Daniel and the attendants to the Emir's office to explain Daniel's condition in Arabic. Once his summary was complete, the physician bowed to the Emir, and departed the room.

"He says your condition is improving. You are putting on weight. This is good," the Emir said.

"What is the word from my consulate?"

"I have not heard from them yet. I send my trust agent with letter to Hargeisa. He has not returned. Phones are too dangerous because Somali's listen to each other talk," the Emir said, tracing a squiggly finger in the air. "We must be most careful, for everyone's sake."

"I understand. And I appreciate what you're doing," Daniel said.

**He continued to eat hearty meals**, soak up the sun, and exercise for increasingly longer periods of time. He had been at the compound for a month now, but there was still no word from the Emir's most trusted agent. Each time they spoke, the Emir explained that a dangerous radical religious faction called Al-Shabaab were hostile to anyone from the West, and they controlled much of southern Somalia. Daniel recognized the name as a militant affiliate of Al-Qaeda. The information alone was enough to placate Daniel's angst. He would rather be patient than get mixed up with Al-Qaeda.

But after two months at the compound Daniel was growing increasingly frustrated. Couldn't the Emir drape Daniel in a full body burqa and drive him to Mogadishu airport where he could take an international flight to a safer country? Or perhaps they could smuggle him in to Kenya, where the people are friendly to Westerners. The Emir dismissed these ideas out of hand, all too dangerous. Given Daniel's experience on the way into Somalia, he was in no position to disagree over the degree of danger, but still, he was increasingly ready to take the risk rather than watch *Cinderella* again, but the Emir insisted Daniel just be patient until the U.N. could send a plane. Perhaps he could work some stress out in the gym, the Emir suggested.

Daniel did. In fact, he was spending a significant amount of time building his muscles and running on the treadmill. If he was going to be holed up here and have nothing else to do, he could at least buff himself up for his triumphant return home.

**He had been at the compound for three months** when the Emir made a surprise visit to Daniel's room. The Emir was flanked by five full-bodied men Daniel had never seen.

"I am sorry for this," the Emir said.

The men flooded in to the room. Daniel backed in to a corner. The first two men grabbed his arms, two took his legs, and the fifth shackled his wrists, ankles, and ran a chain among the two. Daniel pled and screamed.

"May Allah bless you with a good home," the Emir said as Daniel was dragged down the hall.

He was taken to a wing of the compound he didn't know existed. This section was not as well maintained, with peeling paint, only illuminated by natural light and not air-conditioned. The heat between the narrow cinderblock walls was at least 100 degrees Fahrenheit. Daniel and his entourage stopped in front of a door guarded by a cattle-prong armed man, who easily slid open a heavy-iron bar deadbolt. They pushed Daniel into a room occupied by six other men. The room's other occupants stared unwaveringly on the ground, ceiling, or wall. All shirtless, they were all also in excellent physical condition. He recognized the African man he had seen the day he arrived at the compound, the one on the treadmill.

The bolt slid ominously in place behind him.

"What is this?" Daniel cried out. None of the men broke their beaten gazes, but one slowly raised his head, revealing eyes dim with despair.

"We are sold," one man said in a pitifully broken English.

"*What?*" Daniel cried, unwilling to fathom that the seemingly good-hearted Emir had duped him.

"We owned men. They take us to sell at the Bantu Slave Auction."

Daniel need only see the truth on the faces in this unfortunate room. His chest tightened. He hallucinated an apparition of himself smashing his skull against the wall, but there was no suicide in him.

He would live to let these barbarians determine his fate.

**Sayyid sat in a private house** just off Main Street in the Somalia port city of Kismayo, chewing large leaves of khat and drinking imported Kentucky bourbon. Sweat peeled down his impressively muscular frame, dampening his tank top. He peeled his tangerine keffiyeh from his head and let it lie loosely around his neck. He reclined on a dilapidated sofa on an open-air veranda, laughing at everything and nothing with his host, when his phone rang. It was his friend Tak, who reminded him the Bantu Slave Auction was starting soon, and asked wouldn't Sayyid meet him in the street so they could hurry over before it got too crowded?

Sayyid started speaking his goodbyes, before he grabbed a one-pound bag of khat, and sauntered down the exterior steps to the street, where Tak leaned against Sayyid's Land Cruiser.

"I thought you were going to back out on me," Tak said.

"You know I never miss," Sayyid said. Sayyid unlocked the SUV door, and the two men rolled down their windows and they swerved around the pockmarked street. Tak flared two cigarettes in his mouth and passed one to Sayyid. Sayyid let the tube dangle playfully from his lips, exhaling the smoke through his nose.

"So how come you finally decide to come to the Auction with me? What use you have with a slave?" Tak asked.

"Aww, I hear they have a special one for sell today. American journalist," Sayyid said.

"I don't understand. What useful work do these do? Nothing."

"They take pictures and make my story. Then I let it go back to America and he tell them about the greatest warrior, Sayyid. I will be famous and probably do commercials for million dollars on TV. Sayyid will be Kobe Bryant famous."

"Only your trigger finger is bigger than your imagination."

The pair laughed incessantly as they searched for a parking spot outside the Bantu Slave Auction, converted from a cement amphitheater secured with miles of barbed wire and scarred machinegun-toting men. Several of the guards slapped hands with Sayyid as he approached the entrance. One of the men, one with whom Sayyid was unfamiliar, indicated a "no guns" sign just by the portal. Sayyid laughed, lifted his tank top and revealed a fully-automatic Uzi. He released the fabric veil, draping the gun, and then he swirled his keffiyeh over his head and face.

"I am a humble servant of Allah. Surely, if anyone attacks the auction I will serve as additional security for you," Sayyid said.

The younger men looked to the senior guard, who nodded a grumbling assent. Sayyid knew his reputation for perfect violence preceded him, and no one wanted to risk that sort of trouble.

Tak and Sayyid passed through the portal and descended the steps and took seats on a cement bench in the midst of the theater. Sayyid passed Tak the bag of khat, and they began gnashing the narcotic between their teeth, the juices soaked into their blood, and their eyes bulged while they waited for the infamous sale to commence.

Emir Sharif walked to a podium, dressed in a finer collection of shawls than usual, with a stapled sheath of papers in his hand and delivered a summary of the chattel to be sold at auction. Once he'd given a brief description of the men and women he held captive, his agents began dragging the chattel onto the stage, one by one. Many of the attendees were merely gawkers without any real intention or means of purchasing a slave. Depending on the physical shape and genetic success of the individual on offer, the crowd either cheered and applauded or booed and hissed. Regardless of the reception the lot received, each of their faces appeared totally humbled, humiliated, and frightened to death. Sayyid kept his views on the lots to himself, munching on the khat and laughing at Tak's anecdotes. Sayyid quit laughing when Tak asked about Sayyid's younger brother, Yousef.

"Those were the good times when we kids, yes. But look, here now is my man."

Two of the Emir's assistants dragged the journalist onto the stage. He was paler than the pictures of white men Sayyid had seen. The Emir named him Daniel Barnes, and described him as an American Photojournalist. The Emir said he would be easy to keep tabs on, since there are few white men in southern Somalia. Also, he said the man could be used for a homicidal video to be published to the West, or many other uses.

Sayyid started the bidding by raising his fist in the air for the price of $1,000. The bid quickly shot up to $2,000, $3,000, and $5,000 U.S.D. Everyone, it seemed, wanted to bid on the white man. No doubt, he would be useful for many, many purposes, yes. Sayyid bid $8,000, but for the first time had to consider how much he would be willing to pay for the slave. After all, he would be purchasing the man mostly as a novelty. Sure, he hoped the man could bring him world fame, but he realized, at least on an implicit level, that such a result was farfetched.

A wealthy looking Arab bid $15,000. The Emir looked to Sayyid, as the last remaining bidder, to raise the bid at least another thousand dollars. Sayyid peered hard at the slave, who stood staring directly at the ground with muscles trembling. The man was in surprisingly good shape, didn't look as though he had been beaten hardly at all. He had a thick mane of hair, and although he was indisputably frightened, a certain determination shone in his eyes. As Sayyid peered deeper and deeper in to the man, he became intrigued by the contradictions he saw. He saw both a killer and a saint. He saw a man who had lived through much and maintained a fire he knew only in himself.

Sayyid was attracted to strong things. He rose his hand and barked out $20,000. His bid placed, Sayyid shifted his attention to the other bidder, who consulted a litter of his associates.

A piercing explosion reverberated throughout the amphitheater, and soon a dusty smoke began to permeate the air. Sayyid's ears rang for a moment. He had reflexively covered his head with his arms and dropped to his haunches, but he shot up immediately while the rest were bowing for safety and cowering in fear. Helicopters could be heard in the distant air, the unmistakable roar of heavy armored vehicles groaned in the proximity. Lookouts were shouting from the rooftops, numerous injured were wailing in mortal pain. Machine gun bursts punctured the air. Sayyid looked up to see Daniel lying alone, facedown on the stage, the Emir and his guards vanished inside the labyrinthine compound. Sayyid dashed to the stage and with a deadeye blasted the chain ran between Daniel's legs with a single shot from his Uzi and commanded, "Come on," as he led the white man down from the stage, hurrying up the amphitheater steps. Tak close at his side, they ran in hopes of reaching the Land Cruiser before the Ethiopian and TFG forces pulverized the already dilapidated buildings surrounding them, no doubt intent on razing Kismayo to the ground. Sayyid flung open the door to the back seat and Daniel dove in headfirst, but as Sayyid climbed into his seat he watched as a pink mist spewed out the side of Tak's head, his lifelong friend fell limp to the ground. Without missing a motion, Sayyid started the SUV, threw the vehicle momentarily into reverse and sped along an already ransacked and smoldering street. Sayyid peered through the rearview mirror at Daniel who sat upright, his face green and his eyes as empty as a cloud-covered desert night.

**Daniel wasn't certain whether to be glad this strange man** had saved him from that battle zone, or if he would have preferred to have just perished in the mortar, grenade, and machine gun spray that had descended on the place. This man appeared to have abandoned his companion back there to a certain death. If he was so ready to let an acquaintance die like that, how much less sympathy would he show a man who was just auctioned at a slave market? Further, the sudden turns, swivels, and bumps in the SUV were making him sick, seeing as he hadn't ridden in a vehicle but once in the last several months, and that was a luxurious ride compared to this frantic departure.

They motored through bullet-riddled streets before finally escaping in to the wasted expanse of desert. Daniel turned to see the conflagration burning behind them, helicopters hovering over the small city and explosions shaking the buildings like a serving of free-standing jello. After they had pushed several miles into the sand-duned land, the man's erratic driving calmed.

"I am Sayyid. A Captain in the Puntland Coastguard. You were just for sale at the Bantu Slave Market. I bid for you because you are a photojournalist, yes?"

"I am a photojournalist."

"What is your name?"

"Daniel Barnes."

"Daniel Barnes, this is a very American name, yes?"

"I suppose."

"We will return to Puntland now. I have many business contacts in southern Somalia, but the TFG and Ethiopia like to fight with Al-Shabaab, yes? They cause much death when they meet. This is why we leave them so quickly. If we stay, we die like my friend Tak, yes?"

"That man was your friend?"

"Always, yes. But what use is a man once he has taken a bullet through the head?"

"Are you sure he was dead?"

"I have seen many friends die. This is life in Somalia. Friends live until they die. No one cries. There is no use. It would be a sad life if we mourned what is every day."

They plowed through the barren desert for what seemed an eternity, desolate, and uninhabited. Daniel finally discerned that they were following a set of tire tracks cut in the sand, here one moment, swept away by the wind in the next. He was relieved they weren't merely barreling in to the monochromatic desert without navigation. They finally stopped at a speck of civilization, several mud huts surrounding a sole cinderblock building that huddled together under the brunt of the desert sun.

"The fighting is behind us, yes," Sayyid said.

A couple of children emerged from their huts to greet Sayyid, apparently familiar. Daniel opened the truck door and waddled out in to the excruciating heat. He was nauseas and certainly traumatized, if not suffering some unknown physical injury. His wrists were still manacled, and his legs bore the weight of shackles, which impeded him from taking more than the slightest step at a time. Daniel peered out into the vast sandy nothing: an occasional scrub brush and dune, the only objects doting the otherwise bleak horizon. He hurried towards that place where earth meets sky, his metal restraints heating his skin, simmering slightly on the flesh, melding themselves to his form. He gave the pain no thought. In death there was absolution.

**Sayyid bought some lemonade,** but when he returned to the SUV, Daniel was gone. He peered around, and saw Daniel limping out in to the desert void. At first, he thought maybe Daniel was just going to use the bathroom. But when he kept treading beyond the distance necessary for privacy, Sayyid called out to him.

"Um, pardon Daniel," Sayyid called out. "All there is in the desert is desertlarks to pick out your eyes then the jackals will feast on you while you breathe, yes. It is better you come with me."

**Daniel fell to his knees and cried**. Snot surged from his nose. At least it was cool, wet. He heard Sayyid's footsteps pounding on the sand behind him. Daniel gazed straight into the fiery sun. What good are a slave's eyes? What good is life? What good is anything?

"Come with me, Daniel. When we get to Mogadishu, I will buy you a camera."

"Why?"

"I buy you so you can make my story, yes? When you finished, I let you return home so you can tell the world that Sayyid is the greatest pirate, the Somali Robin Hood. Your story of me will put my picture on cereal box like Kobe Bryant. I will be world famous, yes."

It was plausible that an egomaniac would want him for such a task. But would he really let him return home? Daniel wouldn't have to return to the U.S. to publish a story, but perhaps an indigenous Somali wouldn't know that. Either way, it was the only offer of escape he had on the table. Sayyid had saved his life once. Perhaps if he played along, he'd at least be able to live long enough to run into some U.N. personnel, a journalist, *someone* who could secure his release.

"Come now, yes," Sayyid said. He grabbed Daniel by the arm and lifted him to his feet. Daniel raised his manacled hands to his face and wiped the snot and tear stains from his face. "Let's get those chains off of you, yes? You can see Sayyid is a man who acts on word."

Sayyid led Daniel to trunk of the SUV and opened a rusty toolbox, digging for the correct instrument. He tossed around various tools, unable to find the right one, when he said "ah ha," walked to the side of the vehicle and retrieved a pair of bolt cutters from under the back seat. The handcuffs and chains were no match for the torque of the bolt cutter's jaws. The metal slivered from Daniel's appendages flaccid and useless to the desert floor.

"Much better, yes!" Sayyid said. "Now Daniel trusts Sayyid. Daniel will stay by Sayyid because nowhere is there to run. Here, the desert will kill you. In Mogadishu, if you wander the police will find you and they kill you for fun. To think of it, the desert would kill you for the fun, too."

Two little girls carrying glasses of yellow drink skipped up to the men, and pushed a plastic cup in to each man's hand.

"It's lemonade," Sayyid said, taking a big drink.

Daniel stared down in the cup. He had seen Sayyid drink his. If Sayyid was going to kill him, he wouldn't have to poison him. He could simply lodge a bullet in Daniel's skull to put an end to the acquaintance. Daniel drank the lemonade, the heavenly lemonade. He hadn't tasted anything sweet since his arrival in Somalia. It rehydrated him, and his trust in this present master was incrementally growing. This place was an infinite, oceanless beach. The desert possessed a different kind of beauty, one he had never known, equal parts enchanting and tragic.

Nearby, children were bathed in the welded hull of an old Volkswagen Beatle, parked beside a mud hut, a mother pouring laundry detergent into the riotous bathtub of children. Either a large rat or a small pig was smoked over an open fire. Beyond this place there was only inhospitality and desolation, forbidding life for miles. Pre-teenage mothers held their infant babies in arms. Several other abandoned cars were strewn around, left to rust for eternity. On the side of the single cinderblock building, an old Siad Barre poster, the former dictator of Somalia for a generation, was still plastered and scrawled with an indecipherable slogan from the far gone past, frozen history.

After he finished the lemonade, he exhaled a refreshed awe of his surroundings. If Sayyid was being genuine, he was only a job away from returning home. Conveniently, the job he had come to do.

"It's good, yes? You want another?"

Daniel was taken aback by the hospitality. In D.C., he never asked for seconds because he never wanted to trouble the host. But Daniel had been enslaved for some time unknown and if this stranger were going to declare himself Daniel's master, then Daniel was going to accept his hospitality. He was too tired and indifferent to both social custom and death to care otherwise.

"Sure, I'd love another glass."

Sayyid spoke to the little girls in Somali, so that they ran away and quickly returned with two more glasses. Sayyid flipped off a tiny bundle of Somali shillings, and the girls' faces brimmed with smiles before they skipped away holding hands and singing.

"Ok, let us go. You can take the glasses. I buy them, too."

Daniel climbed in to the front passenger seat, and they started in to the empty desert.

"So we have an agreement, yes? You jump the ships with me, and you take the pictures and write the story, yes?"

"Yes, we have an agreement," Daniel said.

Sayyid smiled a large, white, gap-toothed smile.

"We going to make the news," Sayyidd said, leaning over and patting Daniel on the knee. Daniel's impulse was to squirm, but he sat tight. Westerners frequented Mogadishu if nowhere else in Somalia. It was a major city. If he could stay on Sayyid's good side and be given relative freedom, he was confident he would have a chance to escape. And if he didn't find a chance to escape, then perhaps this Robin Hood would prove to be a man of his word.

# *Six*

Daniel and Sayyid motored along the remnants of an asphalt highway, flanked by the suburbs of Mogadishu. They passed through countless checkpoints controlled by armed men, which increased in frequency as they approached the city, and although Sayyid slowed at them all, once the militants saw his face he was readily waved through. Sayyid appeared to enjoy some degree of local celebrity. From what Daniel had seen, not everyone appeared so fortunate. Numerous cars were parked, with the occupants detained at gunpoint while the vehicles were being rifled through. At one checkpoint, Daniel was rather certain he saw several corpses lying unceremoniously, mangled in a ditch. He averted his attention immediately after glimpsing the sight, not so much worried for his own psychological trauma as he was one of the militants would catch him staring, and become angered by his curiosity.

They reached the city during the dusk adhan. The muezzin, by loud speaker from the heights of the tower of the Isbaheysiga Mosque, called the city to prayer. Everywhere, the silhouettes of pious Muslims in the process of rak'ah, or kneeling in prayer towards Mecca, kissing the ground with arms stretched out flat ahead, before rising to the knees to face the sky, each whispering their private penance to God. Somewhere along the drive between the last stop and the present moment, in the midst of the quiet and Daniel's intermittent slumbering, Sayyid had found a small bag of khat and had been chewing nonstop since he discovered it. Some of the juice had oozed down his chin and dripped on to his black tanktop. Daniel decided not to bring the blemish to his attention. Sayyid didn't strike him as the type to send his clothes out to the drycleaners.

"Daniel, you awake! Welcome to Mogadishu, Somalia's great city. We hurry to Bakara Market before close to buy you cam-era."

"Good," Daniel said, stoic faced, his mental wheels racing in to gear. How could this man really trust Daniel not to run away at such a famously large and chaotic market? Daniel clandestinely checked himself, flexing his thighs, calves, hips, quietly testing his lungs for capacity, ready to run, if necessary, for hours. Adrenaline coarsed through his veins.

He was going to run.

He was going to wait until Sayyid became distracted, and then he was going to disappear in the crowd. He would dive in to a trashcan, if he had too. Hell, he would swim through a sewer. He was going to run until he found some sympathetic Westerners to provide him sanctuary until he got the hell out of the godforsaken situation.

The Land Cruiser screeched around the corners of deserted city blocks, leaving a trail of dust behind them as they motored along. They passed blocks of crumbling buildings, carcasses of burnt up automobiles. Resting Somalians, content to chew khat, reclined on a set of well-preserved stone steps, blanketing the area with their robes, their eyes a vacuum of awareness.

They continued through the oblivion.

Sayyid stopped at a tiny café and yelled some anecdotes at men sitting around a plastic table under a Pepsi-Cola umbrella. Khat littered the table. The men's eyes were ablaze and their tongues were thick with words. Sayyid laughed heartily at them. While Sayyid's attention was diverted, Daniel leaned over and pulled on the leather laces of the boots given him by the Emir. He was ready to run. When Sayyid waved goodbye, Daniel jerked inconspicuously against the seat upright. They accelerated forward rapidly.

"We must hurry for the market closes now, at dusk," Sayyid said.

Daniel's heart was beating rapidly. He knew the moment was drawing near. They motored through several darkening blocks, then a haze glowed on the skyline over the horizon. They drove closer and closer until the source of the glow was within sight. Operable cars were parked along the streets. Daniel readied for his opportunity. Within view were multi-colored tents, women wearing burqas, tables littered with spices, khat, rifles, butchered goat, flowers, and garments lined the streets for a distance not estimable. Sayyid stopped abruptly fifty yards short of the market.

"How goes there friend," Sayyid spoke to a teenage boy leaving the market.

"Hello. How are you, the great Sayyid! Will you need me to help you hijack a boat tomorrow? Or this week? Or perhaps I could guard your hostages? Your Land Cruiser is looking nice, but it could use a wash, could it not?"

Sayyid barked a hearty laugh. "Little brother, I am looking for a cam-era for my friend Daniel, a journalist."

"I can find you the very best camera, Sayyid."

"Yes? And a notebook and something to write with, too?"

"Yes, Sayyid. The best pen and notebook. I will find the best and bring it straight to your hotel. Are you still staying at the Orient Pearl?"

"You can find me there."

"I will bring them to you shortly. Camera, notebook and pen. I will bring you the best, Sayyid."

Sayyid waved and they did a U-turn away from the market. Daniel's hopes of escape flat lined along with the diminishing market lights fading behind them.

"What is wrong, Daniel? You wanted to select your own cam-era, yes? Do not worry. If you do not like the cam-era the little man bring, we send him back to get another. It is this easy. Besides, we do not want to walk through the market late at night. It is a most dangerous time in Mogadishu, even with the extra security the businessmen provide."

"Where are we going now?" Daniel asked, trying to conceal his former intentions.

"We're going to meet my gang. We stay at the Orient Pearl sometimes when we come to Mogadishu. They take care of us. Anyone I let stick their hand in my pocket takes care of me in Mogadishu, yes," Sayyid said with a full-throated laugh.

They motored past more unlit blocks of shelled buildings, entire walls of multistory housing units peeled back so the opposite exterior wall of the structure was visible. There was no organic quality to the exposed coils of wires, busted plumbing and shard glass. Mold grew on forgotten furniture. A handful of young boys practiced their aim with a Colt .45, blasting a row of glass bottles lined along a wall. Daniel whiffed the smell of sewage in the air. He laughed that there was a time when that smell would have made him gag. Now the stench reminded him of the living.

Daniel took immediate notice of the contrast between the streets previously passed and the Orient Pearl Hotel. The hotel's lighting alone set it apart from the scores of blocks surrounding it in their bleakness. Lush vegetation scaled the polished stonewalls. Immaculate red awnings adorned the windows and doorways. A steel gate opened and three heavily armed guards saluted as Sayyid entered the complex through a portal into a central courtyard. A litter of porters and valets stood ready to assist at the main entrance, adorned by a large lit canopy. A custodian assiduously wiped smudges from an immaculately clean revolving door. Daniel felt like he'd passed unwittingly through a wormhole and found himself in upscale Europe on holiday with some well-heeled friends who were splurging, even when measured against the notoriety of their limitless means. Hell, even Bally would be charmed to stay at this place.

"Hello Gentlemen, welcome to the Orient Pearl," a valet said to both Sayyid and Daniel, as each of their doors were opened for them simultaneously. Daniel followed Sayyid into the gilded establishment.

"Your friends await you in the Crown Suite, as you always request. Is there anything we can do to be of service to you?" the porter asked.

"Only one thing. Soon a little boy named Mattee will come with a cam-era, notebook and pens. Let him to my room because I request these things."

"Someone will escort him up when he arrives sir," the porter said, performing a slight bow to Sayyid, before guests walked onto the elevator.

"You are going to like my friends, Daniel. The story you write begins with them and me, yes? Where would Kobe Bryant be without his teammates and his coach? Nowhere. Everyone sees this."

"I agree."

"Is good you agree. I remind you, Daniel, do not run from me or big bad will come to you. Sayyid is friendly compared to what many Mogadishian think of gaalo. You stay with me, no one bother you. Out there you alone, maybe you fly away. More likely you get crushed like a little bug scurrying to he knows not where," Sayyid said, accompanying his words with demonstrative hand gestures. He turned and faced Daniel with a serious expression draped across his face. "You understand me?"

"Loud and clear."

Sayyid raised an inquisitive eyebrow.

"Yes, I understand."

"Good," Sayyid said as they stopped in front of a double-doored room labeled *The Crown Suite*. Sayyid tapped on the door. "Knock, knock."

The voices inside hushed, and footsteps could be heard to approach. A deadbolt was released and the door flung open. A young African's stern expression instantly turned to smile.

"Sayyid, you return!" The young man said. The two embraced. Sayyid turned.

"Daniel, this is our good friend Macalin. He shoots very straight with a gun, yes? You will take many photographs of him with his gun. Fierce pictures, like Rocky Balboa. No, Rambo. Yes, the Rambo you will make him look alike."

45

"Sup cuz," a husky white man greeted Sayyid from behind a granite bar in the kitchen, where he was cleaning an M-16 mounted with a scope and shoulder strap. His muscles bulged underneath a tight white v-neck t-shirt.

"Daniel this is Cameron," Sayyid introduced him.

Daniel was immediately intrigued. Who was Sayyid? Who were these men who worked alongside Sayyid? The Cameron guy looks more like U.S. Special Forces than a Somali pirate. These guys had nice digs, hinting at more than just a little success. Maybe he could arrange a meeting alone with Cameron later. The man spoke like an American. Surely he would be sympathetic to the emergency nature of Daniel's condition. Even if Cameron wasn't going to double-cross Sayyid to help Daniel get away, maybe Daniel could at least get a read to determine whether or not Sayyid was a man who kept his word. It would, after all, be tremendous to believe he would get to go home if he wrote the story.

Another young black man burst out of one of the bedrooms, led by his round belly, receding hairline, but undoubtedly toned physique, his movements empowered by hostility. He marched right up to Sayyid, and Daniel quickly discerned the two were related, if not brothers. The resemblance was striking.

"Where have you been? Is there something you have forgotten?" The young man inquired of Sayyid.

Sayyid scratched his head, but his overcooked laughter hinted he was aware of his guilt.

"No, I have just gotten back from Kismayo. See? I have brought the journalist. He will write our stories."

"What?" The young man said. "You missed mosque today. You promised we would attend mosque as a family, and now as it is we will go out to sea without having spoken to our Father as a family. Do you not know how much stress this brings me?"

"I know you are all disappointments with me these days, Yousef. But we were nearly killed in Kismayo, and I come back with the journalist I go for so he can tell our story, and we become famous and rich. Then we won't have to worry about going to sea to make money because the businesses will pay us just for taking a picture with the car, the watch, the cereal. Then we can relax."

"You," Yousef laughed. "You think this journalist is the answer to our problems? You want to draw attention to what we do so the Americans can hunt us, take us to jail? Have you thought of that? That that be their reaction?"

"No. The Americans love violence and greed. They will worship us on TV once Daniel make our story to them."

"If he makes a film about us, the shura is already very angry with you. They know you were not at mosque. They might not let you go to the next raid when we go to Eyl tomorrow."

"The shura always lets Sayyid pirate in Eyl because Sayyid is the best pirate there is. No questions."

"This is your vanity talking. This is haram. No man is the greatest."

Cameron laughed. "I'm not Muslim, so I don't give a shit. Sayyid is the only man I've ever known to get the giggles when the shooting starts."

"Shut up you infidel. You all need to understand. This is not just about money," Yousef said.

"Yes it is, little brother," Sayyid said. He wrapped his arms around his younger brother and swung him around wildly like a rag doll. Then he slammed him down on the soft, feather-stuffed couch. "It is *only* about money. And don't you ever forget that."

Everyone laughed, including Yousef as he lied beneath his brother's muscular curvature. Daniel even caught himself laughing. For a moment, he felt like one of the boys. For a moment, he forgot how deeply intertwined his fate was with these hellish rebels.

A knock came at the door.

"Come in," Sayyid sang, rising off his brother's sprawled body.

47

Matte entered the room, holding a vintage Polaroid camera and a bulging plastic shopping bag.

"Cheese," he yelled, snapping a flash. An undeveloped picture shot out the bottom, and he laid it on the table to dry. Then he unloaded three boxes of film, two notebooks, and a mixed assortment of used pens.

"Good work," Sayyid said, peering down at the contents, turning the camera over in his hands. "How much do I owe you?"

"Mmh, the pencils were three dollars, the notebooks two dollars, the film eight dollars and the camera one-hundred dollars."

"One hundred thirteen dollars for this!" Sayyid said incredulously. "You must rethink this price my friend or risk losing a valuable customer."

"Seventy-two dollars?" Matee squeaked.

"How come you make up this price? Why not you tell me what you pay for it, and I give you extra for Matee's trouble."

The boy's shoulders slumped. He stuck his tongue in his jaw and stared at the ceiling.

"What is it, Matee?"

"Alright. I pay ten for the camera. Two for the film, one for the pens and one for the notebook."

"So fourteen. Here is fifty dollars. Take it home to your mother before you buy khat, that is our deal."

"Ok Sayyid, no problem!" Matee said.

Sayyid flicked through a collection of bills, Euros, Pounds, Somali shillings, and finally United States Dollars.

"I appreciate what you do," Sayyid said as he gave the boy the money.

Matee smiled at Sayyid, clutching the money greedily, then quickly ran out of the room, followed by one of the hotel attendants. Sayyid closed and locked the door following the boy's departure.

"So you're serious about your boy here doing up a story about us?" Cameron asked. He had totally disassembled the M-16 and laid its various parts on the counter. He was scrubbing a squeegee in and out of the barrel of a 9mm Glock.

"Why I not be serious? If no one takes pictures or tells stories how will we ever be famous?"

"It's not about fame," Yousef said.

"Yea, the goal was to make money. Not become a boy band," Cameron said. Everyone turned and looked at him with a total lack of comprehension, as if expecting some sort of an explanation. "You know, like New Kids on the Block? Like Madonna but with a group of boys?"

All quickly dismissed what he was saying as Yankee gibberish.

"What I'm saying is I'd like to go home one day, and if Danny boy here has written up some exposé about our antics on the high seas, that may not be possible."

"Why you want to go back to America?" Yousef asked. "So you can oink along with the other pigs you left there."

"America's not such a bad place. You just let your moms rot your brain with all their preaching and whooping. Wake up. No place ain't much different than another. Well, that's not totally true. About anywhere is safer than here. Hell, Baghdad's safer than this place."

"I like Sayyid's idea," Macalin said. "So what if we never go back to U.S.A.? It's a chance I would take. Besides, I would bet Sayyid is right and the Americans will love our story. They would probably cast us in so many movies that we'd die before we ever made them all. Before it is over, they'll even consider us great Americans for robbing American ships. Americans are quick to forgive. Jesus was all about forgiveness."

"The Americans are pigs," Yousef muttered, but must have realized he wasn't going anywhere with his line of reasoning because his exhortations tapered off into a whiny muttering. He crossed his arms when no one as much as glanced his direction, and resigned to the sofa to weather his prejudice alone.

Daniel loved the exchange between these guys. There was a deep story seam to be mined, he could feel it. Sayyid placed the camera back on the table, and Daniel began examining the tools he had been provided. The Polaroid was primitive, for certain, but there were advantages to having the ability to develop his own photos. For one thing, he wasn't certain he could find a dark room in Mogadishu. Plus he could see the quality of his photography instantly, which in the absence of a digital camera wasn't bad. The pens and notepad would make do. He sat at a round wooden table, mass produced for some civilized market, jotting notes. He hadn't realized how much he missed plying his trade. It felt amazing. Perhaps it felt even better to have a story worth telling unfold before him. This story put Burton's boring tax work in perspective.

"Sayyid, now that you're here," Cameron said. He reached behind the bar, dangling a miniscule something between his thumb and index finger.

"Now we are talking," Sayyid said, wildly swinging his arms horizontally to and fro. "Yes, yes, yes."

Lust exploded in Macalin's eyes.

Cameron dumped the contents of the small package on the granite countertop, just to the side of the disassembled M-16. Macalin and Sayyid huddled around quickly.

"No, no. This is haram! You must not!"

"This is haram, this is haram," Cameron mocked. "You might as well say 'it exists, it exists,' for as much as you use that damn word."

Yousef made no attempt to conceal how this bothered him, his face flush with troubled disbelief.

"Brother, please not you do this to," Yousef shrieked. "Allah cannot forgive apostasy."

Sayyid bowed his chest and shoulders in his brother's personal space.

"You do not make judgment on my relationship with Allah. You do not!" Sayyid thundered.

Anyone who blinked would have missed it, but Yousef slunk, however slightly.

"The gaalo is no good here. This," he said, pointing to the cocaine on the counter, "this is also forbidden. Nothing good will come of any of this. Nothing!" Yousef proclaimed before he marched off into a separate room, the door crashing taut against the threshold in his wake.

The room grew quiet for a minute. Then there was giggling that eventually erupted in to an uncontrollable laughter.

"You not hear about your brother?" Macalin asked. "He is politicking for supreme ayatollah of Somalia!"

Cameron's ribs pulsated, in and out, and he slammed his lunchbox fist against the granite countertop. Sayyid's laughter evolved into a purring howl. Macalin laughed and lifted his eyebrows suggestively, fanning the success of his joke. Daniel's laughter subsided before theirs, and he took the opportunity to snap a quick picture of the gang in a relaxed moment. He took a second picture while he had them all standing around. Recognizing their receptivity, Daniel parlayed the moment in to an introductory group interview. He asked them why they pirated. Each in his own turn said money. Sayyid reiterated he wanted to be rich and famous like Kobe Bryant. Cameron told Sayyid he was dreaming. Sayyid rebutted that once Kobe Bryant was only dreaming, too.

"So how does your business work, exactly? What are the tricks of the trade?"

"Hu?" Sayyid puzzled.

"I mean, I generally know you seize the ships then the owner's pay you ransom, but there must be some specifics that aren't as well known."

"This is what you mean tricks. This is what you write in the story? People like this?"

"Of course."

"Very well. Where should I begin?"

"You could begin wherever you like. How about at the beginning? Tell me about your life. How you first got in to pirating."

"Yes. I was born into tribe of nomads. Then there was no rain for two years, and I was forced into Mogadishu. It was Mogadishu or starve in the desert. Only everyone in Mogadishu starve too. It was no bonanza for sure. Yousef and I got by, though. One day they formed a new Puntland Coastguard, to prohibit the foreign fishing. They train me to shoot rifle, board ship, drive and navigate a boat. They turn Sayyid into a real seaman. See, it was just shepherd work, like I do before. Only on sea instead of desert. Thai, Indian, Yemeni fishing ship were like jackals, and we went chasing them from the fishing ground. I enjoyed the coastguard work. But then they quit paying the coastguard. Men start to quit. But then we use the boat to fish, and when we catch the foreign boats, we fined them. We ate the fish and spent the money. Once, we caught a real nice Thai fishing ship, and its owner pay us $50,000 with us not even ask for that kind of money. We start to think to ourselves is this money is going to keep coming? Then the government take the boat away from us and there was no ability to coastguard. My brother and I hungry again. Then there was a new idea. A man took his fishing skiff out into the ocean and boarded an ocean liner. We took the guns, too. The crew did not fight. The ship was an empty Syrian oil tanker returning from Asia. The owner pay us $250,000 to let the boat and crew go free. We did not harm them. If we harm them, we upset the owner and maybe they not pay us. Maybe they even pay mercenary to hunt us like animal. No man wants this trouble."

"So how do you make the money? How does your actual operation work?"

"Aww, I finish my story. So one day the man I work for, the first pirate, he was killed when he boarded the ship. He had always boarded first, and this time a ship hand shoot him. Bang," Sayyid said with his fingers mimicking a gun. "So Sayyid jump on the ship and shoot the man. Then shoot another. Then the rest of the crew surrender. When we get the boat to port I ask what we do now. Everyone say Sayyid in charge now because the other is dead. You see, that is how I became the Captain. It took five months for the ransom to come this time, and I went in to town some so that my share was reduced. But this was ok because everyone got paid and no one was sad because death in Somalia is a sunset. It brings darkness but happens every day."

Sayyid continued. "We became very good at boarding the ships. My gang then say I was better than the old captain. My methods were new. We use faster boats. We bring RPG. We leave a driver with the boats, so escape is possible. My old captain not do this," Sayyid said, tapping his temple lightly. "But Sayyid think yes, this make the pirating more easy, if success is what we after. One day the Sheikh approached Sayyid after we hold ship for seven months, and he say why Sayyid waste time guarding prisoners? I tell him this is necessary part of the business. The Sheikh ask me how many times I successfully catch the boat I chase. I told him every time. I always catch the ship. He was very impressed and made me an offer. He say if I come work for him, I never have to guard another ship. I just catch the ships and he pay my share as soon as we get to port, immediately. No matter if he get ransom or not. Now how is that deal for Sayyid! I said yes! Now we catch as many ship as there are, and everyone knows we are the best. So you go and tell them!"

Daniel had been writing furiously, trying as best he could to get this all down. The specialization of roles amazed him. It made sense, it was human nature. But he hadn't realized how special Sayyid was, at least according to the man's own account, until now. Sayyid and was the pirate of pirates. They left the housekeeping and bookkeeping to other men. Their trade was blood sport on the high seas. Daniel could not get enough of it. He knew no one else would, either.

"Can I ask you a personal question, Sayyid?"

"Ask me question," Sayyid said, raising his chin to show Daniel his proud neck.

"How come Yousef doesn't party with us? Why did he get angry at you and leave the room?"

Sayyid reclined back in to the arms of his bar chair. He put his hands together in a circle.

"Yousef is very pious," Sayyid said respectfully. "Our parents died when we were very young. They were killed in the war that saw the end of Siad Barre. The tribe discussed what to do. Yousef was too young to be of use in the hinterland, so he was sent to schools. He learned English at UNESCO, but when that program end he was sent to study at Islam school, where he receive most of his education. I stay and work with the nomads. Not all brother learned in Islam school made him easy to deal with. He sees Allah in a way many do not. He sees him intensely. Like a flame, Yousef is afraid if he is not constantly tending the coals he will be burnt. Yes, the school make him that way, but I know he just miss our parents."

"I'm not sure I can ask you this, so if it offends you please don't kill me."

"Go on," Sayyid said, a sinister leer rusting across his face.

"If Yousef is so pious, religious I mean, then how can he justify raiding ships? What if he had to kill someone in the act? Wouldn't that be an offense to Allah, or haram as you say?"

Sayyid's index finger ticked back and forth like a metronome.

"The Prophet himself was often given to raiding. Quran 22:39: Permission to fight has been given to those who are being fought, because they were wronged. And indeed, Allah is competent to give them victory."

Daniel recorded Sayyid's Quranic quote word-for-word.

"You see, life in the desert can be harsh, yes. Death is always awaiting tomorrow. Allah does not expect us to die without fight, so if we must take from other tribes to sustain our own, this is right, yes. When the drought come, pirating is all there was. We are pirates because it is all there is. There is no fast food to apply for. No toilets to clean. No government to give the aid."

Vanity prodded Macalin and Cameron into talking about themselves, after Daneil had given Sayyid's story so much interest. Macalin had grown up in Minneapolis,

Minnesota. His parents relocated there from Somalia before Macalin was born during one of many periods of great unrest in the Horn of Africa. He was raised Muslim, and gently taught about the Clash of Civilizations. The West, the imam testified, was trying to eradicate the Middle East. The West disrespected the law of Muhammad. The West refused Muslims the right to govern themselves by their own law. This is why Islam is irreconcilably pitted against Western civilization. When Macalin was a teenager, an opportunity sprang. Any willing young man could travel to Somalia, train for jihad in the homeland, and fight the rising tide of Western aggression in Islamic countries. It was a call Macalin accepted. He had excelled in training camp, and after Sayyid had become involved with the Sheikh and it came to pass that he needed to replace a fallen member of his gang, Macalin came strongly recommended for his skill and bravery. Under Sayyid's wing, Macalin eventually desensitized to his former religious fervor. Some of the boys he had trained with had gone on to complete suicide bomb missions. He grew quiet after he said this, perhaps ruminating over the thought that he would have met a similar fate had Sayyid's employment not saved him from that exploitation.

Cameron was from Charleston, South Carolina. The man's muscles bulged in his sleeves and around his neck as he related his past. A large tattoo of the North Star on his bicep shone through his white t-shirt. His head was slick bald. Cameron had joined the U.S. Marines out of high school. He served in Operation Desert Storm during the Bush I era. When his four years were up, he got out of the service. He took out a loan to buy a deep-sea fishing charter. For a while, business was manageable. Then there was a slowdown. The activity had merely gone out of vogue. He fell behind on his payments, and the bank repossessed his ship. Beat but not beaten, he took the first job he was offered, working at a restaurant. The people were nice, but the work wasn't fulfilling.

They say bad luck comes in threes.

The IRS decided to audit him. He hadn't paid any of his income taxes from his fishing excursions. His clients had paid all cash, and he thought you didn't have to pay taxes on that. What people do and what they're actually supposed to do were two different things, he learned. It was too late for an accountant's advice to save him. There was talk of criminal charges. He saw a documentary on Somalian pirates, how these guys were raiding these big ships when many of them couldn't even swim. Couldn't even swim.

He knew he'd be useful and that's what gave him encouragement to pursue the vocation in the first place. He'd known a Somali refugee at a seafood wholesale, who had connections back in the homeland. The man put Cameron in touch with a contact in Somalia, Sayyid. Sayyid had been looking for English speakers, strong men with experience, and when he heard of Cameron he volunteered to personally arrange his transportation.

Sayyid liked both of these men because they spoke English, an international shipping language. In the past, when he had employed men who only spoke the native tongue, there were misunderstandings. Unnecessary deaths resulted. Ransoms were lost. Otherwise great work was spoiled by a lack of communication. Sayyid fixed this problem by employing only bilingual men. They attacked ships who shared a language. Common language created efficiencies.

The cocaine supply exhausted around 3am. There was a refrigerator full of beers and packs of cigarettes strewn all about the hotel room, but the remaining khat leaves were dry and stale. Sayyid tried chewing a leaf on a couple of occasions, but discarded the gnawed stem each time in disappointment. He said he would have to wait until Bakara opened in the morning to purchase some khat flown in fresh from either Kenya or Yemen. No one cared much for the Ethiopian khat, he said.

Daniel wrote furiously, speaking only to prompt the storyteller to continue, being as unobtrusive as possible, like a security camera surveilling its perimeter. One by one the men began to drop. Sayyid was the last of them awake. He mumbled that he was the greatest. The greatest pirate. The greatest partier. The greatest Somalian. Daniel noted that once Yousef left the room the subject of haram had not been revisited.

With everyone asleep, Daniel rested his pencil. The able-bodied men littered the room, Macalin and Sayyid asleep on the sofas, but Cameron lied face down on the countertop, his powerful jaws flat against the granite. One minute the husky white man had been railing lines, the next he was unconscious on the cold countertop. His M-16 was still disassembled and the Glock was sandwiched between his waistband and his slightly revealed gut.

It was 5 am. Daniel started thinking quickly. It had never crossed his mind that these men might party so hard they would all pass out, leaving him unattended. He saw a phone in the corner of the room, but he hadn't memorized any country codes and wasn't sure who to call or what to say even if he did get in touch with someone resourceful. Before setting out to Somalia, he had not given serious consideration to being taken hostage.

He could just leave. Walk out the door. Down the elevator. Talk about coffee and breakfast if anyone asked questions. Take his chances on the street. Pray for a break. Get to the airport. If he could just get to the airport.

Everyone was very polite as he passed through the hotel. All smiles and good mornings. The contrast between this civilized enclave and the ruined world beyond its gates was stark. On the streets, there were no other pedestrians or taxis. Even a passing car was rare. He did not know where he was going, only that he was scrambling for freedom, wherever it was to be found.

A sedan with emergency lights mounted on the hood and a bull-ring on the grill sputtered on the road. It was coming in his direction. It resembled a police car, what he thought a police car might look like in Somalia. He waved his arms.

"Hello," a man said from the driver's window. He wore a linen button down shirt and the car had a C.B. radio and a pistol hung beneath his arm.

"Are you the police?"

"Yes."

"Can you help me?"

The man stepped out of the car and walked around the vehicle, standing within inches of Daniel, invading his space. Daniel could smell the man's breath and whatever uncouth breakfast he had forced down his throat.

"Do you have travel documents?"

"No. I'm in danger. You have to help me."

"Are you Muslim?"

"No. I'm, I came here for work. I'm a journalist."

"You are a journalist and have no travel papers."

"Yes," Daniel said, glancing furtively. "I was kidnapped."

The man made short shrift of throwing Daniel face down on the ground. The familiar coldness of steel handcuffs tickled Daniel's wrists before they crunched, notching one click at a time in to the bone. He wailed to stop. The man did not react. He raised Daniel to his feet and dropped him on his belly in the back seat.

They drove a short distance to a large facility within the city. There were barred doors and windows everywhere. Similarly outfitted cars. A machine gun turret. Daniel was turned over to two men at the facility who spoke to him in their native tongue, which Daniel could not understand. He told them he did not understand, but they could not understand that he did not understand.

He was escorted into what was unmistakably a jail, and led to a cell. No one paid him much attention. There was another man in his cell. He was standing by a window, peering out in to a courtyard. The jailers left Daniel with his cellmate.

"What is this?" Daniel asked. "Do you speak English?"

The man nodded yes.

"Then tell me where I am. What is this?"

"Al-Shabaab has us," the man said.

That didn't sound good.

"Why?"

"Why?" The man laughed. "They have me because I am a TFG soldier. Why do you think they have you?"

"I don't know. I was kidnapped, then sold, and then I escaped from a hotel, the Orient Pearl. I was walking down the street when I was taken."

"You were arrested for violating Shariah law. Well, maybe you didn't violate it. But they will punish you by it."

"What will they do to me?"

The man motioned Daniel over to the window. "Come see for yourself."

Out in the courtyard, a man was stretched and bound to a wall, being flogged while several other men stood around watching. Daniel winced at the flick of every lash.

Bad decision of bad decisions to leave the luxury hotel.

"They're going to whip me?" Daniel asked.

"I don't know. It's not the worst they do."

"What else?"

The man laid down and closed his eyes. Daniel continued to watch. A parade of horrors marched past his eyes. They drug one screaming man out to a thick wooden table, where his hand was clamped to the table. The punisher switched weapons, taking a saw this time. The man pled until the surgery started. Then he prayed until he fell unconscious and the ungodly work was finished. When the hand dropped to the ground, his limp body was dragged away.

Another man was given a shovel. This perplexed Daniel, as he watched the man dig a hole at gunpoint. The digging took so long that Daniel lost interest for some time and sat against the wall of the cell, standing and peering out to check on the progress intermittently. The man finally finished his hole, and his captors ordered him into it. Two of the guards made short work of burying the man, to the neck, and then a group of men gathered stones from a large pile and struck the man in the head until there was only a red stain upon the ground.

Daniel's cellmate woke as the sadists dragged a woman outside. A man read aloud what Daniel presumed were the charges. The cellmate translated that she was charged with having music on her cell phone. Daniel counted each of the sixty lashes she received.

"What will they do to me?" Daniel asked.

"Are you Muslim?"

"No."

"It would be better if you were. You are white. They will say you are a spy. Your punishment will be death. There is a small chance they will commute your sentence if you agree to spy for them, but it would require a good argument and depend on their mood."

Daniel trembled. He thought about praying to God, but he was too scared to ask for final forgiveness while a guest in that dungeon. He didn't want to provoke them. He tried to calm himself by remembering good times with Bally and thoughts that he would soon be relieved of the torment of this long-lived nightmare. He was beginning to understand Sayyid's view on death. Once you had become adequately familiar with death, its presence was no longer frightening. It is hard to be frightened of what is so well known, of what is inevitable.

Two guards arrived at Daniel's cell.

"Gaalo," one said.

Daniel rose to meet them. If it was the last time he would walk, he might as well take advantage, even if he was lightening his executioner's burden.

He passed through the same halls from which he had arrived.

Outside the facility, Sayyid leaned against his Land Cruiser. The guards spoke to him in Somali, then they turned and went back in the facility.

"If you run away from me, you steal from me," Sayyid said.

"I—

"Don't even say. Sayyid tell you all truth. Sayyid even trust you. I tell you how them treat gaalo. You see? They let you see? What they do to these people?"

Daniel gulped and shook his head sullenly.

"You see them take the hand? Cut with the whip? They crucify like Jesus, Daniel." Sayyid nailed an imaginary nail through his wrist.

Daniel nodded comprehension again.

"But I let it go. You had to run once, didn't you Daniel? To know you're truly trapped. You won't run again though, will you?"

"No Sayyid."

"I know you won't. It is hard to be feral in a strange land. I break dogs, I break you. You will stay with me because this is where the sun is shine. This is where you eat. This face is the last one you see before you fly home. Do not cross me again or it will be the last face you see any."

Daniel's voice cracked in to a whimper: "I promise you I will never try to escape again."

# *Seven*

Daniel was surprised the gang was so alert on his return to the Orient Pearl, given the previous night's debauchery. Yousef and the others spoke to each other cordially, like professionals. Cameron loaded magazines from a bowl filled with armor-piercing ammunition.

"There he is! Don't worry about Sayyid having to spring you from jail grasshopper," Cameron said. "He had to bail me out a dozen times before they finally remembered me. Still, he's a good man to know." Cameron laughed. His plastic Coke bottle was blackened with tobacco spit.

In a matter of moments, zipped bags were piled by the door and soon a host of attendants arrived for their luggage.

Daniel rode snuggly between Macalin and Cameron in the back seat of Sayyid's Land Cruiser on the road to Eyl. The air conditioner was broken, the men's sweat beaded directly from their pores onto Daniel's skin, but he feared if he shifted an inch, he would upset them.

The drive lasted for hours.

"Hey Sayyid, I think I change my mind about the journalism. He makes the ride very uncomfortable so maybe we leave him here." Macalin said as the gang traversed a sandy plane, devoid of life. Daniel hoped, even tried to look for the sarcasm in Macalin's voice. "Hey how about it, Sayyid? I'll write the story for you. I took, ay um, Anglish when I lived in America."

"Stop this talk. Only Daniel can shoot the camera because you shoot the gun. Do not confuse these roles, yes."

Macalin jerked his arm away from Daniel, before shimmying in his seat to stretch his space, but there wasn't anywhere else for Daniel to go. He was sitting with his legs together and his arms crossed and he had been sitting like that since they left Mogadishu and they arrived in Eyl with him sitting like that.

There weren't many modern buildings in Eyl, or construction at all for that matter. There were some squat cement and mud buildings with Land Cruisers and trailer-mounted boats parked outside. Some ostriches were penned up in front of one of the dumpy edifices. The sun scorched his eyes. Everything seemed to be khaki, as if the democracy of colors had stricken a great, monochromatic compromise. Craggy hills sauntered up before crumbling away beneath the sky's burden. Then they perched on top of a ridgeline and Daniel saw a sea bluer than could be described by Homer's Latin.

They arrived at a dock where great flocks of men anxiously stood around, everywhere. Daniel naturally assumed this was some sort of a pirate headquarters. Sayyid seemed to have viewed in to Daniel's thoughts, because he broke a long silence.

"This is just a marina. Fishermen, mostly. They want pirate work, yes, but they only pilots."

"They don't know how to shoot guns," Cameron said.

"They can shoot," Macalin said. "They just believe it's wrong."

"I don't see the difference," Cameron said.

Macalin shrugged, lines wrinkling across his forehead.

Everyone exited the vehicle and immediately the loose aggregation of enterprising men herded around the pirates. A man of some preeminence emerged from the building adjacent to the docks, and the crowd parted for him as he gravitated toward Sayyid.

64

"Basse," Sayyid said, eagerly wrapping his arms around the man.

"The weather is good today for policing my waters."

"It is the most perfect day for this. Yes," Sayyid said. Then he introduced Daniel to Basse.

Basse owned the marina. He called a few men over and issued orders and soon Sayyid's pirate gang was standing on the dock watching as men fueled and stocked the boats with food and water, while Sayyid and Basse joked about something in the native tongue. Luggage was loaded into the speedboats. Two new men joined the party. The pilots, Sayyid explained.

The boats raced parallel to one another, skipping over the surf towards the oceanic horizon. Cameron stared over shoulder, a certain eagerness about him, clutching his M-16 in his hands with his finger reclining on the trigger. Sayyid snoozed. Yousef fidgeted between his pockets and his duffle bag. Macalin conversed with the pilot, though their conversation was inaudible due to the noise of the boat.

After three hours of plowing through open sea, a pelagic flotilla appeared on the distant horizon. Macalin woke Sayyid, and Sayyid drew Daniel's attention to the sole blip on the two-dimensional plane.

"The navy is here, yes," Sayyid said.

"What do you mean?"

"We have a navy. You not know this. We meet our navy before we raid the ships."

"All those ships are yours?"

"Not mine. The Sheikh's. The Sheikh is the big investor, yes? He pay all the operation. He have a many network for Sayyid to use. A very smart man," Sayyid said.

Sayyid's statement drew Yousef's attention, who nodded unqualified agreement.

Soon they boarded the largest ship, a seventy-foot yacht that had been commandeered by a group of pirates during a Sheikh-financed heist. The owners of the yacht were accidentally murdered, so the Sheikh was left with only the magnificent boat as a bargaining chip. Sayyid explained that he hadn't wanted to bring the wrath of the French down on him for the death of the yacht's owners, as the French bore a reputation for violent responses to pirate raids, so he decided to just keep the boat. He devised this plan to use it as a mothership from which to attack distant vessels. Sayyid explained it was a most profitable decision for everyone involved, as these long-range boats increased the pirates' range of attack exponentially. An M-2 Browning machine gun lie ready, camouflaged underneath happy umbrellas red, yellow and blue, ready to spit death. Lying next to it were two RPGs and a nasty looking African snarled.

The discipline exhibited by the rest of the pirates aboard the mothership was impressive. Although he wouldn't have called them uniforms, they all wore the same make of t-shirt. The apparent commanders were a man and woman dressed like affluent sea travelers. The gang met with them in a dining room rigged with laptop computers, navigational equipment, sea charts, and satellite telephones. It was a sophisticated, floating headquarters. Sayyid shook hands with the patron, clothed his well-tailored suit, and everyone took a seat around a large dining room table.

"What game have you got for us today, Quimbly?"

Quimbly unfurled a chart on the table. "We are here, about 300 miles out of the international shipping lane. A Saudi oil tanker the *MV Sirius Star* is cruising at 10 knots without convoy. They are returning from Europe unloaded, so they can travel up to 18 knots. We have a different plan this time. Instead of chasing them like Indians from behind and shooting until they stop, we put you out in a life raft in the middle of the shipping lane. Cameron will lie in the boat and use an emergency mirror to attract the attention of the ship. They'll see he's alone and white and send out a dinghy."

"What about the rest of us? Cameron cannot take the boat by himself."

"Yes I can."

"Ok, Cameron can," Sayyid said. "But he shouldn't have to. This dangerous, yes."

"Let me finish. Cameron won't have to. You'll all be in place. Everyone else will be in camouflage. When the dinghy approaches, everyone else will go underneath the

66

water, and breathe with a hidden snorkel built in to the raft. Cameron will hold them up first, then you will all jump out of the water on his signal, and take the dinghy. Then use those hostages to negotiate your way on the oil tanker. We understand the oil alone is worth $100 million."

"Why don't we just do it normal?" Sayyid asked.

"Well, obviously we wouldn't put the extra thought in if there weren't other impediments to consider. This ship has been retrofitted. Steel doors guard the bridge. Electrified fences cover all the freeboard. Water cannons. Noise guns. Tear gas. This boat's a floating nightmare."

"We lure the bees out of the honeycomb without their stingers," Sayyid said.

"Something like that," Quimbly said.

"When do we get in position?" Yousef asked.

"In one hour, be ready."

"Wait, what about my journalist?"

Quimbly looked hard at Daniel, regarding his presence for the first time.

"No one has told me about this. The Sheikh has said nothing. I think he should stay here until you return. Perhaps he can enjoy your story after its success is secure."

"No, he must come. This is his purpose."

Quimbly sighed, as if he had expected Sayyid to insist.

"He can lay in the raft with Cameron. Perhaps two shipwrecked white men will look more convincing than one."

"Good."

"Wait a minute. I don't know I want to be lying in any raft with him when they come up to the boat," Cameron said. "What if he does something to tip them off? I'll be the first man shot."

"Daniel not do anything, will you Daniel?" Sayyid said.

Daniel nodded eagerly.

"The sooner I get the story, the sooner I can get to work making you guys famous back home," Daniel said.

He didn't know why. Maybe he would try to signal the Saudis. Maybe once he was aboard the ocean liner the plot would go wrong, and when the pirates retreated he could hitch a ride to safety. Now there was an escape plan! He'd even have a daring tale of escape for everyone back home, even the raw material for a commercial story.

"Daniel," Sayyid inflected his voice as if he had a special read on Daniel's thoughts. "You know if something goes wrong on the raid, you are the first to die. You know this?"

"I want it to work out the most. It's my first raid, after all."

Macalin tried to hold back his laughter, but he infected Cameron and soon everyone was laughing. The matter was settled.

They spent the next hour relaxing, eating, lounging around, dressing in the same yellowy fabric the life raft was made of, except for Daniel and Cameron who were supposed to be discernible from the oil tanker's bridge from afar. When it was time to go, they boarded a fishing trawler, which sped them out to the international shipping lane over the curve of the horizon, about 20 nautical miles from where the flotilla drifted. The gang climbed into the little life raft, with weapons, emergency provisions and a satellite phone, to sit and wait. The fishing trawler left a gentle wake as it cut through the ocean, vanishing over the horizon.

The life raft bobbed up and down one to two feet on the breast of the ocean. The sea breathed just like an animal. There were two shades of blue. The sun bisected the ocean like a surgeon's scalpel. An occasional fish jumped and splashed in the ocean, but he rarely caught sight of one. He had never been in such close quarters to the pirate gang. They smelled terrible, despite having been given all that time at that fancy hotel, time to shower or rinse up on the mothership. They all still stunk, but no one else seemed to notice their confluence of odor, so Daniel kept his sentiment to himself. He wasn't exactly in a position to critique the pirates.

A long, dim square moved in to sight on the horizon. It grew larger and larger as the minutes elapsed. Cameron dug the emergency mirror out of his pocket and began practicing his manipulation of the sun.

"How long must we be underwater?" Macalin asked.

Sayyid put his finger to his lips. "We must be in the water for at least half an hour. Actually underneath the boat we will not need to be for longer. Only once their dinghy approaches should we have to go underneath the boat."

No one questioned Sayyid's logic. Everyone was preparing now. The divers checked their emergency floatation devices, locked and loaded their guns, checked their knives, checked everything, strapped and restrapped everything if for no other reason than to have something to do other than get nervous in the moments leading up to the siege.

"It's time," Cameron finally said.

Daniel's blood raced. He dug the Polaroid camera out of a dry bag. The black pirates all laid down in the life raft and pulled yellow veils over their faces so that they would be invisible at a range.

Daniel imagined himself dying in every manner imaginable, death by shooting, strangulation, broken neck, blunt force trauma to the head, knife in the gut. He simultaneously felt the pain of all those exits. He suffered it all contemporaneously with the suffering of losing Bally. He was a dead man, but at least in the afterlife there was absolution from the agony.

Once everyone was in place, Cameron began reflecting light as best he knew how on the bridge of the ocean liner. He was patient with this, and persisted for half an hour without any sign of results. The ocean liner drew much closer to the life raft. They were positioned perfectly in the middle of the shipping lane and when the colossal ship was only three or four miles away, Daniel saw a dinghy lower from the ship to the sea.

"Roll out, boys," Cameron said.

The black pirates gently edged over the side of the boat, one by one, none making excess moves. Daniel felt confident the precautions taken precluded the prey from having any clue what trap awaited them.

The three heads were still bobbing above the water when the second dinghy hit the water. Cameron put away his mirror, digging through the dry bag for a flare gun. He pointed it towards the sky and the flare climbed towards the sun, scrawling red smoke across the sky as it rocketed.

"Two boats now, boys," Cameron said.

Daniel snapped a picture of the men floating in the water, and squirreled the picture away in his dry bag. The three divers submerged, no longer visible. When the dinghies were within photographic range, Daniel began snapping pictures of the rescue. The lead dinghy killed its engine fifty meters from the life raft and began floating straight towards them. One man crawled to the bow.

"Shipwrecked are you?" The little Arab man yelled, perched there like a cat, his English more polished than expected.

"Fishermen from Australia," Cameron spoke with a conjured accent. "Damn cook on board was a drunkard and sunk the whole damn lot of it. Got another raft floating around out somewhere. Lost the rest of the boys last night. God pray for them," Cameron said.

"We can put out a report for them once we return to the ship. Let's take care of you two for now," the Arab said.

The dinghy pulled caddy corner to the raft. The second dinghy stood back some hundred meters, uselessly. Daniel took another picture of the rescue dinghy. While he was putting the picture in the dry bag, the Arabs began shouting frantically. The weight of the raft shifted and in one solid motion Cameron had leapt from his back to the dinghy, brandishing his M-16 in the faces of the terrified rescuers. Shouts came from the other dinghy. Sayyid, Yousef and Macalin jumped from the water and were on the dinghy in a flash. The other dinghy started back towards the ship. Cameron subdued the 3 mates by the time Sayyid and the others had joined him. Daniel was the last one to board. Macalin doubled back to grab the supplies and satellite phone. Then they steered the dinghy around towards the ocean liner.

Macalin and Yousef fired warning shots at the second dinghy. It stopped in the middle of the sea before reaching the ocean liner. They corralled the boat and boarded it, perhaps one-third of the ocean liner's crew were under their control. The ocean liner had stopped to permit the dinghies to be lowered. Now it was surrounded by its own commandeered satellite vessels. All of the hostages were transferred to one dinghy, left to remain at sea. Cameron stayed with the hostages, while Daniel and the other pirates approached the ocean liner in the second dinghy with a lone hostage. When they raised the ladder to the ocean liner, the pirates yelled for the electrified fence to be switched off. If it wasn't, they threatened to toss the mate held captive to an electrified death, and every other hostage by implication. The fences were powered down, and the hostage was the first to board. He was ordered to hang on the fence while each pirate and Daniel climbed, one at a time, over the deactivated fence. They started towards the bridge when a bullet pinged off the metal deck just before them.

Holy shit.

In the middle of a gunfight clutching a Polaroid camera.

Everyone threw their backs taut against the wall. The hostage took the opportunity to run for it.

"Let him go," Sayyid said. "He served his purpose. Yousef, you go around the other side, keep your radio on volume low. Um, Macalin you go with him. Give him cover. Daniel, you stay with me. I hope you are getting the good pictures. The pictures tell the story, yes?" Sayyid said.

Daniel nodded dumbly. This shit was too real. Sayyid wasn't even breathing heavily. His muscles were relaxed. He stood there inches out of sight of a sniper's bullet, and yet there wasn't a twitch of hesitation in his body. Cameron had said Sayyid was fearless and Daniel had witnessed it twice now. Life, to Sayyid, was a chip that on any given moment might be gambled with impunity. Daniel searched himself for any comparable purity of courage, but it wasn't there. Daniel was scared. Thoughts of how to distinguish himself from the attackers as a mere reporting journalist occupied his thoughts. Daniel wasn't eager to be slaughtered along with the pirates once matters turned intractably hostile.

There was gunfire in the distance, on the other end of the boat. Sayyid whispered into his radio. Yousef responded that they had killed two mercenaries. The last one told him there were only two gunmen, just before he died. Sayyid told Daniel to follow as they hurried along the deck, until they reached a set of stairs and ascended towards the bridge.

Yousef and Macalin were waiting for them when they arrived. The captain, first mate, and two ship hands were sitting in the corner with their arms wrapped around their knees, their hands bound in zip ties.

"Good work pirates," Sayyid said gleefully. "We have taken another ship!"

"There's still crew out there. We don't know how many," Macalin said.

"This is details. We ferret them out when we get back to Somalia. Tell Cameron the news. We get him on board along with his hostages, and then we have plenty stock for the Sheikh to bargain."

Daniel stepped around, as would a neutral observer, instinctively snapping pictures and recording mental notes to write down as soon as the photographic fodder was preserved. Sayyid instructed Macalin to help Cameron come aboard while Cameron participated via radio. Macalin set out to accomplish this.

Daniel noticed an unbound crew mate hiding in the shadows of a place where a piece of navigational equipment formerly occupied. He met Daniel with benevolent eyes and placed his index finger to his lips. At first, Daniel feared for the man, feared he might do something brazenly stupid. Then he thought, the fight for this ship isn't over. Who knows how many crew are aboard? Who knows what other plans they have for retaking the ship? Wouldn't they want the pirates to think they've won and let their guard down, before the armed resistance struck back? It seemed plausible. Besides, if Daniel told them about the hidden man he would likely be sentencing him to death. He looked away and continued taking pictures. Sayyid and Yousef relaxed a marked degree once they saw the other hostages being unloaded from the dinghy. Daniel looked in to the shadow and saw the hidden man holding a gun. Daniel gulped, jerked his gaze away quickly. He was startled to lock eyes with Sayyid.

"What is wrong, Daniel?" Sayyid asked.

"Nothing. It's just, first pirate raid, you know."

"I see. You are scared of death." Sayyid barked a hollow, sinister laugh.

The hostages were approaching the bridge, so Sayyid turned his back to unlatch the door, and Yousef was equally distracted, watching the few hostages they had caught on the bridge.

Just as Sayyid opened the door, the hidden man leapt out of the shadow, firing his pistol and striking Sayyid in the shoulder. Sayyid turned and popped the Trojan horse with a single shot through the heart. The man's handgun raked across the metal floor until it idled by the wall. The body struck the ground with a definitive thud. The room became so quiet he could hear the blood ooze from the man's body.

"Damn," Sayyid said as he glimpsed down at his arm. "The pig grazed me."

Cameron burst in the room ready to kill, disappointed to learn the action was over. Macalin shepherded the rest of the captives inside. They filled half the room.

"What happened Sayyid? One of them sneak up on you?"

"Yes, but he did not sneak up on us at all," Sayyid said, as he examined Daniel. "He knew he there, yes. Daniel was to let me die."

Yousef kicked Daniel's legs out from under him. Daniel's face smacked against the cold unwashed metal floor. Yousef rolled him to his belly and zip tied his hands behind his back, dragging him the few meters to the hostage pool, his face skidding against the ground along the way.

"Maybe you need to learn what side you want to be on," Yousef said, spitting on Daniel's face.

Sayyid did not restrain his brother. No one did.

The pirates spoke Somali, only speaking English when Cameron was concerned. This didn't appear to bother Cameron who was relaxing in the window with his rifle slung around his neck, staring out at ocean.

Sayyid finally walked over to Daniel. Daniel stared at the fabric of Sayyid's boot, from where he still lay against the metal floor.

"You would let Sayyid die."

Daniel said nothing.

Sayyid kicked him in the ribs. Again. And again. Daniel tried not to exhibit pain. He'd broken a rib. He wanted to cry, but he muffled his whimpers. He feared if Sayyid lost any composure, the pirate would squeeze Daniel's life from him.

When Sayyid let up, he craned his neck until a joint popped and he rejoined his band's conversation circle. Daniel wondered whether he would soon be for sale again at a slave auction or executed and left to rot somewhere unspeakable. He couldn't contemplate an alternative fate.

**The next day they harbored the oceanliner** off the coast of Eyl. They anchored less than an hour before an SUV pulled a boat trailer along the beach, and soon the boat was motoring towards them. There were four armed men and the fifth was dressed in white robes and dawned a red and white keffiyeh around his head and wore dark aviator style sunglasses. The man had a silky handlebar mustache and a pencil-thin goatee. The man held a black wooden cane adorned with brass handle forged to resemble a cobra. The man greeted Sayyid first. They conversed in Somali, then Sayyid spoke to Macalin. Macalin cut Daniel's zip tie loose, and beckoned him to leave the hostage pool and join them.

74

"He wants you to take pictures. Write about this," Macalin said. Daniel massaged his wrists, picking up his camera from atop navigational equipment. Sayyid stood shaking hands with the Arab, both smiling and posing, while Daniel snapped two pictures.

"This is the Sheikh," Sayyid said. "He is the investor. He runs the operation."

The Sheikh nodded with a proud smile slashed across his face.

"Come," Sayyid said. The Sheikh's men relieved Sayyid's gang from their guard duty. The Sheikh, Daniel, and the rest of the pirate gang trod out to the deck of the ship, from where the Sheikh arrived. Daniel gazed out over the beaches of Eyl. They circled the ship, inspecting its contents and conditions. The Sheikh seemed pleased to have the distinguished oil tanker in his possession. Once the cursory inspection was completed, Sayyid's band and the Sheikh lowered themselves into the Sheikh's speedboat and returned to the coast. During the ferry, Sayyid reiterated his business arrangement with the Sheikh. Sayyid and his men capture the boats, and the Sheikh pays them up front and handles the rest. Daniel scribbled the information as best he could, given the palpitations of the ocean.

Once the speedboat was beached, the Sheikh's men set about refastening it to the trailer. Meanwhile, another well-heeled man stepped out of his vehicle. He ended a phone conversation as the Sheikh approached with his bandits. The well-heeled man's wrist was handcuffed to a briefcase. The Sheikh took a key from his pocket, releasing the case from the man's care. The Sheikh thumbed the combination and opened the case. It was stuffed with $100 bills. Sayyid grinned and laughed merrily.

"A beautiful relationship it is, yes!" Sayyid said. He breathed into his hands. "The sight of it always seems new, yes!" Sayyid took the case and briefly displayed its contents to the pirate band, also all smiles, before he shut it and secured the latches.

"A ride back to our truck?" Sayyid asked, as he draped a familiar arm around the Sheikh. The Sheikh didn't strike Daniel as a man who liked to be touched, but he permitted Sayyid's advance. Sayyid was too valuable to rebuke.

"Yes, as always. But I have an invitation to extend," the Sheikh said.

Daniel was intrigued by the man's curious accent, one he had never heard. Daniel examined the man thoroughly, but discerned various elements that did not sum to a single conclusion.

"We are having a special exhibition at the Coliseum in Mogadishu. I had hoped you would accompany me as my guest of honor. We have an extravagant array of entertainment planned for the evening. Bring your new gaalo as well. We'll see no harm comes to him."

# *Eight*

"Sayyid, we're leaving," Cameron yelled across the gang's suite at the Orient Pearl. Shower water tinkled in the bathroom, and steam wafted through the cracked door. Sayyid hummed a nomadic folk song as he bathed. When Sayyid didn't reply, Daniel shrugged. Cameron was clearly frantic about missing the games. Daniel had watched him count and recount a fistful of gambling money before he filed all the faded and wrinkled bills in to a zipper bag and stuffed the bundle in his waistband. "He'll never be ready. The hotel can give him a lift."

Macalin and Yousef agreed. Macalin nodded to Daniel before the pirates disappeared in to the hallway.

Daniel had showered and dressed for the Sheikh's event some time ago, but he was obliged to wait for Sayyid. Before Sayyid stepped in the shower, he told Daniel if he left the master bedroom he could expect to have his throat slit. Today would be very important for the story, Sayyid explained. Sayyid spoke those words through the lit of a sarcastic smile, but Daniel didn't want to further antagonize the man whose life he left at risk on the *MV Sirius Star*. Between then and now, both Macalin and Cameron told stories of other slaves Sayyid had purchased to serve a niche purpose and were released once the job was complete. They shuddered at the memory of one slave's fate that failed to satisfy Sayyid's requirements. That slave, ominously enough, was a journalist. Daniel didn't probe the particulars of that story, having understood its implications. Sayyid told

Daniel once he joined them on three or four pirate raids, experienced the exploits of his private life and produced an acceptable written draft with pictures, Daniel would be permitted to return to the U.S.A. Sayyid certainly loved his freedom, and Daniel amused himself with recent memories of Sayyid's antics over the course of the previous days. He stowed all his pens and notebook in a rucksack, and started to count the number of exposures the Polaroid had remaining, when Sayyid emerged from the shower ass naked and dripping wet.

Daniel laid his camera aside and shielded his eyes with his arm.

"Could you put a towel on?"

"You are cheeky for a slave, yes."

Daniel peeked across his shielding arm to see Sayyid had pulled on a white cotton robe.

Sayyid took a silver tray loaded with khat from the mini-fridge and sat it on the bed. He sifted through the leaves until he found a near-perfect specimen, and set to work gnawing.

"Cameron," Sayyid called out.

"They've all gone."

"They leave us?"

"They called for you, but I guess it was too loud in the shower."

Sayyid appeared slightly hurt his friends had left him. Prior to the pirate raid, Daniel would have viewed that situation as an opportunity to escape, but now he was so humbled by everything that had happened since arriving in the Horn, that he wasn't up to the risk. He had no money, no bearing for how to get to the airport. He had first-hand knowledge of the magnitude of the local police brutality, and a well-founded suspicion that Sayyid had hired the hotel attendants to make certain his slave didn't lose himself again in the streets of Mogadishu. Maybe once Daniel wrote an acceptable story Sayyid would reneg on his promise to release him, but Daniel decided he would wait until he was betrayed before he risked any other avenue to return home.

Minutes later Sayyid was dressed in a loose-fitting linen shirt and tailored black slacks, as polished as Daniel had seen him.

The two rode the elevator down to the lobby and by the main entrance Sayyid asked the head valet to retrieve his Land Cruiser.

"I sorry sir, but you friends requested the truck, and leave. I thought you give permission. I won't make mistake again." The head valet wore a lapel pin that read The English School, Eastleigh, Nairobi in miniscule letters. Daniel wondered what the man studied in school, whether he had played sports, if he ever considered returning to Kenya.

"Let's no worry, yes," Sayyid said, shrugging off the opportunity to exhibit anger. "Can we get a lift to the Stadium?"

The head valet frowned once more.

"I sorry sir, but our cars all gone with guests to the Stadium. If I know the Sayyid want a car for the Coliseum, I would have drive you myself."

Sayyid strummed his fingers across the valet stand, then struck his fist through the air as if inspired by his own gestures.

"We will walk, yes," Sayyid announced.

"Sir, but you cannot walk there with time to see the spectacle."

"We not walking around the battle zone, we're walking through it, yes."

"Sir, I suggest this idea is bad," the head valet said.

Daniel nodded agreement with the head valet.

"Bullets only kill weak men, yes," Sayyid said. "And lucky for Daniel I will protect him," Sayyid said and launched into a hearty chuckle as he started out the door onto the street. Daniel looked the pirate over to see whether the pirate was strapped. Sayyid's Uzi bulged slightly underneath his white linen shirt. There was some comfort at the sight. They passed through the walled courtyard, through the opened gate with the guards at salute, and they walked along the dusty post-apocalyptic street.

"Are you sure this is a good idea?" Daniel asked, as they both sauntered along through the mixture of equatorial heat and air pollution.

"Mogadishu is my second home. I know these streets, yes. Today there be less fighting because of the event. Yes, most be watching the event or relax for day of comfort. Some will watch the line or fight, but Sayyid is meaner than anyone in Mogadishu. If they shoot at us, they shall have an event themselves, yes?"

Sayyid's logic didn't comfort Daniel. The right machine gun could mow them down before they had time to register what was happening. A sniper from a distant window could take shots at the two with impunity. The murderous pierce of a bullet could steal their lives before its heinous laughter was heard. What threat would two pedestrians present to a sniper hidden comfortably in his citadel?

They cut through a few mortar-shelled buildings, careful not to fall and cut themselves on the exposed rebar and glass and other hazards lurking in the pulverized neighborhood. The blackened, burnt up hull of an ancient Chevrolet El Dorado lay permanently situated in the middle of a street, a spontaneous monument to perpetual civil war. A desiccated dog's carcass lay huddled against the remnants of a cement wall, cooking for perhaps a third or fourth day, the few sinews of muscle left tenderized to jerky. Daniel took pictures of these scenes for the collage he would inevitably assemble; their combined force the milieu for his story.

They entered what at first appeared to be a junkyard, filled with disabled school buses, but on closer inspection Daniel realized the buses were used to transform the space in to a maze, the buses arranged to produce whimsical corridors through the field.

"This is always fun for me," Sayyid said as they wandered past the long ago looted windows of buses resting on cinderblocks, the hoods, windshields, and metal sheathes of trim removed for employment elsewhere.

The place was ideal for an ambush. A rogue assassin could be lurking anywhere; a gang of greedy burglars might be lying in wait. Having already snapped a picture of the labyrinth, Daniel pushed the camera underneath his shirt, driven by the paranoia, that to a desperate Somali the camera might be worth murder.

"Let's see, I do not remember this section," Sayyid said. He glared around bemusedly.

"Sayyid, this place is making me really uncomfortable. Can't we just go back the way we came and walk around the whole thing?"

"And not make the fun use of the maze? We beat the maze, yes."

"Sayyid this place is a death trap."

"Haha the bus maze is the last place someone hurt us in Mogadishu. Al-Shabaab build this for children. TFG and Ethiopia know this. No one would molest this place. Aw, here I remember the secret," Sayyid said as he boarded a bus. Daniel followed him inside the sweltering automotive shell. A meal could be slow cooked in the thing. They walked the length of it, where the rear emergency door was connected to another bus, and when they exited through its primary door a straight and narrow corridor greeted them.

"See, Sayyid solve this puzzle always," he said, tapping his temple.

They walked another mile until Stadium Mogadishu loomed on the horizon. Cars, horses and camels littered the periphery. Daniel snapped pictures of the tailgating, if you could call it that, men drinking from canteens fashioned from animal bladders, flavored water sipped through straws from Ziploc bags, sausages whose meat originated from unknown origins skewered over open fires, rancid belches, yelling, clamoring for tickets, a young girl squatting and shitting right in the middle of the road.

Affixed in measured increments across the peak of the circular stadium waved countless black flags of Al-Shabaab. Serious faced men brandished five-foot long belt-fed machine guns, dispersed throughout the crowd, careening backwards to support the weight of their life-snatching devices. Dogs barked everywhere. Beggars approached Sayyid for money. He distributed a few small denomination Somali shillings, to their overwhelming praise and gratitude. Sayyid smiled as they spat their flattering words at him.

They arrived at the entrance, where security was beefed to a critical mass. Armed men reclined against the galvanized gate, creating a second perimeter of flesh and threatened violence. Sayyid presented his tickets in the form of a signed letter to the gatekeeper, while the security detail eyeballed Daniel with snide reprehensibility.

The gatekeeper called for security, and a small cadre detached from the otherwise listless bunch and approached them with a certain troubling intent gleaming in their eyes. Daniel took an involuntary, frightened step backwards. He glimpsed at the scene behind him. Doubt clouded his mind. He acknowledged foot speed would be no match for the swiftness of the men's bullets.

One of the men nodded at Sayyid, and Sayyid permitted them to lead.

Daniel exhaled. They were escorts, not executioners. They entered the Stadium and Daniel found himself shoulder-to-shoulder with the full-spectrum of Mogadishian society: some men in tailored suits, others in shepherd's robes, excited teenagers in rags, throwback nineties Nike swooshes the safest symbol of conformity. Some went barefoot, while others wore thong sandals or shod their feet in tennis shoes of various conditions. A vendor sold barbequed lamb. Another bottled water. No one in sight chewed khat and the ground was remarkably devoid of the discarded stems that litter the other busy avenues of Mogadishu.

This security detachment led them up a set of stairs into a stack of Somalia's version of luxury suites. The vast remainder of Somalis sat in the open air on tiered cement bleachers. Those black flags flapped in the breeze above the crowd.

In the suite, a boisterous bunch was already in the swing of celebrating the festivities, eating on a giant roasted lamb surrounded by a variety of local vegetables. There was no alcohol in the room as Stadium Mogadishu was the headquarters of Al-Shabaab. Though Al-Shabaab quietly granted Sayyid and his band leniency to break the moratoriums imposed on them by the strict imposition of Shariah law, even Sayyid showed deference to religious law when visiting the nerve center of the quasi-government organization. By following the rules, Sayyid stayed on friendly terms with his employers.

Macalin, on the other hand, appeared to be pouring himself an illicit drink in the corner of the room from a smuggled flask, contrary to better judgment.

Yousef was talking to the Sheikh by the glassless window overlooking the Stadium. Cameron feasted on roasted lamb, sitting alone at a round table that could have hosted up to a dozen, shunned by the others because of his suspiciously colored skin.

Sayyid rushed over to the Sheikh and the affiliates clasped hands. All were in good spirits. Sayyid beckoned Daniel over to snap a picture of the duo. Daniel removed the camera from underneath his draping shirt, raised the instrument to his eye and beckoned all to strike a pose, but when he clicked the shutter there was a noticeable lack of mechanical activity. He pulled the camera from his face and turned it over in examination.

He was out of film. He said so and apologized. Sayyid and the Sheikh separated, and Sayyid began fuming.

"I bring you here to record, to document. Today is special, it does not happen but very not often. Without pictures, there is a story without belief. You not believe today without the pictures, yes."

"What exactly is the event today?" Daniel asked, realizing for the first time that everyone had been somewhat vague about the day's programming.

"Today is the blood sport, Daniel. Today they host the Roman games. There will be fights of a Somalian variety. We bet and talk yes, but today is where I wanted you to get the pictures. Without the pictures, they not believe how fun the Mogadishian can be, yes."

Sayyid scoffed and lamented and insulted Daniel some more until he grew tired of the activity and left Daniel. Sayyid reignited his enthusiasm for the day as soon as he joined another conversation circle. Daniel followed him, trying to appease the man he had so clearly upset, the man on whose whim his freedom, his very existence, hinged. He followed close by Sayyid's side, hoping to capture some good fodder for the story. He also hoped to ease Sayyid's doubts about his ambition to complete the project by standing close by and being attentive.

Once, Sayyid stopped abruptly as he moved through the room and Daniel bumped into him, causing Sayyid to slosh and spill his drink. Daniel cringed. Sayyid examined his shirt, but it was unspoiled. An ungreeted acquaintance of Sayyid's stood there speechless, fear for Daniel written in his jaundiced, dark eyes. Sayyid started to speak, but swallowed his anger. Then the pirate turned his back to Daniel and initiated a conversation with the dark eyed man.

Daniel took a deep breath. He felt like he was trying to swim to the surface from underneath a large body of water without knowing which way was up.

There came a time when a great gong sounded and a man rode out into the center of the arena standing on the bed of a smoking pickup truck and made an announcement that the games were to begin shortly. He spoke a prayer to Allah and then the truck exited the arena. Everyone took his seat in anticipation of the commencement of the first competition.

Daniel stood in the back of the room when the stadium grew quiet, and everyone watched the central court of the walled arena in rapt attention. A truck pulled in to the center and deposited a bale of palm fronds and grass. When the truck was gone, a separate gate opened. A litter of oryx, a type of antelope, with long straight horns that run diagonal from the head of the animal and point towards its tail, gradually entered the arena. They sniffed around shyly, intimidated by the man-made surroundings but allured by the bounty of food only a few meters in front of them. Tender voices commented on the beauty of the animals. Daniel locked onto a nearby conversation in English between two traditionally-robed Arabs. He discerned they had traveled from Saudi Arabia for the occasion. They speculated what would happen next. Would the oryx be the predator or the prey? Daniel started to scribble some questions and observations in his notebook when the audience erupted.

A great yellow lion emerged, strutting into the arena. The oryx stammered back towards the door from whence they had come, but that exit had long since closed. A groomed mane hung from the lion's face, its powerful haunches bulged and deflated as it moved towards the oryx with a killer's intent. Its skin wrapped tight around its ribs, the beast starved over the past few days in anticipation of the great feast. It ran its tongue along its lips. Dinner was served.

Four of the oryx huddled together against the door, whimpering, trembling. It would have been a most pitiful sight had it not been for the one, dominant oryx standing rigid in the midst of its likely destruction. The alpha buck. It would rather die than quiver in visible fear. No doubt pulled straight from the wild. The father of great progeny.

The lion stopped ten feet in front of the dominant oryx and roared. Everyone sat on the edge of their seats.

The dominant oryx lowered its head and surged at the lion.

The still more agile cat sidestepped the frontal attack and circled around, keeping the game within his visual periphery.

The rest of the oryx disentangled themselves now, looking on in disbelief at the fearlessness of one of their own. They spread out in a more sensible defensive position. Daniel thought he saw the lion take a step back. A second oryx lowered its head and surged toward the lion, but the lion had seen this attack before. The lion sidestepped again and as the less speedy oryx passed, the lion struck the oryx with its paw across its brow, slashing its razor claws across the oryx's eyes and face, down its cheek. The oryx wrested free before the lion could pierce its jugular, but judged from its chaotic jerking and tragic moaning, the oryx may have wished it had let the lion finish its work.

85

Daniel's eyes were dry because he hadn't looked away from the action, hadn't blinked. Everyone else gazed quietly, afraid if they diverted their attention even for the briefest moment, they might miss the definitive kill.

Daniel overheard the two English-speaking Arabs exchange a bet, 7-1 in favor of the lion. The Sheikh intermittently argued and shook hands and exchanged money with a counterparty sitting next to him, a Somalia, to be certain, wearing a fine navy blue silk suit but none of the traditional adornments of Islam or the area. Rather, he had the pedigree of an international businessman, but something told Daniel that the man was something less. He was the type of man who would readily attend an event such as this, among the company of terrorists and pirates.

The combination of action and audience was exciting, spontaneous and raw.

The dominant oryx darted at the lion, too quick this time for the lion to sidestep the entire attack, suffering a blow to its exposed torso. The lion stumbled backwards as the oryx quickly retreated to a safe distance. Another oryx, however, immediately bowed and bum rushed the lion again. Then again. The last oryx to enter the fray lunged gawkily forward, clumsily exposing all of its underside. The lion reached into the air and opened the oryx's belly with the ease of unzipping a windbreaker, the innards splattering out on to the ground, like dumping out a can of beans, the vital organs still vaguely attached to the vessel like balls tethered to a string.

The audience gasped and cringed. It was a ghastly sight that seemed to signify a major shift of momentum in the course of the fight. The three suddenly seemed no match against the lion, and it appeared to recover instantly from the previous blows, as if prior damage was trivial.

One of the Sheikh's agents brought him a duffle bag, and the Sheikh opened it and stacked bundles of currency on a table and shook hands with his counterparty. The Sheikh's large wager was so spectacular it distracted from the main attraction. Daniel heard the two English-speaking Arabs discuss the wager. The one who had taken the lion from the beginning said the Sheikh was out of his mind to risk such a large sum on three oryx. The other suggested that perhaps the Sheikh was privy to some information that had not been revealed to them. His friend conceded that maybe this was so.

The dominant oryx took another pass at the lion, but failed to make contact.

The oryx herded together now, gathering strength in their numbers. The V-formation appeared intimidating. Surely the lion would have to rethink its strategy.

Daniel shuddered in surprise as the lion lunged forward, into the litter of antagonistic oryx, all claws drawn. It punctured the flesh of two oryx, both of them wriggling, screaming, trying to kick but lacking the range of motion to counterattack the predator. The lion grasped on to their backs, mauling them, while their knees buckled one after the other, tumbling to the ground. The fallen oryx whined pitiful death cries.

The dominant oryx avoided the assault and stood at a safe distance, watching helplessly as the life bled from its last two comrades. They writhed on the ground while the lion continued to maul, big balls of flesh flying through the air, blood squirting everywhere. Both the oryx and the lion were painted red. The audience's cheers blended with the lion's roar as the oryx were silenced.

The dominant oryx snuffed and shuffled its feet, kicked dirt, yelling in its wild tongue. It had seen enough.

The dominant oryx galloped at the lion, who, craning to chew a piece of flesh from a deposed victim's neck, was caught off guard. The dominant oryx knocked the lion from its ken. The lion struck the cement wall, shook its head to regain composure while the oryx, squandering no advantage, rammed the lion again. And again. Like a hammer it continued to strike the disoriented lion, and the cat began leaking its own blood for the first time. The lion rolled to its back and looked as vulnerable as it had when the oryx leapt through the air with its head lowered down, neglecting to utilize its visual facilities, and the lion rolled to safety. The oryx struck the naked dirt, head first. The oryx faltered, collapsed, and stuttered to its feet once more, blinking and coughing, apparently concussed.

The Sheikh and Sayyid were cheering at the top of their lungs. The Sheikh wagged bundles of money in the air. He turned to his counterparties and doubled his bet. Daniel wasn't able to comprehend the current stakes, but he was certain they were rising.

The lion and oryx circled one another. The oryx was disoriented, the lion having nicked one of its artery. Both were battle weary. The audience was on it feet. Throughout the stadium, hands waved and were contorted into fight gestures.

"Dilo, dili, dilaan!"

The oryx leapt at the lion again. The lion stood on two feet and swung at the oryx with both claws as the oryx's head collapsed into the lion's breastbone. The lion stuck its claws in to the oryx's ribs. They fell to the ground, together, the oryx on top of the lion. Daniel looked closely, and saw the lion's front right paw entering and exiting the oryx's rib cage over and over, with the speed of a prison shanking. The oryx took a final breath and fell limp on the lion's indefatigable chest. The lion finally rolled the dead oryx off itself, triumphantly circling the arena to secure its position from any malingering survivors, then settling in to feast on the fallen torso of the dominant oryx.

Most of the crowd cheered, while those who had lost their money on the oryx slumped in their seats. The Sheikh was one of the dejected minority. The large bundles of money the Sheikh had placed on the table were raked away by the counterparty. The man being still unknown to Daniel, he couldn't help but to wonder his story.

Sayyid leaned over to comfort the Sheikh, but the Sheikh brushed him away. The Sheikh sat there sullenly for a moment. His money courier tried to garner his attention. When the Sheikh's face emerged from his hands, he dispatched the money courier, who made short shrift of returning with even more of the Sheikh's money. Daniel began to wonder where the incessant gambler secured these large sums of cash.

After the stadium crew had coaxed the lion out of the arena, a few of them dragged the oryx in to a single pile and lit them on fire.

The oryx pyre served as a sort of intermission, a time when much of the audience left their seats for a refreshment, the restroom, to stretch their legs or socialize across the stadium. The last thirty minutes had been intense, and the spectacle required a cool down period to cleanse the pallet, to reset the audience's adrenaline before the next major act.

# Nine

An employee of the stadium entered the suite and passed out programs. Initially, Daniel had thought the schedule of events was left to surprise, but after he glimpsed at the indecipherable text, he realized he had seen several of the men holding copies of the program earlier. Only he, a slave, had not been privy to the day's scheduling. He wasn't really surprised. He was, after all, still feeling out the contours and customs of the position he had found himself occupying in this strange society. Still, it would have been useful to provide the journalist with the day's itinerary, even if it was printed in Somali.

As the audience meandered back to their seats, a small fenced area was set up in a corner of the arena. Several cages of chickens were truck driven out to the mini-arena and deposited nearby. Two men, each taking a chicken by the neck, made a lap with the birds around the stadium, giving the audience a fair look at the birds. The Sheikh resumed his betting, though he did so in smaller sums. Many left their seats, having chosen to converse in the corridors rather than sit and watch cocks striking each other, with bloodied beaks, to the death.

This was the halftime show.

A cadre of men entered the suite, dressed in gaudy military uniforms with guns slung about, surrounding a man dressed in an impeccably tailored suit. The well-dressed man was escorted towards the Sheikh, where the men sitting near the Sheikh, except for Sayyid, were made to move. Daniel burrowed his way towards this meeting until he was within earshot of the discussion. They exchanged the usual pleasantries, thanks for inviting me today, no thank you for gracing me with your presence. Daniel gathered the man was the President of the Transitional Federal Government of Somalia. Daniel was rather surprised to see the two men talking cordially amongst one another, considering Al-Shabaab and the TFG were locked in a brutal civil war. Following the short exchange of pleasantries, the conversation immediately shifted towards business.

"Be that as it may," the President said. "You cannot keep with the pirate raids from TFG controlled territory. The United Nations, the community of nations will not continue to condone it."

Sayyid scowled from his seat nearby, but the Sheikh admonished his employee to hush.

"Pirating is good for us. It is good for Somalia. Now I understand it causes you some small headaches."

"It causes me massive headaches! I am trying to develop a country from dust! In two weeks' time, I have the Secretary of State of U.S.A. visiting. What will I tell him? He will ask me if I allow pirates and what will I tell him? If I say no, and he know I lie, they will give us no funding. What pirates make a year is a drop in the bucket compared to friendly U.S. aid."

"A desert lark in the hand is worth two in the scrub," the Sheikh said.

"What are you talking about?" The President asked.

The Sheikh called over his money courier, and at a sprint the man had returned with a stack of manila envelopes, bundles of the Sheikh's money bursting from within.

"I cannot take this. This is graft!"

"It is tax dollars. I pay you tax dollars for our operations. No one calls this graft. Now you can build a school or pay a doctor. I do not know what you do with these tax dollars because it is beyond my business," the Sheikh said with a wink, his attention circling the vicinity, expecting everyone to nod in agreement with his statement. Everyone did, except for the President's guards who stood at attention, expressionless.

The President acted infuriated, but a plain-clothes associate of his leaned in, whispering in his ear. The President not only calmed down, but listened with grave attention. Only then, the associate backed away.

The President turned to the Sheikh.

"One day the piracy will have to end if Somalia is ever to be taken seriously."

"On that day of appointment, my piracy will end. You have my word," the Sheikh said.

The two equals stood and bowed to one another before shaking hands. Then the President and his cadre of security escorts left.

What a strange meeting. Weird he thought mere graft strange in the midst of all this, but still. He seriously wondered whether or not the President had sincere misgivings about taking the money. In a country with few bright lines, whether it was a bribe or a tax payment hinged on what the money was spent on. He also wondered whether the conversation had been a routine colloquy or a serious discussion that might have ended any other way.

The series of cockfights commenced and ended and even more bundles of the Sheikh's money were carted away by the counterparty. The man, who no doubt usually enjoyed fruitful investments, was becoming rankled at his mounting losses. His agent brought him a duffle bag with a quantity of money approximating his entire losses up to that point. Then the Sheikh and the counterparty began their negotiation.

Fierce speculating filled the room. Daniel sought out the two English-speaking Arabs, who had served as his window into the action, but they'd abandoned their seats. His curiosity hit such a height that he finally caved and tapped Sayyid on the shoulder and asked him. Sayyid winced when he turned to see his disobedient, incompetent little slave pestering him. Daniel spoke softly and made it quick.

"What's next?"

"Elephant fights."

"Aren't elephants endangered?"

"No," Sayyid said and scoffed. "They overpopulate the Somalia. This fight is a service, yes."

"Oh."

Sayyid's face relaxed. Thank God. Most others' attention diverted to the large bet the Sheikh was placing on the table.

"You like to know a secret, yes?"

"Of course."

"The Sheikh knows one of the elephant has suffer an internal injury. The other is given a narcotic to make brave, yes. He, how do you say, hustle this other man," Sayyid said, chuckling. Sayyid clasped his hand on Daniel's shoulder. Daniel trembled a bit, half expecting one of the violent blows he knew Sayyid capable of, but Sayyid didn't harm him, and Daniel's adrenaline subsided as he realized Sayyid's hostility towards him was thawing.

A cheer erupted. Both turned, watching the Sheikh and his counterparty shake hands, a mountain of bundled cash stacked on top of the table.

"The Sheikh bet $250,000 USA dollars on the red elephant," Sayyid said.

It was an astonishing sum to have bet in Mogadishu, a city where a million people live on $1 a day. It was equivalent to the annual income of 685 people.

There was some scrambling around, people gathering snacks and drinks until a conch horn echoed throughout the stadium, and everyone in attendance rushed to find his seat. It became apparent this was the big event, the spectacle of spectacles. The Sheikh had manipulated a wealthy gambler into accepting a large bet on the last contest of the day, and now thanks to some tampering stood to win double what he had lost throughout the course of the preceding minor skirmishes. It was a classic hustle.

One of the doors to the arena was opened and a tusked elephant painted blue gaited out in to the arena. Everyone greeted the mighty beast with their bellows and cheers. The enormous beast stood still in the center of the arena, overtop the exact place where the oryx carcasses had been burnt and subsequently scraped away.

The crowd stilled. The opposite gate jostled, then flung open. The red elephant charged out, to the adulation of the crowd. Even from where Daniel stood, he saw the blood vessels cracked in the red elephant's eyes. It was breathing deep, heavy breathes. The mortal combatants locked eyes. The collective heartbeat of the audience sped to a sprinter's pace.

Daniel could not believe what he was seeing. But sight these days seemed like a debunked theory that no longer possessed its predictive power. It didn't matter whether he could adequately process the information around him or not. All of his senses told him this was happening. He scribbled down this thought and tried to turn his mind for more insight, certain it was there, if he could just dig and haul it to the surface of his consciousness.

The elephants circled one another, then the red elephant charged. Before they collided, they both rose on their hind legs and locked trunks. The red elephant disentangled its right front foot from the mess, and began punching the blue elephant in the face. Daniel couldn't believe his eyes. He had no idea elephants fought like that.

The red elephant struck the blue elephant until it lost its balance and toppled to the ground with a quaking thud that was felt throughout the stadium. The red elephant, rather than seize the advantage, immediately returned to two feet and let loose a battle cry. The beast was a true showman. Daniel was beginning to surmise it had been assiduously trained to compete in this spectacle. The untrained and drug free blue elephant didn't stand a chance against this conditioned war machine.

The blue elephant recovered its feet and bawled a rebuttal war cry.

The bleachers were on the verge of exploding.

Daniel understood well why Sayyid had been disappointed he expended the film prematurely. This scene was epic. This was the type of D-batteries in a sock journalism the people would pay for and buzz about back home. Without the Sayyid connection, a journalist couldn't just casually scalp a ticket outside the stadium and settle in to the bleachers to enjoy the day's entertainment. It was being held at Al-Shabaab headquarters. This entertainment was presented for the benefit of insiders alone, a company outing. Daniel hoped to God that Sayyid had exaggerated the scarcity of such events, hoped he would be able to photograph similar spectacles on a future day. Judged by the hysteria of the spectators, however, he doubted he should see such a show again. He had the impression the event was just as new to the audience as it was to him.

The blue elephant and red elephant locked trunks again, braced on all fours, engaged in some sort of illogical tug of war, wrestling for position, both pushing and pulling and trying to determine where or how the adversary might submit.

The blue elephant released its grip and tried to take a step back, but the red elephant charged it relentlessly. The red elephant smacked its opponent with its trunk, before lunging forward with its right front foot, punching the blue elephant on the nose. Blood oozed from the brow of the elephant, bisecting its eye and filtering across its cheek, dripping on the ground.

The crowd roared, could not have been more elated.

The red elephant turned away from its adversary to bathe in the crowd's adulation. Perhaps it wasn't as well disciplined as he had thought. The red elephant exposed its broadside to the blue elephant, and the blue elephant leapt to its feet in a furious start and smashed its ivory tusks into the red elephant's ribs.

The red elephant shrilled, trotted away and turned to face its adversary. The skin hadn't been pierced by the jolt. Daniel's vision wasn't what it once was, but he could have sworn he saw the red elephant spit flecks of blood. Perhaps the red elephant had suffered some internal damage. But maybe the blood was from the blue elephant or wasn't blood at all.

The red elephant, without warning or fear for its own safety, lunged its ivory tusks at the head of the blue elephant, striking it in the face in an apparent attempt to blind it.

96

He missed, however, and the blue elephant quickly snaked its trunk around the red elephant's left ivory tusk, penning its trunk underneath. The blue elephant leveraged its position and began punching the red elephant in the face with those large parkbench fists. The red elephant heaved to escape, but each time it tugged to get away, the blue elephant just pounded it back down.

The crowd roared.

The red elephant struggled to escape, but finally fell limp, unconscious.

The cheers deafened the air. The blue elephant reversed, then sprinted forward and lunged with its right tusk towards the skull of the red elephant when the fallen stammered to its feet and pushed the blue elephant to the ground. The red elephant maneuvered on top of the blue elephant, and started stomping it into a non-entity. It stomped and stomped. Occasionally it would direct a shot to either the face or a weakened rib. It penned the blue elephant down with its great trunk.

There was an element of certainty, of finality to the moment. The Sheikh was grinning for all in the suite to see, palms open reaching for the sky, grasping for the treasures awaiting him in heaven. Everyone talked rapidly with his eyes locked on the death show.

The red elephant was dancing, pattering those great feet with tons of force on its brother's poor broken body. Then it howled to the sky. Its feet went motionless. Without warning or cause, the red elephant collapsed to the side of its brother.

The quiet chattering around grew increasingly hushed as suspicions raised. The red elephant just lied there. The blue elephant gradually hobbled to its feet. At first it started away, but once it met a cement wall and perhaps remembered there was no escape, it returned to its fallen brother. The blue elephant raised its mighty right foot and hurled it down like Zeus's lightning, splitting the skull and splattering the red elephant's brains across the dirt battleground.

There was silence, followed by a polite, subdued applause.

The Sheikh threw off his keffiyeh, revealing a mostly baldhead adorned with long erratic tufts of greasy black hair. He pulled at these tufts and screamed in to the sky like a mad man who's lost the object of his monomania.

"Aiiiiiiiii! Fuck Noloshayada!"

The Sheikh's counterparty began gathering the mountain of currency notes.

"No, no," The Sheikh yelled, rushing to stop the man. He pulled the man's hands away from the table. The counterparty stood back, security uncertain of how to react because despite the Sheikh's social standing in the stadium, it appeared that a bet should still be honored. Security was conflicted by custom on the one hand, and the Sheikh's power on the other. Daniel watched as the Sheikh's wishes were repelled by the limit of his authority. Sayyid wrapped an arm around the Sheikh and beckoned him to accept the loss of his wagers with honor. The Sheikh was feisty for a moment but under the further restraint of Sayyid, he eventually regained his cool. Once he was calm, Sayyid released him and the Sheikh touched up his robes and delicately wrapped his keffiyeh around his head and face.

"One more bet," the Sheikh asked.

"But the day's events are over. There is no further spectacle for us to bet," the counterparty said.

"Then we shall make one." The Sheikh briskly walked to the window where he surveyed the greater arena, before his attention magnetized on Daniel. Daniel gulped and took a step back, wondering why his impulse to hide had failed him.

"We'll bet on the white man," the Sheikh said. Daniel searched about for the exit, but two large armed security detail quickly took him by either arm and lifted him from his feet.

"This is my slave, yes. He cannot serve his purposes for me if he is dead," Sayyid said. Daniel was disheartened by the lack of conviction in Sayyid's tone.

"If he dies, I will pay you double for him."

"I pay $10,000 for him, yes." Sayyid fixed his eyes hard on Daniel. A calmness, and acceptance of circumstances overcame Daniel. He laughed to himself. From day one, he had never seriously thought he would escape Somalia alive. An immediately approaching death would merely release him from weeks and months of cruelty and horror of being trapped in Somalia.

"Ok, $20,000 for the slave," the Sheikh said.

Cheers roared in the suite.

Soon the loud speaker made an announcement. Daniel had no idea what the announcement said, but he assumed it said that the Sheikh was providing bonus entertainment.

Soon, Daniel was being dragged down the stairs, retching along the way as spectators stood in crowds trying to catch a glimpse of him, some cheering, some hissing and booing, until he was led down a dark private corridor, into the underbelly of the arena, where he was taken into a preparation room. The expansive basement was lined with a wall of cages, and he was left in the first one empty. It stunk of a decrepit barn. The audience clambered with an excitement on the bleachers above him that shook the roof and the very foundations of Stadium Mogadishu. Far from Daniel on the opposite side of the macabre hall was a wall of game's tools: shovels, swords, shields, various harnesses, and rakes. All of it dangling uselessly out of arm's reach. Daniel was at a loss to determine how to perpetuate his own survival as he struggled to think at all. The terror was shutting off his ability to think.

Soon a rather muscular man was led to a cage, just down from Daniel, with one empty cage separating them. The man looked raw, more like a beast of the sands than a human being. Like a dumb oxen that only knew how to complete a single task. He stood with his face toward Daniel, peering across the lone empty cage. Daniel could see him breathing heavily. The man wanted to kill him, to crack his arms from his torso and bash him over the head with them. Daniel didn't know how to protect himself. He didn't know how to fight. Perhaps if he had taken the time to learn Somali, he might have bluffed the man into submission, or otherwise talked his way out of the situation. But it was too late for learning. He laughed at the possibility he might have ever learned a language as complex and foreign as Somali. If this was it, then why not laugh?

"Quit laughing like a lunatic, yes," Sayyid said, materializing in the staging room.

"Sayyid, please. You've got to call this off," Daniel said. But Sayyid was accompanied by the Sheikh, the counterparty, a cadre of security, and Cameron. The Sheikh and the counterparty began discussing the contestants in Somali. Daniel was examined first. Then the gamblers strolled down to examine the other specimen. Cameron was the only one to linger by Daniel's cage.

When he thought no one was looking, Cameron beckoned Daniel to lean in close and handed him a sharpened piece of scrap metal, a shank.

"Gotta look out for our own skin in this country," Cameron said, tapping the flesh on his arm. Then he winked at Daniel and strolled on to the black man's cage. Daniel quickly tucked the shank in his waistband. Cameron must have bet on me, he thought with a wicked, subdued smile.

In front of the black man's cage, the Sheikh and his counterparty shook hands in agreement. Sayyid strutted back to Daniel's cage.

"The Sheikh has placed his wager on the Somali. It has been determined that since you are a runt, you be given the advantage of a staff to even the fight, yes."

One of the Sheikh's cadre of security approached Daniel and presented him with a five-foot shepherd's staff. It was sturdy enough to fend off his opponent's blows, if not too bulky to make it a clumsy weapon. Daniel wasn't certain the staff would save him. He wasn't certain it would even the odds at all. He wished to God he spoke Somali so he could confess both how weak and unprepared he was.

One by one, Daniel and his adversary were led to opposite sides of arena's staging area, to wait by a large door that could only lead to the battleground. Daniel stealthfully checked to make sure the shank was secure. It was. The sting of the cold, jagged metal gave him some relief. Still, he wasn't prepared. No one ever told him murder was a prerequisite to being a journalist. He was no longer covering the story; he was the story.

He wasn't sure he had the spirit to kill. His thoughts drifted to Bally, who always occupied some corner of his mind. At least she wouldn't be here to see him murdered in front of thousands, after having not even put up a fight. Then again, a spectacle like this *would* be something to go viral on the Internet. Perhaps those in attendance would be the first to see it, before it was watched on computers around the world.

The large gate was flung open, and Daniel was admonished by a gang of men to walk out on to the battleground. Boos and hisses struck him from the bleachers on all sides.

"Dilo nin gaalo!"

He looked up at the suite where he formerly sat. He saw the Sheikh, sitting in the front by the window, leering down at him. He wished he had helped himself to some of the roasted lamb. He could have used the energy. He should have assumed, that sooner or later, he would be locked in a death struggle.

A gate on the opposite side the arena flung open. Daniel clinched his staff. His adversary, a native Somali, sauntered out in to the sun to the roar of an admiring crowd. The muscles of his unclothed torso bulged, his sweat glinting in the light. His pearl white smile was demonic, far too pleased to be instants removed from either killing or being killed.

The adversary's fanfare dwindled and the chant recommenced:

"Dilo, dili, dilaan!"

The adversary started in a sprint at Daniel. Daniel held the staff over his right shoulder like it was a baseball bat. He had never been very good at baseball, however, and he started his swing too late, so that the man had ample opportunity to form tackle him, hugging his legs, lifting him to the sky before hurtling him towards the ground. Daniel bounced twice before his body came to a sore rest. The man stood and entreated the crowd to cheer louder. With the crowd's interest at its apogee, the adversary turned to Daniel and signaled for him to stand. Daniel scratched around for the staff, but it laid a good ten feet from where he splayed across the battleground. He shimmied his stomach to feel the shank still lodged in his waistband. He hobbled to his feet, the shank giving him an illusion of confidence.

The adversary charged at Daniel again. Without the staff, Daniel simply covered his head with his arms. The adversary dispatched Daniel back to the ground with a clothesline. Daniel tasted the dirt in his mouth, that dry earthen and eternal taste. The substance he came from and to which he would soon return. He wished he could have seen Bally just one more time. Told her how he felt. Even if he had failed, well, he should have reasoned that in death, everything fails.

Daniel cringed when the adversary rolled him to his stomach. He thought that was that. But the adversary began spanking Daniel on his ass. The crowd erupted in laughter.

The adversary was going to humiliate him first.

The adversary alternated between spanking and stiff concussive blows to the skull.

Daniel thought he heard a female voice call out, "stop the fight," in an English tongue, but he wasn't exactly blessed with the leisure of surveying the crowd to match a face to the voice of his sole supporter. Blood bubbled from his skull. The man was battering his ribs now, too, making it last, prolonging the inevitable. He felt something loosen inside him that wasn't supposed to loosen. His consciousness became spotty. The camera reel was beginning to skip slides. The adversary bent down and bit a chunk out of Daniel's neck, narrowly missing an artery. Then he resumed pummeling Daniel in the ribs.

The adversary was his chaperone to Hades.

After one of the blows, Daniel felt the shank pinch his stomach. How could he keep forgetting he had it there? He hadn't known what he would do with it, but now it was quite clear. Daniel had no more mercy to dole out.

"Dilo nin gaalo!"

The adversary laughed along with the crowd, spanking Daniel's ass. The mixture of laughter and death orders was the most frightening opera he had witnessed. An orchestra of demons played their scythes, maces, and knives to a crescendo, anticipating the imminent outer-body experience of Daniel Barnes.

Everything turned red, and he heard only sirens. As the man's spanking hand left his butt, Daniel reached for the shank and rolled on top of him and shoved the blade deep in to his adversary's gut, then again between a set of ribs. Daniel gritted his teeth, twisting the knife into the man's breastbone.

The adversary cringed as if something had been released from him that could never be recaptured. The crowd grew quiet with uncertainty. Hovering above his adversary, Daniel spat his own blood on the man's, still twisting the knife in his ribs. Daniel's expiration of bloody mist increased to a steady trickle. The cacophony of spectators roared once more. Daniel's vision went black. Then all he could hear was his own breathing. Then there was nothing.

# Ten

"Stop the fight," Caitlin yelled.

The Somali spanked him, exhorting the crowd to cheer him on as he intermittently battered and humiliated the white man. Then the Somali straddled the white man with the intent to finish the ordeal.

"Stop the fight!"

Most around her spoke no English, were unmoved by her words, but a couple of men glanced her way. Were they suspicious? She pulled her robes tight, nervous she be discovered a woman in a man's world. Still, it was the climax of the fight and everyone's attention was magnetically attracted to the death struggle. A shock rang out through the crowd when the white man rolled to the top of the Somali, thrusting what appeared to be a concealed knife into the man's ribs. Blood shot through the air like oil spouting from a derrick. Silence fell over the crowd as the white man twisted the blade with a heave of his whole body. Even from where she sat at a great distance, in the silence she thought she heard the Somali's ribs crack. The white man's entire body was covered with maroon syrup. Then he just crumpled against the ground, exhausted.

Her medical training instinct betrayed her. She raced down the steps, jumping the fence, sprinting across the arena. In triage, she reflexively allocated her energies where they might provide the most benefit. On closer examination, the Somali was certainly going to die. The white man had stuck him with the knife in the heart. The puncture wound to the heart only precipitated the pace of blood loss, rhythmically squirting with what few heartbeats remained.

She turned to the white man. His injury was not as major as the Somali's, but he was badly beaten and rather lifeless. Bruised all over. Concussed, no doubt. He might even enter a coma, if he wasn't given adequate treatment immediately. She checked his vitals. They were weak but present. She positioned his limbs to assist the flow of blood throughout his body, and stroked a caring hand through his scrub of greasy hair.

A gang of men, lead by a muscular Somali, shadowed over her. They grabbed her by the arms and snatched the white man from the ground, one of them carrying his depleted body in his arms. She screamed and shouted to be let go, to let her to treat him. But the muscular arms were too much. She eventually quieted down. There was little she could have done to treat the white man without proper facilities and medical instruments.

The gang led her and the injured white man to a Land Cruiser, parked in a well-guarded parking area. She felt mild relief to note the presence of another burly white man in their presence, but when she looked to his eyes for comfort, he gave none. They all packed in to the vehicle and sped away from the emptying stadium.

The driver scolded the rider in the front seat, but the other two men, including the burly white man were silent. She couldn't quite make out what they were saying because she had trouble focusing on their conversation. Too much of her attention was fixed on the ailing white man.

When all grew quiet it donned on her to be worried for her safety. Who were these men? Why did they take her? Where were they taking her? She couldn't recall being this anxious in her life. Images of rape and murder flashed through her mind. The white man's cold demeanor, the one sitting next to her, seemed to confirm her greatest fears. They were going to forcibly fuck her then lop her head off without a gram of remorse, before moving on to other recreation.

# *Eleven*

Caitlin was tremendously, though not completely, relieved when they arrived at the modernly trimmed Orient Pearl Hotel. The valet showed an excessive amount of deference to the Land Cruiser's drive, and the other hotel attendants made quick work of delicately gathering the body of the bruised white man.

"Where are you taking him?" She asked.

"He is a friend of ours, yes. You are a nurse, yes? Then you will come care for him," the muscular black man said, definitively.

"Now wait just a minute. You and your friends practically kidnapped me. I need more of an explanation," she was saying when the burly white man who had rode in the Land Cruiser wrapped a bulging arm around her, and slapped his palm over her mouth.

"Practically. *Practically?* I assure you, you are very kidnapped," The black man laughed. "You will learn to talk with some lady manner, yes."

They rode the elevator to the top floor of the hotel. As before, she continued to be bound at the wrists. The white man led her down the long corridor, in to the palatial suite, tossing her forward on to a bed. She reared around like a cat to face her assaulter, ready to defend her dignity. But the burly white man just laughed. Then he told the attendants to place the injured white man on the bed next to her. The black man, the driver, walked in to the bedroom.

"My name is Sayyid. This man who lay here is Daniel. He was made to fight today, but not by me. He is, he become a friend of mine. You are nurse, so you care for him, yes." Sayyid said. Then the bedroom door closed and what sounded like the fixing of chains and a lock on the other side rattled before footsteps led away from the bedroom and a soft conversation could be heard in the distance.

She instinctively turned to the white man, Daniel. How had he ended up here and gotten mixed up with the heathen crew? And who were they to be able to afford such opulence in Mogadishu? These questions would have to remain unanswered while she applied her attentions to caring for this poor, battered man. As she examined him closer, she determined he was somewhat attractive, in a damaged sort of way. He was more of a man than those granola-fed doctors back at the WHO compound, anyway.

**Daniel awoke several hours later**, at night, to find himself alive and comfortably tucked in to a bed among the familiar trappings of the Orient Pearl. He heard breathing. Someone else was in the room. He worriedly searched the room, still traumatized from the death struggle he was rather certain had occurred on his last consciousness, when he spotted a WASP'y angel slumbering on a settee in the opposite corner of the room. The light in the room was dim, but from what he could tell she had fair skin, freckles, hypnotizing blonde hair, and an abundant chest. He wrested a hand free from the covers and felt for what was blocking the pores on his forehead. It was a bandage. He shimmied where he lie to sense that he had similar bandages stuck to multiple areas of his body. He felt a row of makeshift stitches on his left forearm and wondered where else on his body had required such attention. It was nearly a moment for celebration just to be able to wiggle all of his appendages and feel them present, blood circulating, a working central nervous system. The elation at having his entire body intact momentarily overcame his feelings of guilt at having taken another man's life to preserve his own.

The woman began to rouse, disturbed by the commotion on the other end of the room. She opened those big blue-green eyes and peered at him, without moving at first, then she stretched her limbs and gradually careened forward until she was on her feet and standing over him. She seemed to be studying him.

"Are you the one that patched me up?"

"Not voluntarily," she said. She laid the back of her hand against an uncovered swath of his forehead, then repeated the procedure on herself.

"Who are you?"

She took two defensive steps back.

"Who are you? Your friends kidnapped me and locked me in this room with you. I—I don't feel inclined to provide you with any more information about myself."

"Listen," Daniel whispered. "I'm a journalist. I was kidnapped, I don't honestly know how long ago. I was sold and eventually ended up in the hands of these pirates."

"*Pirates*," she shrieked.

"Shhh!" He sat bolt upright in the bed. "The phone," he whispered. She jolted across the room, before remembering she had earlier tried this herself.

"It's dead. I mean it isn't connected. They've locked us in here. That's what I was trying to tell you. I was at the Stadium. When you were injured I rushed to help you."

"How are you here now? How do you know them?"

"They grabbed me when they grabbed you. They brought me back here. The one, Sayyid, told me to care for you. He gave me a first-aid kit, and they locked me in. I patched you up as best I could."

"Who are you if you aren't with them?"

"My name is Caitlin. I work for WHO, the World Health Organization."

Daniel leaned back, the pain from his battered body testing his awareness.

"What are you, a spy?"

"I'm a doctor," Caitlin said, her voice tinged with annoyance.

"Oh right. That's the best news I've heard in a while."

"You were seriously kidnapped?"

"I came here to get a story on Somalian pirates. My sailboat to Eyl was seized by a group of unscrupulous third wave pirates, and I was sold to some sheepherders in the hinterlands. Then they sold me to a slave auction. Sayyid picked me up there. He's been relatively kind to me, that is until he let his boss talk him into having me be the bonus entertainment."

"Will they—hurt me?"

"I don't know. They beat up on me occasionally, but it's usually retributive. I've managed to put them in harms way a couple of times. You know, when I aim to escape. But will they rape you? I honestly haven't seen them around women."

She threw herself onto the chair, sobbing and trembling. Daniel jumped to his feet, walking across the room on trembling legs. He put one arm around her and stroked her head.

"I shouldn't have said that. I don't think you're in danger, but I mean this is Somalia and you must have appreciated the dangers before you came here."

She cried some more and Daniel had no further words to comfort her. He had spoken the truth, but false promises of safety weren't going to keep her safe. She needed to know she should remain vigilant. She needed to be aware of the danger so she could protect herself.

A telephone rang in the other room, which got Caitlin's hopes up. Daniel saw this and realized how naïve she was. He actually winced at her misplaced optimism.

"I would settle in," Daniel said.

"My people will be looking for me. The WHO has connections all over Somalia."

"I wouldn't count on it."

The chains rattled on the other side of the door, and Sayyid entered the room.

"Doctor Caitlin Cordon," Sayyid said.

"How do you know?"

Sayyid held up her WHO identification badge.

"You will not stay here long. This is my favor to you for fixing my property, yes. But a girl like you should know better than to wander in to dangerous events, yes! Now. I will ask of you one small favor before I return you to your work."

"What?" Caitlin asked. Daniel noticed her wringing her hands behind her back, fearing the worst.

"We have ay, um, hos-pit-all that we would like for you to visit. There are many sick and wounded there, yes. You can help them."

Daniel was as surprised as Caitlin appeared to hear Sayyid's request.

"Why don't you just bring them to the WHO hospital?"

"This is a good question, yes," Sayyid said, stuyding her. "The answer is difficult, but for you to understand these people have religion that they do not believe in Western doctor or they have too much hate for the West to use the service. But if you come to this hospital, we not tell them about the West, yes? They ask question, you just let me explain you a jewel eyed Muslim or something. You won't mind this."

"If that's the bargain, then I would be obliged to help as much as I can."

"I'm going too," Daniel said, standing, haphazardly this time, deprived of energy. When was the last time he'd eaten?

"After all this Daniel, you disappoint me again, yes."

"What? Why?"

"You think if you go to the hospital you can escape, yes? You believe you find exitman."

"No I thought I might get some proper medical treatment."

Caitlin shot him a sour a look.

"You know what I mean," Daniel said, alternating his attention between Caitlin and Sayyid. "I need X-rays. Plus I'm in a lot of pain. I need Vicodin. I'm dehydrated. There I could get an IV."

111

Sayyid examined Daniel suspiciously.

"What are these things you speak of? You try to trick me? This not a modern hospital full of English doctors, this is a sick ward full of the suffering. You will find no modern conveniences there, this is the reason for the doctor to come, yes."

"All the same, I'd like to go." Daniel could see Sayyid was about to call enough with Daniel's requests, when Daniel summoned a trump card. "I'd like go for the story. You know, show the public service angle. Tell the Americans what a good guy you are."

Sayyid scratched his chin. Daniel had never seen him do this before. Sayyid stared out the window while he scrubbed those chin whiskers.

"Ok. If there is extra care for you to a have, then you get it. I take you because you fight well, not because you are a good journalist. You are a bad journalist, Daniel. How do you make my story without film?"

"Maybe you could get me some more film?"

"Need need need. IV. Vicodin. Film. *Cameron*," Sayyid yelled his comrade's name. Cameron appeared in the doorframe. "Daniel has hurt himself. You see this. Do you need all your back pills?"

Cameron disappeared, reemerging a few seconds later, tossing Daniel a rattling pill bottle.

"Three of those and you won't feel anything Dannyboy," Cameron said.

"Thanks," Daniel said.

"Now you have pills. Now you have no need to go to hospital."

"That's not true. Get me some film and I can take. . ."

Sayyid interrupted him.

"I get you film, you waste it on dead dogs and old cars. What to take picture for? Do you even know how to write a story? Maybe if you tell me an agreeable story I will take you to the hospital. Otherwise, I may decide you are not able to piece a story at all."

Sayyid fingered the grip of his pistol.

Daniel swallowed hard.

112

"I'll tell you a story," Daniel started. "There was a flock of sheep that was terrorized by wolf attacks. It came to pass that one sheep's lover died in one of these attacks, and at her funeral her lover vowed to stand up to the wolf, to protect the sheep, even if it meant his death. Either way, he would not live another moment in fear. When the wolf next attacked, the brave sheep threw a lucky punch and killed the wolf. The flock celebrated him as a hero. Shortly thereafter, however, the hero sheep was killed in retaliation by a gang of wolves, who attacked and killed multiple sheep. After the sheep had had time to calm and bury their dead, they determined to fight back, to seek out the wolves and kill them. The clumsy sheep blundered at first, but became increasingly apt at killing wolves the longer they hunted. Over time, the wolves began to flock together and cowered at the sight of a single sheep. The sheep grew fangs and claws and their once white coats turned matte black for stealth, and the scared wolves lost their will to sharpen their fangs and claws, and their coats turned white and fluffy from fear. Eventually, it no longer made sense to call the sheep 'sheep,' and the wolves 'wolves,' because their roles were reversed, so that the two different animals switched names."

"Is that it?"

"Yes," Daniel said, his voice trembling.

Sayyid leaned forward, gripping his pistol and leering at Daniel until the man appeared sufficiently terrorized, then relaxed. "The story you tell is acceptable. I will send for film, then we go to the hospital together." Sayyid turned to walk out of the room. "One thing Daniel. The stories you will hear at the hospital will be much worse than the destruction of a flock of sheep. You will hear the loss of entire families, villages. Of people harmed not in rage but tortured for entertainment. You will see new horrors. Are you sure you would trouble yourself with this? For you, I give this choice."

Daniel looked at the handsome doctor, and coupled his lightning bolt interest in her with his own hopes of escape.

"Yes, I'm sure."

113

"Good. Also, Daniel, do not let us forget who is the sheep and who is the wolf. There will be no trading names for you."

**The place Sayyid took them** was more an impoverished hospice than a hospital. Denizens sprawled all along the outside wall of the mighty cement and steel structure. Signs of previous shellings and small-arms attacks were present, but it stood erect with a poise that suggested it suffered no fatigue. It was a building constructed to endure ages. Still, a lack of maintenance left the fortress reduced to a state of squalor. Bloody bags, feces, possibly severed human body parts were discarded through the windows. They passed through the entrance to enter a long hallway lined with army cots squeezed in along both walls, the sick and dying moaning in the shadows. A couple of nurses worked with the sick, taking their time as they moved between patients. The nurses seemed little concerned. Most of these people looked like they were reclining to board an arriving flight to the afterlife. Daniel saw a gauze lying in a baseball-sized cavern on a young girl's leg, soaking up blood and puss, no doubt infested with bacteria. The sight made him want to retch. Daniel searched the length of the hallway, earnestly wondering when the spectacle of horrors might come to an end, perhaps they would stop in an office or sanitary compartment of the building.

Sayyid saw Daniel casing his surroundings.

"Do not think of escape, Daniel. This is a facility of Al-Shabaab. There is no escape here. If you leave my side, I will put a bullet in your brain. Now there is suffering enough without me having to keep watch of you, so no make me mind you of these threats. My heart aches here too badly for," Sayyid trailed off as he leaned down and addressed a man, who was jaundiced and very ill although the cause of his illness was not readily apparent. While Sayyid and the man conversed, the Doctor gave the man a cursory examination. Daniel stepped back, framed and snapped a picture. While the two were with the man, a Somali in a white coat approached them, and Sayyid stood, greeting the man with deference. Then he introduced Caitlin to the white-coated man, who was the chief of the hospital and its only doctor. Caitlin and the chief struck up a conversation immediately, and the chief had a nurse bring Caitlin some medical instruments and supplies, so that she might divide some of his day's work and make some rounds on her own. Neither of them wasted time getting to work, as the situation was chaotic; new patients were continually rolling in to the facility. Others, the helpless, were given a dose of pain medication and sent away to die at home.

While the doctors worked, Sayyid ambled in to the area where the children were grouped. It was a slightly cleaner section of the facility than the rest, fresh cream paint stuck on the walls and more sunlight penetrating through the cleaned windows. The children cheered a bit when it was understood he was a pirate. Daniel remembered Sayyid's chief purpose for employing him, to make the pirate famous like Kobe Bryant. In a country like Somalia where organized sports are few and celebrity idiosyncratic, a successful and wealthy pirate could attain the status of an icon. Sayyid was strong, brave and happy. He was all too ready to spend some time brightening the day of these children, away from indulging his own hedonistic pleasures.

Daniel took pictures of Sayyid going to the children's beds, hoisting a smaller one to the sky, so she could see the horizon from the Sayyid mast. He told a tall tale of defeating a foreign navy in a battle at sea. When Sayyid started to part their company, the children cried out in a plea for him to stay, but he assured them that if they paid him a happy goodbye he would return soon and perhaps even with a present.

"Nabadeey!" They yelled with crescent smiles stretched across their faces.

Daniel naturally assumed they would be leaving, but Sayyid ventured in to another wing, this one housing the elderly. He knelt down beside a select number of them and prayed a Muslim prayer for deliverance from poor health, strife, and a future filled with happiness.

Daniel took more pictures.

Sayyid finally returned to the main hall and thanked Caitlin for tending to so many, but informed her that it was time they go because he had other appointments and he wanted to honor his agreement and return her to WHO. The chief walked from the other side of the long corridor to say farewell to Sayyid, when Sayyid presented the man with a bundle of U.S. currency wrapped in a rubber band.

"For supplies," Sayyid said, summarily.

Sayyid was beginning to write the story himself. He wasn't just an open-sea thug. The man was a robin hood. In a country with little other opportunity, he hadn't chosen to be a highway robber; the situation in Somalia had chosen his profession for him. Daniel flipped to a clean notebook page, held it to the wall, and scribbled these thoughts and other descriptive observations for inclusion in his story. Sayyid was turning out to be more than a one-and-out article: this was book material.

As they reached the main entrance, a kindly old imam entering and striking up a conversation with Sayyid, although Sayyid kept looking out at his Land Cruiser and looking at the clock mounted on the wall behind the imam. The imam began by cross-examining Sayyid, condemning Al-Shabaab but admitting they did a good thing by maintaining the hospital, as retched as it was, but soon the chief was in the conversation as well and he showed the donation Sayyid had made and explained that Sayyid had brought along another doctor to assist in medical care for the day and a reporter who was writing a story on Sayyid and Somalia. The imam drew Daniel aside and told him that Islam did not approve of Al-Shabaab, that Al-Shabaab was the curse not the solution to the strife in Somalia. He said that it was heresy for the radical militants to act in the name of Allah when they maintained such unholy alliances with Al-Qaeda and other gangsters. He said according to the Quran that only Allah had authority to judge for violation of Allah's law. Allah's law and man's law are separate, and each should judge violations according to his own dictates.

Daniel agreed.

Eventually Sayyid's manners wore thin and he thanked the imam for educating Daniel on these fine distinctions but he pushed his charges forward, out of the hospital waving goodbyes as they climbed in to the Land Cruiser and wasted no time driving away.

"Daniel I know you think WHO has soldiers and will free you if you get message to them, but I will kill you right in front of them. They do nothing. They keep peace, not make war. Remember this. I grow tired of reminding you of these unpleasantries, yes."

Sayyid turned to Caitlin.

"You too, Doctor."

Caitlin nodded. Her attention fixed on Daniel from the back seat. Daniel could feel her looking at him. Perhaps it was pity? No, that wasn't all there was. There was something magnetic in her gaze. An element she couldn't resist. Could Caitlin have a thing for him?

He certainly found her attractive. He certainly hoped she would pass on information to WHO that he was being held hostage and forced into servitude, even if his conditions weren't exactly antebellum. A thought of Bally flared in his mind for an instant and extinguished as quickly as they had flamed. How the hell was a woman like Caitlin in Somalia? Where else could she possibly be? She had to be here, somewhere dangerous and alive, untainted by shopping districts and first-world pretention, where real life happened beyond the rectangular frame of the television after having been blessed by studio executives, where she could work, live, love and die. Where she could meet a man like Daniel, and he could pursue her with the handicap of ridiculous circumstances, overcome slavery to overcome her resistance, subdue her emotions and wrap her fingers in his hand to call her his own.

"This is me," Caitlin said. Sayyid braked by a sprawling structure with electric fence, barbwire, a minefield, and M-16 toting guards. She leapt out of the car without even a goodbye.

Daniel's heart sank. He had been dreaming. She hardly knew he existed. She wasn't going to help him escape, she couldn't give thought to every moronic journalist that lost his way in Somalia and didn't know how to get home. That was his own fool errand. Don't get yourself into something you can't get yourself out of.

Two guards came rushing at the SUV.

Caitlin had told them.

She had rushed to try to save Daniel, while Sayyid was distracted. Sayyid slammed on the accelerator. Daniel peered out the window as Caitlin locked eyes with him, or so he thought, as Daniel was rapidly driven away from her, a girl who had manipulated a situation as best she could to try to liberate him.

But now they were racing the bomb-shelled roads of Mogadishu, and the WHO compound fell out of sight.

# *Twelve*

The Sheikh's next job for the pirates was to rob a train. The Sheikh had credible information the regionally powerful Ethiopian government was delivering a regular under-the-table payment to the President of Djibouti for an unrestricted license to access the sea across their national border. Ethiopia's landlocked borders were considered by many to be its largest impediment to total regional hegemony.

The attack was unconventional and Sayyid lodged protests, but ultimately the Sheikh gained upper hand in the discussion by disclosing the prize was a horde of gold bullion.

The plan was simple. The gold bullion was to be loaded aboard the train in the capital city of Addis Ababa. The pirate gang would board at Dire Dawa, Ethiopia. The Sheikh expected Ethiopia to transport the gold under heavy security. At the international border, however, the Ethiopian military would remove itself and permit the President of Djibouti's personal security detail to take possession of the gold. The Sheikh's informant in the Ethiopian government had no way of knowing when the Djiboutis might remove the gold from the train once they took possession. Therefore, it was imperative the gang locate the gold while it was in possession of the Ethiopian military, but wait until the Ethiopians surrendered the gold to the Djiboutis, and take it from the presumably weaker

Djibouti security force as soon as the change of the guard left the prize vulnerable. If the Djibouti were able to offload the gold before the gang could locate it, then they had failed because the gold would be rapidly lost in the vast, unfamiliar Djiboutian territory.

Once the gang had the gold in their possession, they would need to hurry directly back to Somalia where Djibouti has little influence. If Djibouti misplaced their property, the Sheikh believed Ethiopia would not make the matter its concern. Ethiopia would take the position that it had satisfied its end of the bargain. Djibouti would be forced to permit Ethiopia the benefit of the easement even though the payment had been lost. Next time, Mr. President would be more careful. No international body would call foul because the legitimate use of Ethiopian funds was going to an illegitimate pocket. There was no risk of retaliation because the Sheikh's affiliation with Al-Shabaab made him a more dangerous man than the peace-touting President of Djibouti.

In exchange for the unusual risk, the Sheikh was willing to give the gang 30% of the gold plus whatever else they might loot from the train. Sayyid argued the offer was low because he had no expertise in the matter and for all he knew it created great risk. The Sheikh argued that he was increasing their compensation exponentially. Sayyid argued that he wasn't used to operating in a hostile foreign country. The Sheikh nudged his offer to 50%.

"If you don't take this offer, then I'm giving the job to the other crew. They're less capable than you, but more loyal. If I offer it to them, they will likely succeed. But if your group handles the matter, I know for a fact the gold will be recovered."

Sayyid accepted the Sheikh's proposition. The Sheikh's other gang was a rival to Sayyid, plus he hated that they were such mindless radicals. Sayyid believed they were connected to Amniyat, Al-Shabaab's ruthless secret police, notorious for carrying out midnight executions.

"Now Daniel, you will see that the Sayyid can rob anything," Sayyid told Daniel after the meeting, explaining the unspoken nuances of the matter, so Daniel could preserve the information for the story.

They gathered munitions and other supplies from a weapons cache in Eyl, then flew in a private charter plane to Hargeisa, Somalia. Daniel was impressed by his brief visit to Hargeisa. There were bus routes, uniformed police officers, children dressed in school uniforms walking the streets with their mothers, an absence of gunfire, erect buildings of sound structure and money changers with relatively unguarded mounds of currency stacked on the streets. This was what he saw while they drove across town, from the airport towards the Somaliland-Ethiopian border. In order to bring heavy weapons in to Ethiopia, it was necessary for them to make a clandestine border crossing. Four miles from the international boundary, they were dropped in the middle of a clumpy, dry dirt valley. Daniel thought that if it were to rain while they trekked across the powdery dirt, they would be trapped like insects on fly tape.

A rise in elevation was discernible to their west. How high, Daniel couldn't know. He wondered how far they would have to hike. How they would respond if they were found walking through a wasteland with heavy arms near an international border? There was more likely to be a shootout than an explanation.

The men hoisted their packs on their shoulders. Their rifles were checked for ammunition, then draped over a shoulder. Sayyid waved goodbye to the SUV, and the five men started their hike across the desert. They trudged for an hour over the bedrock before Daniel infiltrated the silence.

"Where are we now, Sayyid?" Daniel asked.

"This is no place," Sayyid said as he checked his hand-held GPS unit for the third time in as many minutes of the hike.

"Surely it must be someplace. How does our ride on the other side know where to pick us up?"

"It's near Tog Wajaale," Yousef said. "It is known where we are to be picked up."

"But?"

"Please, Daniel. I know it your job to ask the questions, but save your strength. This is a long hike. You exhaust us with these pointless questions, yes."

Daniel had learned when it was time to shut up. Since the gladiator experience over a week ago, he had been exceptionally well received and looked after by Sayyid. He needed the special treatment, too, for when he recalled the scene, the taking of the man's life, his hands began to tremble, his thoughts darken. What scared him most was the insight that he trembled not at what he had done, but at how little it had affected him. Now that he had started, would he be able to stop? Would he kill again? If so, what would be his victim's offense? Would he be able to reserve his death dealing for those who threatened his own life, or would less offense spur him to action? How would he ever know for certain the limits of what violence he was capable? Images flashed through his thoughts of Bally, at the stranger he murdered, a courthouse and a trial, prison, black ink scrawled on his arm and a forgotten way of life.

"You're learning," Sayyid said, lifting Daniel out of his inner turmoil.

"What?"

"You not taking all your pictures of dry rocks, you save them this time. For the good moment, yes."

On a few occasions over the past week, Sayyid had sat down to answer Daniel's questions and to proof the draft of the story Daniel was working up. Sayyid's enthusiasm for Daniel's work increased the writer's optimism that Sayyid would ultimately be a man of his word and release him. Daniel's camera was loaded with fifty exposures. He was hopeful that if the train raid was successful and the gold recovered, that Sayyid might be in such a good mood that he would assent to Daniel's return home. Because of these feelings, Daniel wanted to play his cards carefully on this raid, not frustrate or endanger anyone. Still, he was haunted by the anxiety that the event last week had forever changed him to the point that he was no longer fit to return to the civilized world.

The hike was taking hours. They walked four miles in Somaliland and another four in Ethiopia until they reached the outskirts of Tog Wajaale. There came a time when

Sayyid told everyone to hold up, and they all unloaded their packs and sat and rehydrated and joked. Daniel was confused by the absence of a road. The only habitation they had passed was a squat mud hut on the distance over a mile away. Daniel watched as Cameron leaned in and gave Yousef a wet willy. Yousef jumped when the wet finger penetrated his ear canal.

"In the name of Allah, why you do this?"

Everyone laughed.

"This is haram! The silly play is haram! It also endangers us in this hostile country!"

"Relax brother," Sayyid said. "This is just a horseplay. There is no danger. Look around. The only danger we are is to ourselves."

"Allah will no tolerate this foolishness! I will not let this apostasy stand!"

"No one said anything about Allah, brother," Sayyid said.

"An insult to me is an insult to Allah! You must know this."

"You hold yourself in pretty high esteem these days," Cameron said.

"Every time someone toy with you does not mean Allah has been desecrated," Sayyid said.

"I attend the mosque. I attend the Islam school. Do you get degree brother? And why do you side with the infidel? This is why we do not work with infidel because they disrespect our God and turn brother against brother!"

"Alright," Sayyid said dismissively. "Let me call our ride so we not vulture food, yes?"

Yousef's flared shoulders slumped and he crouched on the ground, well away from Cameron, and crossed his arms peering out in the distance. His orange keffiyeh flapped in the wind, like a desert fire.

**Despite the lack of visible landmarks,** an SUV followed by a tail of smoke soon appeared on the horizon. Everyone stood, dusting and stretching. Yousef avoided eye contact with the group.

Sayyid took two steps towards his brother, but then stopped himself and batted a waving hand towards his brother's back.

They tossed their packs in the back of the vehicle along with Daniel, who rode penalty box. Then they started off. The driver took them to the small village of Tog Wajaale. The main street consisted of a series of one-story cement buildings fronted by tarp-covered retail stands. A camel caravan entered town, two of the more curious camels in the vanguard, sniffing the retailers' wares, being shooed away, their shepherds buried in the midst of the herd.

The gang's driver suggested they have something to eat. Sayyid asked if they could get something quickly. The driver said they could and led them to a favorite café. They ate beef tibs, with gomen and injera. All the men drank Coca-Cola except Yousef, who drank bottled water. After they finished eating, the uneventful journey to Dire Dawa continued. Desolate plains. Battered, unmaintained roads. Cactus. Near desert conditions. An occasional car sped by. Macalin collected and concealed all the rifles in a field hockey bag. Cameron removed his double-breasted outdoors shirt and pulled on a field hockey polo jersey. Soon everyone was wearing them.

"Put this on, Daniel," Cameron said.

Then they were all wearing the jerseys. The pretext for their trip. The reason for carrying the bag of feigned field hockey equipment. These fellows had some tack after all, the capacity for subterfuge, not all full-frontal assault like they're made out to be in the movies.

Dire Dawa is the second largest city in Ethiopia. Craggy, dusty cliffs loom over a lush, river-fed garden valley. There's a downtown, suburbs. Regular life. It all felt foreign to Daniel. Unreal. As if piracy were a practical, routine life, and working behind a desk for eight hours a day were some exotic occupation.

124

Button-down shirted Ethiopians exited office complexes. Network-building over drinks. Dates transpiring. Camel-drawn rickshaws. Dusty and unrenovated, but authentically desirable. Self-confident. Not striving to be like every other place. Daniel seemed to recall learning in a history class that Ethiopia was the only African country never colonized. He hoped that illustrious military history didn't portend the results of the mission ahead.

The train station wasn't particularly special. A yellow brick two-story façade, a red roof. Flies buzzing around a lonely camel tied to a post outside. "Chemin de fer Djibouti-Ethiopen," a sign read in Roman alphabet underneath the Arabic scrawl Daniel couldn't read. Daniel watched as Cameron and Macalin checked their concealed pistols on their hips before departing the SUV. The bags were unloaded, and Daniel was surprised to see everyone give the driver such a scripted goodbye, as if they were departing the company of their father, or a revered field hockey coach. Once the strained goodbye was complete, they mounted their backpacks and proceeded to enter the station.

"If you do anything, if you move as much as five feet too far away from me, then I will shoot you dead, yes. I will kill anyone who try to stop me for shooting you dead, yes."

Daniel nodded and gulped. He wasn't sure whether he believed Sayyid would endanger himself in a foreign country just to honor this threat, but the man was dangerous. Daniel believed, he wanted, he needed to believe that if he captured good enough pictures on this trip, then Sayyid would honor his promise and allow him to return home to tell the story.

Inside the station, a cat's litter of Ethiopian soldiers lingered around the station. Rather than stand at attention, three of them sat on a bench reading a newspaper while the one in the middle turned the pages. Their brown wool uniforms hinted at having been once pressed, but were wilted in the heat.

Another soldier was sitting on the floor, asleep, with an aged Kalashnikov rifle laid across his lap. The other half dozen were standing around in a smoking circle, laughing or gasping in astonishment, depending on the turn of the story being told. None of them paid any attention to the team of field hockey players that just entered the station. Cameron was a little old to be on a school team, but his muscular athleticism was probably enough to overwhelm any but the most attentive skepticism.

A malfunctioned clock permanently announced the time was 3:12. Daniel wondered how many travelers it had caused delay, or greater problems. How long had it been broken? Why hadn't it been fixed?

A train arrived a few minutes later. Three dozen or so exited the train before the gang filed aboard. The scene was regular enough. Rows of seats occupied by women, children, the occasional male business traveler. Lint-ridden, wool fabric seats, witness to years of thankless use. No soldiers in their car. Macalin heaved the field hockey bag into the overhead storage compartment. After the burden was relieved, he looked to Sayyid for approval. Sayyid gave it with a single, definitive nod. Then they all took their seats as the train began to amble its way out of the station.

The conductor came by checking tickets.

"Playing field hockey?" The conductor asked, having read the English script on Macalin's field hockey polo. "The St. Bartholomew School, I've never heard of it."

"We were in town for a tournament. We play international."

"Funny, I played field hockey in my youth, and I don't recall a St. Bartholomew School ever playing us. I actually don't recall there being a tournament this time of year in Dire Dawa. I'm a native, myself, although I moved to Addis Ababa years ago."

"It was an exhibition tournament, actually. Might call it a training camp. There weren't any crowns at stake. Just preparation and exercise really. You Ethiopians really know how to play," Macalin said.

The conductor gazed at Cameron. Daniel thought he might say something, but apparently wasn't able to fish from his consciousness what had caught his eye.

126

Apparently having exhausted his knowledge of the subject, he left them to continue his rounds.

There weren't any soldiers in their car, or the next car. Daniel hoped the Sheikh had been provided good information. He hoped they had gotten on the correct train.

Daniel caught Yousef staring at him while he was glimpsing around himself, and he realized he had been fidgeting, being too observant. Yousef terrified him more than anyone. The way he always believed he acted in God's best interest. That sort of deluded certainty was frightening, really.

Daniel reached underneath his seat, unzipped his book bag and took his spiral notebook and flipped to the first blank page. He needed to write something to focus his mind and calm himself. He wanted to exercise discretion, so he determined not to write about pirates. In the past, besides writing for work, his second greatest interest had been drafting letters to Bally. He wrote her name on the top of the page. Writing usually came so naturally to him once he had chosen his subject, but oddly he couldn't think of anything agreeable to write. Hadn't she chosen to accept a life with that bastard, Burton Woods? Wasn't Bally generally a disagreeable and selfish? Her taste in music was horrendous. She'd slept with so many people he knew. Her career in undermining women's self-esteem was contemptible as murder. She was dust compared to Caitlin Cordon. He was somewhat jarred to find himself having these unusual thoughts, but what qualified as normal these days?

Next to Daniel, Cameron shimmied in his seat uncomfortably. Granted, the torn, dust covered seats didn't live up to first-class expectations. Daniel watched as the big white man plugged his ears with headphones. He wore mirrored sunglasses, resting his head against the seat as though he might be resting his eyes or even asleep. But Daniel could see the big man's eyes open wide from the sides of the glasses, intent and alert as ever. Yousef sat alone in the row across from Cameron and Daniel, and Sayyid and Macalin sat directly behind Daniel.

The train picked up steam, the route well on its way. Macalin and Yousef were debating which hotel was their favorite in Ethiopia. Daniel, unable to construct a love letter to Bally, fell prey to eavesdropping on the conversation of the men behind him. Suddenly, their conversation turned from hotels to whether or not the surveillance should begin.

Macalin stood and plodded up the car, towards the engine. Then he disappeared in the vestibule. Daniel slid the notebook back in his bookbag. Who knew when this might go down? He understood the international border wasn't supposed to arrive for approximately another two hours, but his intuition told him he needed to remain alert. He consciously tried to let himself relax, but given the situation he couldn't comprehend how to release the tension.

Macalin returned. He handled his nose, obscuring most of his face as he passed the few aisles before he reclaimed his seat. Daniel was all attention again.

"Two soldiers in the car in front of us. Three more cars up there's a whole squad, a dozen or so. Access beyond that point's prohibited. There's only two cars ahead of it. One of them is the treasure car," Macalin whispered.

"Maybe both of them are treasure cars," Sayyid whispered. "Maybe one of them is a hornet nest. Who is to say which is which, yes?"

Cameron had slyly removed the ear bud from his left ear to hear the report. Across the way, Yousef had his arms crossed, his face contorted in irritation. He had excluded himself from the group, and now he was angry for being left out of their conversation. The little brother just couldn't win. He wouldn't let himself.

The train skittered along. A few people came aboard and a few got off at the various whistle stops along the route. The conductor passed back through the car a couple of times, searching for free riders. Daniel watched as a young man boarded the train at a humble train station in a minute village, only to be ferreted out by the conductor a matter of moments later. Daniel hoped the conductor would allow the man to stay. Under different circumstances, Daniel might have considered purchasing the man a ticket. As it stood, he didn't have any money and such an attention-drawing action might get him killed. Helping the man remain on the train might get the man killed, too.

"I'm only going two more stops," the man pled as the conductor led him towards the exit.

The conductor pointed towards the station, and the man disembarked.

When the train stopped at Adele, Sayyid announced they were only 32 kilometers from Dewele. Macalin left his seat and ventured towards the front of the train again. The remaining pirates all held each other's attention in a triangle of focus. Daniel made certain his bag was zipped up tight, except for the camera, which rested on his lap. His mood was calm, but his palms were moist with a deluge of sweat.

Fifteen short minutes later the train braked to a grinding halt. They were in Dewele, the last Ethiopian stop before crossing in to the Djibouti border. A smell of diesel lingered in the air, the engine having become increasingly fatigued as the journey progressed. There was a large departure of passengers, mostly the women, children and family crowds. Most of the suits sat still, hardly noticing the train was at rest. Daniel turned his attention out the window. A crew of four, sleek suited men came walking in unison through the station. "That's them," Sayyid whispered to the seat in front of him. Each of the men had a radio bud curled into an ear. None of them were visibly armed, but each wore his jacket a bit oversized, permitting plenty of room to carry concealed firearms. Two of the four men carried a leather duffle over his shoulder. Daniel didn't have to exercise much imagination to guess what danger lurked in those bags. Daniel also mistakenly assumed they would be boarding the train *after* it had crossed in to Djibouti. Granted, their boarding now made more sense so there wouldn't be a break in armed security of the gold. So would the Ethiopian soldiers disembark in Guelile?

The four men walked along the platform, passed the pirates, towards the train car harboring the squad of Ethiopian soldiers. No one else, including the Ethiopian soldiers, exited the train. The engineer nudged the train to a start. Daniel looked to Cameron for answers, but he appeared perplexed himself. Daniel glanced over his shoulder at Sayyid, who sat stoic. Weighing his options in that calculating mind of his.

# *Thirteen*

The train was away from Dewele when Macalin returned. The pirates communicated with subtle eye contact as Macalin, who was wringing his hands, dropped into the seat beside Sayyid. The two whispered inaudibly at length, frequently shifting their attention outside the window. The train chugged past a tokenly militarized border crossing, complete with a watch house for each border along with a chain link fence that ran a mile in either direction. The train made no pretense of stopping as it zoomed past, shoddy gates raised on the side of both territories.

When the train began to slow before the Guelile stop, Sayyid and Macalin's conversation ceased.

Sayyid jumped into the aisle.

"Well, are we doing it or not?" he asked, without regard for who heard. Yousef nodded assent. Cameron grunted assent. No one bothered to poll Daniel's opinion. Macalin jumped and ran ahead of everyone, disappearing in to the forward train car. Then Cameron and Yousef leapt to their feet and pulled their pistols.

"Everyone sit where you are and no one will get hurt," Cameron said. Yousef echoed the statement in Arabic and Ethiopian.

Sayyid took the field hockey equipment bag from the overhead compartment and distributed the AK-47s. There was a cry in the train car, but Cameron raised a calming index finger to intersect his lips.

Armed and ready to go, they invaded the next car.

Daniel brought up the rear, camera in hand, two pictures deep before their first serious confrontation in the forward car. Two soldiers were taken by surprise. Cameron had taken the lead, and the soldiers surrendered their weapons before Daniel even made his way across the gangway connection. Suddenly, Sayyid wailed, veering backwards, holding his eye, his rifle out of his hands, suspended to his side by the sling. By the time Daniel realized a vigilante passenger had struck Sayyid in the face, Yousef had the man kneeling before him.

"You strike my brother!" He screamed, his face red, his breathing deep and irregular. His pupils were large enough to permit a semi-truck to pass. "Tell me a line from the Quran!"

The man slumped to his knees, quivering with his eyes cast towards the ground and his hands on the back of his head.

"Tell me one line infidel! I shall not strike my brother, but recite to me one line!"

The man began crying.

"Recite me!" Yousef roared.

There was a deafening explosion. Maroon misted across Yousef's face, causing his eyes to flinch in a way the mere noise of a gunshot could not. Daniel surveyed the train car. All the passengers were hunkered down, hands overhead. Except in the heat of the moment, Cameron had turned his attention away from the soldiers, and a passenger had seized his rifle and put a bullet directly through Cameron's chest. The hulking white man lay on the floor, eking away what little life there was left. A cherry-sized sucking wound pulsated on his chest.

Daniel wanted to jump, to help Cameron, but his fear took control. Daniel stepped back in to the safety of the vestibule, which he never fully left. Through the window, he watched the rest. Sayyid and Yousef laid their weapons on the ground and raised their hands to the air. Both soldiers were on their feet now, pointing their rifles at the chests of the two remaining pirates. Cameron was laughing. Death was the great joke. One of the soldiers took the radio from his hip and barked an order in to its receiver.

It was over for the pirates.

Cameron was dying.

Sayyid and Yousef captured.

Macalin alone no match for a dozen plus soldiers. Macalin would likely stand down, hide, and return to Somalia and hope to return with reinforcements before his pirate partners were executed. If he could get to them before they were executed.

Daniel was struck by a haunting thought. They were all wearing the same field hockey jersey. The soldiers would undoubtedly comb the train for other conspirators, once the obvious combatants were rounded up. Daniel would be captured and executed along with the rest of them. No Bally. No Dr. Caitlin Cordon. No possibility of a return home.

Suddenly a red tint was cast over all, and sirens screamed.

He marched back to the gang's original seats, passing rows of passengers trembling in their seats. He hardly noticed a Djibouti beauty peering over at him, her black skin accentuated by a head-dress of gold and pearls that chandeliered across her forehead, nose and eyes. She was strikingly beautiful. He rifled through the field hockey bag. She shuddered when he removed a single 9mm Glock from the nylon. Daniel dropped the clip out of the bottom of the gun, like he had seen done on TV a million times before, checking to make certain it was loaded. Then he put the clip back in the gun, pulled on the barrel, popping a bullet in to the breech. He made eye contact with the girl for a brief moment. He wanted to shoot her in the head for looking at him like that, with such terror. He wanted to extinguish the terror.

Then he walked back in to the forward train car.

Two shots thundered, deafening the air. Daniel looked to watch the two Ethiopian soldiers slump dead to the ground, a bullet in each of their chests.

He held the gun extended in front of his chest, smoke oozing from the muzzle, when Sayyid patted him on the shoulder, shattering Daniel's trance and clawing him back in to the present moment.

"Good work, journalist."

Daniel lowered his pistol from attack position. Then he dropped to tend to Cameron, appearing to lose consciousness.

"He's dead," Sayyid said.

Daniel looked hard at Yousef. If it wasn't for the kid brother's inability to control himself, Cameron might not have died. Or at least he wouldn't have died when he did.

Macalin appeared in the train car, looking at Cameron crumpled on the floor, with sad eyes, before taking the AK-47 from around Cameron's neck and brandishing it himself.

"Report?"

"Take position," Macalin said.

Yousef went in to the rear vestibule. Macalin shooed away the passengers in the seats by the forward vestibule, training his rifle on the door. Sayyid blended in with the rest of the civilians, choosing a seat next to a middle-aged lady dressed in a multi-colored kemi. Daniel dropped in to an empty seat beside an older lady wearing an outfit similar to the beautiful girl he had just considered killing. Their similarity of dress snapped Daniel's thoughts back to the present moment. His breathing returned to normal. He realized he had killed two soldiers. He clutched the pistol in his hand. He had killed again. It was happening. He was out of control, he was a killer. No, no, he tried to tell himself. He'd only done it to survive. But he wasn't so certain of the truth, as he sat there while the woman examined his wildly evolving features.

Cameron threw a final fist into the air, gasped his last breath, then lie there discarded in the aisle, dead.

"Are you a pirate now, Daniel?" Sayyid asked. A few of the cowering passengers risked peeking, couldn't help overhearing the exchange.

Daniel looked hard at the Glock in his hand. He had perhaps a dozen shots left. He was terrified, a sort of terror one feels before undergoing a surgery with mortal consequences. Unlike surgery, however, he was required to assist this operation if he was going to live.

"I'm with you," Daniel said.

His meddle was tested soon, when a soldier followed by a detachment of his brethren opened the door from the forward vestibule and entered the train car. The moment the lead soldier came within sight, Macalin leaned in to not more than a handshake's length with his rifle and splattered the combatant's brains like a bursting water balloon filled with maroon paint. Blood went everywhere. Shrieks pierced the air. The woman sitting next to Daniel started slapping the exterior glass wildly, frantic to escape. The Ethiopian soldiers clamored, all wanting to fight back but none wanted to die or risk killing his innocent countrymen by firing indiscriminately into the civilian-filled train car. There was a wolf among the sheep and it was a situation for which they were inadequately trained.

**The situation became a standoff.** Time passed. The train shuddered, squealed along the rails. Perhaps the engineer caught wind of what was happening and pushed the engine to hurry along to the next town, to get reinforcements, to get his own neck out of danger. His own life his only interest, incidentally co-aligned with the interest of all his passengers.

Without interest none of it meant anything.

Unseen gunshots rang out in the forward car. Daniel looked to see Sayyid and Macalin hanging tight.

Yousef had somehow managed to get behind the Ethiopian soldiers.

Sayyid charged the vestibule, covering himself with rapid fire, shouldering the wall next to Macalin when his clip was empty. Two Ethiopian soldiers stumbled backwards, discharging their weapons into the forward car. Sayyid smashed a bullet into each of their heads at point blank range, the soldiers crumpling to the ground in a mess of themselves, of fitting wool uniforms and scattered brains. One of the soldiers' malformed bodies laid on top of the other, his blood cupped in the upturned shoulder chevron, until it pooled and spilled into the floor. The smell of recently butchered meat began to permeate the air.

"Don't shoot," Yousef said in close proximity of the vestibule door, in the kill zone.

Sayyid raised the muzzle of his gun to the air and permitted his brother to join them in the car.

"The next car is clear," Yousef said.

"How did you this?"

"I was in the vestibule when I saw an emergency ladder to the roof of the train. I walked along the roofs and snuck in behind them."

"Are there more?"

"I killed only four. You killed two more. So there's at least a few more Ethiopian soldiers plus the Djibouti guys. Perhaps many more," Yousef said.

Would they continue to fight, or would they abandon the mission after having lost one of their own? Daniel wondered whether their few men could reasonably expect to overpower an army and seize the gold.

"Let us not show tender now," Sayyid said.

"What about him?" Macalin asked, tilting his head towards Cameron's wasted body.

"He is not a concern any longer. The Ethiopians will see his remains are cared for. A respectful people are they, yes."

Sayyid spoke his words a moment before he surged towards the forward car, rifle butt wedged in the crease of his chest and shoulder. Yousef quickly fell in behind his brother on his right flank with his finger resting on the trigger. Macalin waved for Daniel to follow. Daniel stood there dumbly with the Glock dangling in his hand at his waist.

"Are you with us or what?"

Daniel said nothing. He stared in disbelief at the carnage around him, unable to accept the role he had played. He wanted to wish them good luck and return to his original seat. Daniel laughed that they had asked him his preference at all, like the opinion of a slave mattered.

"If you aren't with us you're on your own. When this train comes to the next stop, there's going to be so many soldiers and police you won't live to count them. This isn't America, brother. Here, they kill killers on sight. That's their recipe for justice."

Macalin was right. Daniel was glued to the situation now, a principal to the crime.

An explosion rang ahead in the distance.

"We won't come back for you," Macalin said.

Daniel nudged forward, but froze again.

"Ok, have it your way," Macalin said and ran in to the next forward car.

Alone and without a compatriot, Daniel shook off his lethargy. He could sort out his feelings later, but for the sake of the remainder of the mission he was a pirate. He had killed and if he were captured here his crime would not be forgiven. He believed that.

He followed Macalin in to the next train car.

Macalin was already at the next vestibule ahead. Daniel ran passed the aisles to catch up to him. People were screaming, crying, praying, saying goodbyes on their cell phones. Daniel opened the vestibule door. A hand immediately reached out, snatching his wrist and pulling him to the ground. Macalin hunkered onto the ground next to Daniel. Sayyid and Yousef were across the way, discussing strategy.

When they were finished, Sayyid produced a tiny mechanic's mirror on the tip of a telescopic pen, extended it to full length and held it to the window of the vestibule door, glimpsing what they were up against. He managed to hold it there for six or seven seconds before a bullet splintered through the glass, and a hailstorm of bullets punctured through the door and ricocheted throughout the vestibule. One round struck a fire extinguisher, which surrendered its extinguishing agent in a hissing cloud. Macalin, with his hand covered over his eyes, dislodged the extinguisher from the wall and tossed it through the broken vestibule window toward the soldiers. The shooting continued for another few seconds. Sayyid pulled a grenade from his cargo pocket, pulled the ringed pin with his teeth, waddled over to the window in a crouched position and tossed the grenade towards the opposite end of the forward car. Four seconds later an explosion rattled the train, breaking glass. There was a hellish howl of screams. A new wind, hot and sandy, gusted through the train. Sayyid pulled the pin on another grenade and tossed it. When the shrapnel exploded, the train rattled again, only there were less screams and a conspicuous absence of breaking glass. A blink after the second explosion and all the pirates were on their feet, AKs and Uzis pumping metal projectiles forward indiscriminately, aiming at everything that moved.

One by one the pirates stood in that vestibule doorframe unloading a full clip of ammunition before dropping in a huddle to allow the next of his men to fire. First Sayyid, then Yousef and Macalin. Daniel didn't volunteer his services, and no one expressed disappointment at his lack of participation. When Sayyid jumped up for his second round, he declared the room cleared. Nothing was moving. If anyone was able, they were wise to remain still.

Sayyid marched passed the aisles of dead, military and civilian. The seats at the opposite end of the car were totally dislocated from their original fixtures. The rest were riddled with bullets and glass and blood and shrapnel. Sayyid pulled on the forward vestibule door, the one they believed might be the treasure car. It was still locked.

"Don't do it," someone on the other side yelled. They repeated similar warnings in French, Arabic and Ethiopian.

Light shone through the bullet holes in the roof like suspended rain. The arid desert air gusted in the train car, drying Daniel's eyes and his mouth. The unholy smell accompanying it burned his nostrils, made him want to puke. He felt like peeing.

Sayyid shouldered the wall, just parallel to the door. He raised his Uzi and blasted the doorknob from its screws.

"Don't do it," the voice yelled again from the other room.

Daniel was peeking out from the behind the vestibule and Macalin. Yousef was in the rear of the forward car, covering his brother from a safe distance. Daniel pumped his foot on the ground, wringing his hands. He fully expected an entire company of soldiers to pour from the car ahead in full-body bulletproof armor. Sayyid turned to face the entry and plunged his boot through the door, breaking the doorframe to the ground.

Sayyid's Uzi butt immediately returned to the crease of his shoulder, but he didn't fire. There was an eerie silence. Yousef moved forward to secure Sayyid's old position as Sayyid disappeared into the forward car. Macalin filed in and Daniel tagged along close behind.

"Come here!" Sayyid yelled. Everyone sprinted forward. In active battle situations, Sayyid's commands carried the authority of an omniscient host. Daniel was the last to enter the previously restricted train car that more than a dozen Ethiopian soldiers had died to protect.

Situated in the car were two full-size Humvee pickup trucks. There was a tarped cargo in each bed. Once the whole gang was in the train car, Sayyid pulled back a tarp to reveal a pallet of gold bars. Daniel watched as Macalin's eyes widened before he immediately snapped back to securing the perimeter.

"Where are the Djibouti?" Macalin demanded.

"You feel that?" Sayyid asked.

"We're slowing," Yousef said.

"Look at the car ahead of us," Sayyid said.

Everyone looked. The first train car and engine were pulling away. The Djiboutis had decoupled the cars to save their own skin.

"What if it's a trap?" Yousef asked.

"Then we will confront it on arrival, yes," Sayyid said. "Load up."

Daniel was a little perplexed by what Sayyid meant 'load up,' but Macalin climbed in to the driver's seat of one of the Humvees and Yousef hopped in beside him. Sayyid heaved open one of the train's heavy iron cargo doors, open to the reeling volcanic plateaus flickering by at 70 km an hour. Macalin turned the ignition, revved the engine, cranked the armored vehicle in to gear, and jumped it off the train.

Daniel couldn't believe his eyes. He ran to the opened door to watch as the Humvee bounced hard against the desert ground, skidded around in a doughnut, and came to an abrupt halt, before kicking up a cloud of sand and racing parallel to the train.

"Get in Daniel," Sayyid said, climbing into the driver's seat.

"I'm not sure I can do that."

"There is no question of whether. It is escape or stay to be execute. There is no other. You are a killer now. Do not let fear kill you."

Daniel reluctantly climbed in to the cab, and suddenly his visual facilities were capturing more movement than he could process, making him dizzy, before they violently collided with the unbending ground. Daniel's head and left shoulder struck the ceiling of the vehicle, the seatbelt slapped his shoulder uselessly. He cried out as Sayyid spun the steering wheel around in a wild manner, before whipsawing straight, cutting a diagonal line away from the train with Macalin driving beside them, the sun careening towards its western bedroom on their right outside Daniel's window, and they sped at peak velocity back to the Somali border.

"Stop the car," Daniel said. "I'm going to vomit."

"There is no stopping now. It would have been better if we had killed the Djibouti's. Then no one know who has done this or to where we escape, yes. But as it is, they will tell their government. The police and military will look for us without question.

Lucky Djibouti has little resource for such an operation. Still, we are unsafe until Somalia. You puke in the truck if necessary."

Daniel leaned his head out the window and evacuated his stomach. The beef tibs from earlier didn't taste much different coming up than they did going down. When Daniel was finished, he rolled the four-inch thick glass window closed.

"You did good today, Daniel."

"You really think so?" Daniel asked, his voice tinged with sarcasm. His hands trembled, unwilling to grasp responsibility for the lives they had terminated.

"Today was your best day, yes."

"So are you going to let me return home?"

"Maybe, yes or no."

"What does it depend on?"

"Well, you no finish the story. But you save my life. But you also risk my life. I like you Daniel, but I know not what to do with you. So I think we go ask the shamaness."

"The shamaness?"

"I go to her for the difficult, important questions. We no tell Yousef because he think she infidel. True, she is not in line with the Muslim way. She is from the, how do you say, old school? Her rel-ig-ion pre-date Muhammad by a millennium of millennium."

"If she says I should go home?"

"Then you shall return there again, yes."

"If she says I should die?

"Then I kill you."

# *Fourteen*

They drove straight, stopping only for gas, until they reached the Orient Pearl in Mogadishu. The Sheikh was at the hotel with his other pirate gang, the one Sayyid despised. The *true* believers. The ones that brainwashed young boys in to carrying out politically motivated suicide missions. The ones who had instigated the U.S. drones to drop bombs and forced Ethiopia's hand in launching an offensive against Somalia. The ones who were ruining it for everyone. They were Al-Shabaab's secret police, a Somalian Gestapo, and they had a name: the Amniyat.

The two Humvees came to a sliding halt in the secured courtyard. Sayyid jumped out of the military truck and began discussing the arrangements for the vehicle and their cargo with a hotel attendant. Meanwhile, the Sheikh strolled up, starting and stopping, towards the vehicles until he was within conversational distance of Sayyid. The patron faintly resembled a drunken Buddha.

"The mission was a success."

"I told you over the phone we got the gold."

"Success! Praise be to Allah," the Sheikh said in song, clasping his hands together in prayer, gazing up towards the hazy, cloud covered sky.

"No, praise be to Cameron. Who died for this gold. And praise be to Yousef, Macalin, Sayyid and Daniel who risk life for this gold."

"You'll watch yourself," the Sheikh said, curling the tip of his silky mustache between his fingers.

"I'll watch nothing," Sayyid said. "But my own skin."

The two men stood square to each other. Daniel wasn't certain what was about to transpire. He hadn't expected the two men to exchange hostile words, considering the mission was complete. Sayyid almost appeared upset at having lost Cameron, but the pirate had barely flinched when his friend Tak was shot right in front of him. Did this represent some shift in character? Or was there something else going on here, underneath the surface?

"Get the gold," the Sheikh ordered the rival gang, the Amniyat. They were four members. They divided into pairs, each approaching a Humvee.

"What is this," Sayyid said. "You get half, I get half."

"I thought we agree to 30%?"

"You know we say 50%," Sayyid said. He snatched his Uzi from his waistband, pulling back on the barrel, arming the weapon. There were small cuts on his face from broken glass, abrasions ran the length of his arm, and other people's blood covered his shoes.

The Sheikh held up his closed fist to stop his men. He examined Sayyid for a moment from behind those mirrored sunglasses, ones similar to the style Cameron had worn on the last mission. The Sheikh began nodding his head.

"I remember now," the Sheikh said, wagging a playful finger at Sayyid. "We agree to 50%. The Great Sayyid said it would be a difficult mission, could he have fifty percent? The Sheikh said yes, of course, fifty percent. And it looks as if you were right, Sayyid. Aren't you missing a man? The fat white man?"

"His name was Cameron," Sayyid said. The pirate firmed his grasp on the Uzi. He jerked his head to look at the opposite pair of rival pirates approaching Macalin and

Yousef. Yousef was watching his brother with anger and confusion intermittently flashing across his face.

"I suppose that was his name. It's a dangerous business, isn't it? Best not to get too attached to our co-workers. Can cause you risk for yourself, I suppose."

Sayyid shook for a moment, like he was wrestling with two mutually exclusive feelings, and one would soon conquer the other and dictate his subsequent actions. Sayyid raised his Uzi, pointing to the opposite Humvee.

"That one is yours," Sayyid said. "Now get Shongola out of my face." Sayyid pointed the muzzle of his Uzi at the head of one of the Amniyat. Not taking Sayyid's lapse in gun safety very amicably, the man quickly drew his pistol, training its sight on Sayyid. An eerie silence befell the surroundings. Daniel stood frozen. The attendants stood frozen. Yousef and Macalin stood frozen. Even the insects and vermin disappeared from the scene. With force matched against force, Mogadishu momentarily became serene in the center of the tension. The breeze conducted its rounds and the sun inched incrementally forward across the sky.

The Sheikh raised his cane, placing its tip on Shongola's wrist, forcing his aim low to the ground.

"We've gotten what we've come for. Now it's time for us to let our friends rest. Fatigue and the sight of death make a man restless, " the Sheikh said.

Sayyid nodded agreement, his better senses coming back to him, returning the Uzi to his waistband. Then he called one of the hotel attendants over.

Shongola mechanically holstered his pistol.

"Call Jacchil," Sayyid told the attendant, who flipped open a pad to scribble instructions. "He is with Dahabshiil. Tell him to come with an armor car because Sayyid like to make a large transfer. Tell him I in the Crowne Suite here."

"Yes sir," the attendant said, before he ran away to carry out Sayyid's order.

"Macalin, do you mind to stay with the truck until the money transfer can arrive?" Sayyid asked. Macalin was already drinking a beer at a table the hotel attendants had dragged over from the café for him.

"What do I tell them to do with it?"

"Tell them to make the usual transfer for Sayyid," Sayyid said, then turned to Daniel. "Come. I need to discuss with Yousef what I do with you."

**In the suite, Daniel was locked in a bedroom** like many times before, while Sayyid and Yousef unwound from their latest raid.

"I don't understand why you need to leave with him, alone," Yousef said. "What if the Sheikh has another big job? Or the Ethiopians, what if they move further into the city? These are perilous times brother, we do not need to be separated. As things are, if Ethiopia catch you, they treat you like prisoner of war."

"I am entrepreneur."

"A pirate entrepreneur. I don't think they'll grant you pardon, especially when they find out who's pirate you are. The most dangerous, is not these your words?"

"Look, brother. I am just going to see a counselor about," Sayyid whispered, but Daniel could still hear him through the thin walls. "Look, we short a man with Cameron dead. But Daniel, he save us. He could replace Cameron. I need to know what to do with him. If he a fighter, then he fight with us. If he a danger, then I--" Sayyid made a shooting noise.

"I don't like working with the whites, brother."

"I know you feel these things, yes. But Daniel speak the good English, and he very close to telling our story. Once our story is out there, it change the way the world see not just us, but Somalia. Somalia will be taken seriously. The wrath of Muhammad will be taken seriously. Now I am not for sure whether Daniel is the cure or the cancer, but this is why I must speak with an elder chief to discover this."

"Then I'll go with you."

"No, you must stay here. This one thing I must do on my own, yes."

"Why?"

"Why? Someone must stay here to make certain the gold transfer is to work. We fight hard and lose much for this to let it blow away with wind, yes? Macalin I trust, but my brother is the very best I trust. Yousef never betray me," Sayyid said.

"When will you take him?"

"In the morning. We will not be gone longer than three days."

A knock came at the door, it opened and feet pattered in. Daniel strained to look through the crack in the door, but saw only abstract light.

"Dahabshiil has been contacted sir," said an unfamiliar voice. "They say it will take them 1 to 2 days to arrive with the sort of security your transfer requires. Until then, the manager of the Orient Pearl is pleased to offer you all the security services it has at its disposal."

"Thank you," Sayyid said.

Feet pattered away, and the door closed.

"See, I need you and Macalin here to play guard until the Dahabshiil can secure the money. The hotel I trust to help, yes, but any one man might get big ideas if he allowed to snoop around that truck. Ha, that truck alone is worth a man's hands. So, you see, I go and speak to elder if Daniel is capable of pirate or not. If he is, then by the time I get back we have our full group and be ready to work again. You stay here and get money transfer so we no have to worry about it. See how this all work?"

"Ok. Just be safe out there."

"Yes, yes," Sayyid said, the two brothers audibly embracing, various metal contrivances and weapons clanking against one another.

**The next day Daniel was suited with a backpack** full of provisions, food, water, hiking equipment. He was starting to think Sayyid had an affinity for the wilderness, an unwitting deep ecologist. They ate a large breakfast at the rooftop restaurant and bar, called the Oyster Bed, overlooking the pool and smoldering Mogadishu. Sayyid chewed on large slices of mango, the juice drizzling all over his fried eggs and toast. Daniel had a sausage biscuit, banana and coffee. The coffee here tasted divine. Coffee was originally cultivated just across the way in Ethiopia, and he speculated his cup was the product of some ancient tree, descended from the line of originally farmed beans, grown to perfection through generations of meticulous cross-breeding and careful fertilization. He could almost taste the bitter history of the region in the crude, earthen kick.

Once lunch was finished, they left immediately. Daniel rode shotgun in Sayyid's Land Cruiser. He skidded that SUV around one decimated city block after another, turning up the volume when he found a folk music station, laughing as he spun that wheel around sometimes with too much sport and bravado for Daniel's comfort, out of warzone Mogadishu. Daniel wondered whether he was really being driven to meet a mysterious Shamaness or to his final death.

"Why did you tell Yousef you were taking me to a see an elder? I thought you said something about a Shamaness?"

"I tell you the truth. The Shamaness is not acceptable to Islam doctrine. Muhammad born 610 A.D. The Shamaness religion come before Muhammad. Thousands before. Her religion exist before Somalia was a land. Before mosque or western church, there was the Shamaness. Yousef would be very very angry if he knew I go to seek the counsel of the Shamaness. He report me to the Amniyat and have me tortured, yes. Many nomad still go to her, to seek the path. The city Muslims no understand this."

"So you were serious, when you said if she thinks I should die you will kill me?"

"She is wise old bag, yes. This is why we take the trouble to see her. If I no take her advice, then why trouble to see her?"

"What hope do I have?"

"I not want to kill you, Daniel. I want to see if you fit. But I cannot know this and you cannot know this. That is why we must ask the Shamaness. Then we will know if you worth freedom or a bullet. Yes?"

Daniel gulped. He really didn't like having the matter of his life determined by some witch doctor way out in the sticks who was generally frowned on by the city types. Still, looking at the relatively carefree Sayyid, swinging the steering wheel wildly, telling jokes, always adventure seeking, taking time to help orphans and injured; he was damn glad it was Sayyid who was having him appraised and not Yousef. Daniel had seen first hand the treatment Yousef's religion dealt nonbelievers. He laughed at the thought of Sayyid's voodoo jungle lady determining whether he lived or died. Like his fate mattered. None of this was real.

"How did you and Yousef turn out so differently?" Daniel asked.

"This is a good question, journalist. Both our parents were killed in 1991 during the Civil War," Sayyid said, a gradual somberness creeping into his tone. "They put us both in the Islam school after that. I knew it was my duty to take care of my little brother. I wasn't interested in all the preaching and praying, so I quit the school and started hustling, so we could eat and not have to rely on other peoples. Yousef could learn the religion, I could keep us fed and wearing clothes. I stole some so they send me for times to my ancestor tribe. They nomads, they teach me many things about shooting, nature, herding, raiding, living from land. Maybe some of this even was knowledge. They first introduce me to the Shamaness, who say I would be a great warrior. My tribesmen were excited when she say this, but I wasn't so sure. I just wanted to make money, to make me and my brother's life better. Maybe I thought I would go to America and play sports, be famous and make the money. I guess where we different is Yousef want to make life better for all Muslims, he struggles for many more than I do, yes."

"Were there ever times when you didn't get along with your brother?"

Sayyid laughed. "When do we get along? Yousef is my greatest pain in this life. But he is my brother. He is my only family. There was one time I had enough for Yousef's preaching and condemning my behavior, so I quit talking to him for long time. But then I was under much inspection for a theft I committed where a man suffered death at my knife. I needed acceptable work, but there was none. One day a man was looking for boys who spoke English to act as clerk. I knew Yousef spoke, so I went back to him and allowed him to vent his anger at me. Then I ask him if he teach me English. So, I can't say the school has teach him nothing."

They were quiet for a while after that, listening to the folk music while Daniel thought about Sayyid's past, speculating about the facets of his childhood that molded him into who he was. Sayyid mentioned they were driving all the way to northeastern Somalia, towards Bosaso to the Cal Madow Mountain Range, where the Shamaness made her home. Sayyid didn't slow at any of the Al-Shabaab checkpoints as they approached. He just kept his foot on the gas and let his trail of dust storm where it may.

They eventually passed from the sandy, rocky terrain of the semi-desert towards a higher elevation. They sporadically passed thickets of African Junipers, with goat and camel herders resting by the oasis in the shade. Eventually the desert moisturized and turned into grassland, and after miles of driving a lonely road through a vast savannah replete with grazing giraffe and wild goat, mountains jutted heavenly on the horizon. Sayyid slowed his driving to account for the curving, up and down road that led through the foothills of Sanaag. Clouds formed overhead and a light rain developed into a downpour, so that at the bottom of a particular foothill, the road was washed out and the men were made to second-guess their route. A tree had fallen over the rocky, gnashing waters of the steep mountain ravine. Sayyid calculated the river flow would remain static for at least a day, and he determined it was time to go on foot. They backed the Land Cruiser up the foothill until Sayyid located an acceptable thicket of underbrush just off the road, and he cut a hole in the vines and small trees and bushes until the Land Cruiser fit inside like a custom-made garage. Then he camouflaged it as best he could and they left it there.

Sayyid studied the tree fallen across the gushing waterway, judging it to have fallen in the last couple of months. Still sturdy. He made Daniel go first, since he was still, after all, his slave. Daniel dropped his pack to the ground and shimmied across the tree on his belly, arms and legs wrapped around the trunk to provide maximum support. The bark scraped his skin, splintered under his fingernails, and the tiny limbs rubbed dark lines of resin across his face. As soon as he stood on the opposite side of the ravine, with a vicious deluge pulsating between he and Sayyid, his first thought was to run.

He laughed.

He looked around at this genuine jungle, mountain ridges enclosing the sky all about him, exotic animal noises singing, crying all around, poisons no doubt sprayed about his path in the form of vines, underbrush, and venomous animals. Where was he going to go without Sayyid as a guide? Out here, he was as good as dead without Sayyid.

Sayyid launched a cable of rope across the river, and Daniel fastened it to a nearby tree. Sayyid strung the packs on the rope, and once they were secure, Daniel pulled them across to dry land. Once all that was complete, Sayyid took the rope in his hands and walked the tree with the ease of a gymnast walking a balance beam. Where Daniel had gotten all cut up and had to endure his anxieties, Sayyid's crossing was a cinch. They mounted their backpacks, and continued along the muddy dirt road. Sayyid checked his watch.

"If we walk hard with few breaks, we should be able to get close before dark. I don't want to walk much longer after dark, yes."

They walked along that muddy road for hours. They passed no traffic. Daniel asked for breaks early and frequently, and although Sayyid indulged him at first he eventually compelled them to trudge at a strenuous pace, uphill and downhill, a few miles an hour with those thirty pound packs weighing on their backs.

The daylight had dimmed when Sayyid turned them off the main road, and up a narrow, hardly discernible game trail.

"Are you sure this is it?"

"See the cliff here, the squat waterfall there. This is it, yes. I never forget this place. I come here every day, in my dreams."

151

They forged on through the jungle thick. Crickets played the violin, teasing cats purred on the perimeter, wet leaves struck Daniel in the face as they trekked along. A tenth-of-a-mile along the new path, and Daniel couldn't perceive any evidence of a trail. He lodged protests with Sayyid.

"I have been here many times. How many times you come here? Ten? Two? No, I know. None. You never been here so let me be the guide, yes?"

Daniel couldn't argue with his logic. They were both exhausted, and Daniel didn't want to back Sayyid into a corner, especially since Sayyid was leaving open the option of executing Daniel in the forest.

Soon they arrived at the foot of a rocky hillside. A narrow trail wound upwards, along the circular edge of the rise. Daniel leaned his weight against the rock face as the distance between himself and the forest floor below diverged precipitously. They walked through the dark until they peaked above the forest canopy, with little light remaining on the horizon, the sun's work finishing for the day. The pink glow captured Daniel's attention, so much that he lamented not having the time or the pastel crayons to draw it. Remembering the Polaroid, he snapped his fingers. He fumbled through his bag as the pink haze on the horizon was quickly dissipating. He found the camera, raised it to his eye and snapped the picture.

"Daniel. You wasting my film again?"

"Look," Daniel said, pointing to the horizon. "It will be worth it."

Sayyid nodded, but said nothing. He rifled through his own backpack until he held a small yet powerful flashlight. He shone it on the rocks, here and there, like a searchlight, resting on the place where a narrow pass was cut right into the otherwise sheer rock face.

Daniel tripped along behind Sayyid for a moment before he stopped and found his own flashlight. When he shined it on the rock, he fell backwards, startled by the images confronting him. On approach to the Shamaness's dwelling, there were peculiar carvings in the rocks, of a strange race with oblong-shaped heads, that took to subjugating

152

humans. Tending indigenous people in the fields, supervising them in workshops. Images of the strange race forcing humans to breed with them. Finally, there was a carving of a giant human crushing the skull of one of the strange race as his crown fell to the ground in a dark pool of his own blood, while the remainder of the strange race fled to the sky. In the final depiction, the humans stood with their hands raised above their heads in celebration. He had no idea what it could have signified, but it was old, based on evidence of its age, where centennial roots gnarled through and bisected one of the depictions. If the drawings were less than a hundred years old, Daniel surmised, they would have been carved over that elderly tree's roots.

"Come on, Daniel, we almost there. You can admire the place after we talk to the Shamaness. There is much to come."

They curved around a switchback carved into a steep precipice, the pass not more than a foot wide for a stretch of ten feet, with a drop of at least several hundred feet. This bottleneck made the place easily defendable. Once beyond the precipice the ground widened, and there were statues made of hewn bones from assorted animals, grotesque dream beings standing sentry over the final walk towards the cave rising just in front of them. The cave glowed purplish-orange and there were mists oozing from its interior. Daniel found himself following on Sayyid's heels. While Daniel was petrified with fear, Sayyid appeared as relaxed as ever.

When they were within a few feet of the mouth of the cave, Sayyid stopped.

"Yoo hoo, Shamaness. It is your Sayyid come to see you." He repeated himself in several different tongues. An owl spoke to them in the near vicinity, and the trees rattled, though there was no wind. Daniel stuck his hands in his pockets to conceal his trembling. The alien light from the cave dimmed, and Daniel's thoughts could only focus on getting the hell out of there.

Then the light of the cave flared, so that Daniel and Sayyid shielded their eyes. Once the intense light dissipated, they lowered their arms to observe the forest still, the light from the cave static, and a camel-skin robed Shamaness standing before them.

# *Fifteen*

Sayyid addressed the Shamaness in a variety of languages like they were old friends, but she rarely responded and when she did it was in a tongue with which Daniel was unfamiliar. He wasn't even certain she spoke a formal language, but rather some amalgamation of indigenous tongues. Her hair was silky grey and well-kept and reflected what little light illuminated the surroundings. Other than her hair, all Daniel could perceive of her features were her eyes, which seemed old and wizened. She began to touch Sayyid's body, not in a recognizably formal approach, but in the manner of a longed-for lover, his chest, his neck, his buttocks. She snapped her tongue and clicked her teeth at him, wrapping her arms around his waist.

"Stop it Shamaness you make me blush in front of Daniel."

She released Sayyid and turned her attention to Daniel. He trembled in the darkness. She held his forearm up to what light there was and examined his white skin. She clicked her teeth as she followed it up to his bicep and shoulder. She dropped his arm and reached between his legs and cupped his testicles. She snapped her tongue excitedly, when she found those, and Daniel involuntarily smacked her hand away from his genitals.

Then she clicked and snapped furiously, jumping back towards Sayyid.

"She says you must let her complete her examination to determine whether or not you are spoiled. If you not permit examination, then she just assume you spoiled."

Daniel tried to drop his defenses. The Shamaness returned to him, albeit more carefully, deliberately this time. She didn't examine his genitals again, having already checked those, but felt his waist and put her ear against his heart, and held it there while it thudded uncontrollably. After she examined his toes, she jumped and beckoned them both inside her cave.

She invited them to sit cross-legged with her on the floor of the cave. She sat facing them, reading tealeaves in clicks and shouts. She broke small animal bones, examining the fractures, ordering Daniel drink the marrow. He did as he was told.

The Shamaness began either praying or singing. Daniel wasn't actually certain what she was doing. Perhaps she was having a conniption or a psychotic breakdown. He noticed for the first time that a vapor seemed to be seeping through the rocks, permeating the air. He felt light headed. The Shamaness continued to indulge them with her alien incantations. For a moment, Daniel thought he saw the candles in his peripheries levitate, but when he turned his head they rested on the ground, melted to the rock. The Shamaness reached into a leather pelt and dusted Daniel with flour. She began repeating herself rapidly, the same ten-syllables clicking across her tongue, an eerie breeze originating from some hidden subterranean corridor of the cave, flickering the flames and causing Daniel's hair to stand all over his body. Fright bumps covered his arms and legs. Fear overwhelmed his skepticism. He wanted to leave, run actually, but he was at a loss for autonomy. Unquestionably there was nowhere to go from here.

The Shamaness stood and started dancing while the two men remained seated, cross-legged. Her camel-hair top fell to the ground, exposing unusually firm breasts for an old outlander who made her living foraging the land. In another instant, she was completely naked, pulsating, swinging and swaying her hips around the room, those candles flickering, revealing glimpses of her toned stomach, firm thighs, conditioned biceps.

She leaned in towards Daniel, and before he could react she had kissed him on the mouth.

He was surprised to feel his lips pucker against hers. She held a wooden bowl to his lips, and in clear English said: "Drink."

He opened his mouth and took a drink of the bitter, sedimentous concoction. He started to cough, then choke, but she returned her lips to his and his reaction was soothed.

Then she stood, with her unmanicured pubic hairs dangling before them and said: "You are brothers if before sunrise a meteor kisses the North Star."

Then she gently draped her fingers across both men's faces, closing their eyelids.

When Daniel reopened his eyes he was sitting next to Sayyid, only they had been transported from the cave to the edge of a cliff, overlooking an expanse of forest illuminated by twinkling stars. The air was rarified, no longer laced with strange incense and candle wax and other indescribable vapors.

"How did we get here?"

"We drove from Mogadishu."

"No, that's not what I mean."

"Quiet your mind, Daniel. Focus on the sky, the earth, and your soul inside. Tonight you need to pray to the sky, for if its will is not satisfied you will not live for lunch."

Daniel remembered what he thought the Shamaness had said: if a meteor kisses the North Star before sunrise. Had she spoken English the whole time? Or had the entire experience been a hallucination?

They sat in silence for a long time until Sayyid initiated a conversation. They spoke long and wide, about many things, from childhood, to food and music, and women. Daniel told Sayyid everything there was to know about Bally. Sayyid told Daniel about a girl he had loved once in Mogadishu. Sayyid told Daniel about how he would meet her in a park, during the last two years of the Siad Barre era, when times were peaceful, and they would go for walks and swim in a pool and eat ice cream. Then there was the Civil War and peace in Somalia was destroyed until this day. Daniel asked Sayyid what had happened to the girl, but Sayyid ignored the question.

Daniel was afraid he had upset Sayyid, but Sayyid soon pressed Daniel for more stories about Bally.

Daniel told Sayyid about how they had been just friends for years, but elaborated on all their adventures together.

Sayyid laughed and smiled at some of the stories. He made a circle with his left index finger and thumb, stroking his opposite index finger in and out of the hole. He said Daniel should have stuck it in there. He said this is the only way to mark a territory, to stick it in there. Daniel sighed, and agreed. They told bar stories and talked about soccer. They each discovered the other shared a passion for soccer. They talked on and on for hours.

The dawn was beginning to make way for the day. Daniel was growing increasingly nervous. They hadn't seen the sign the Shamaness told them to look for. Daniel peered over, discreetly, to see that Uzi bulging in Sayyid's waistband. Would he really use it? After all they had been through? After all this bonding? The pirate was crazy enough to drive them all the way out to this remote jungle to ask the advice of an erotic, heathen cave dweller. Why not shoot Daniel? Hadn't Sayyid shot a slave before? Wasn't killing Sayyid's forte? What if they did just have a nice conversation? Did that mean that Sayyid would shirk the Shamaness's directive and let Daniel live? It seemed unlikely.

A fuzzy orange glow appeared on the horizon. Sayyid had been sitting with his eyes shut for the past few minutes, breathing methodically with his nostrils turned up into the mountain draft.

When the sun crowned on the distant tree line, Daniel said his final prayers. Lord, watch over my sister. Let Bally live a happy, peaceful life. May this strife in Somalia come to a peaceful resolution. May I have done some beneficial work on this Earth. Grant me access to your kingdom, dear Lord. Daniel spoke in this Christian lingo he knew not that he possessed. He looked around at the swaying trees and fluttering birds, a vast appreciation for it all in his heart. Even for Sayyid, his executioner, he was glad to have met him. Sayyid was the only truly fearless man he had ever met, and although Sayyid would soon lodge a bullet in his vertebrae without remorse, he felt his life was more complete for having met him.

Sayyid yawned, stretched his arms and stood.

"Well, that's it, yes?" Sayyid said.

Daniel clinched his jaw and closed his eyes.

This was it.

"Hello, Daniel, are you awake? You can't do this asleep."

"I'm not asleep. Just do it. Just do it."

"I'm not going to carry you out of the forest on my back. You'll have to walk, yes."

"What?" Daniel said, opening his eyes.

"We leave now. I see the meteor kiss the North Star. Did you not?" Sayyid laughed. "I should think you would have stayed awake to watch for the omen to save your life. You are perhaps not fit for this world."

Daniel didn't know whether Sayyid was toying with him. He decided he'd rather clear the air than have this hanging over his head for the unforeseeable future.

"I was awake all night. I didn't see it."

"It was there. Surely I don't question my own eyes."

He was being honest, Daniel thought. Either Daniel had really missed it, Sayyid thought he saw it, or Sayyid had decided because of their bonding that he wasn't going to kill Daniel.

"You gather the things, and I will say goodbye to the Shamaness, yes."

Daniel gladly gathered their belongings and made ready for the hike out. Sayyid returned suddenly, without the Shamaness.

"Let us go."

"Is she not going to say goodbye to me?"

"She had nothing to say to you. She tell me one last thing. I owe you one large favor, to cement our brotherhood, to make amend for owning you as slave, yes. You can think this over."

They carefully edged around the steep precipice switchback, passed the haunting rock carvings, starting down the game trail.

"What kind of favor? I mean, what magnitude are we talking about here?"

"Whatever you want."

"I mean are we talking dinner or like freedom to return to America?"

"Freedom? Freedom you have, brother. You are a free man, yes."

"You mean, like to go home?"

"Yes, yes. You are no longer my slave. You save my life. The Shamaness say we are brothers if the meteor--"

"Yes, I was there."

"Then don't ask questions when you have already answer, yes?"

"Ok, but when we get back to Mogadishu, you'll drive me to the airport and that's it?"

"Yes, yes," Sayyid said. "I still like for you to write article. You did come here for article in first place, yes?"

"Yea, that's why I came here."

"So this is no problem. We both want article."

"I promise I'll write the best article you've ever read."

Sayyid nodded, but seemed a little sad.

"Is everything alright?"

"I just think before maybe you would stay, but now I see you eager return home to U.S.A."

"You would really consider letting me join your gang?"

"You save our life, Daniel. The Shamaness say you are my brother. But a man cannot be made to fight. It would endanger everyone. What you do next is your choice."

**Daniel called his kid sister Freda** as soon as they returned to the Orient Pearl.

"I told whoever this is to quit calling me!" She screamed. "It's not funny!"

"Freda, it's really me, Daniel. Look at the number." There was a moment's silence on the other end of the line. "Listen to my voice. Just hear me out. This is your brother, Daniel. I was given an assignment to travel to Somalia to research an article on the Somali pirates, when I was kidnapped. I was sold as a slave. A few days ago, I saved my most owner's life and in return he's granted me freedom."

"Daniel," Freda said, with a broken voice. It was clear she was distraught.

"I'm ok. Physically speaking, I'm ok."

Freda was sobbing in to the receiver. "We . . . thought. . . you . . . were . . . dead," she said. She was uncontrollable.

"I'm here. I'm alive."

"We . . . mourned . . .you."

"I'm sorry. I'm sorry."

Daniel held the receiver to his ear while Freda's sobs gradually subsided. He needed to talk logistics if he was going to get home. But when she dried up, the first thing he asked about wasn't the logistics of getting from Dulles to Georgetown.

"How's Bally?"

"After you disappeared, I spoke to her once. It's been seven months, Daniel."

"What's happened?"

"I know you always had a crush on her."

"Is she already married?"

"She and Burton had a small ceremony in the Caribbean last month. She called me the night before the ceremony, to ask if there had been any news."

In that moment, the only thing that existed in the world to Daniel was Freda's news. There was no emancipation. No multiple killings by his own hand. No war zone. No crimes committed for and against. There was a singularity of loss, and nothing more. Nothing less. The whole time in Somalia he had wanted to return home, and now he was struggling for a reason to leave. What had journalism ever gotten him? Some allowance? The profession had cost him the love of his life, lost him to the slave trade, left his life in peril multiple times.

Journalism had given him nothing.

He had nothing.

A nonentity.

"When will you be coming home?" Freda asked, a new chipper quality to her voice.

"I'll have to consider the options," Daniel said. He stared across the suite at Sayyid, who had originally left him his privacy, but now sat across the room from him, studying him. "I love you Freda. Tell everyone I'm alright. I've got to go now. Talk soon."

"Wait."

But Daniel hung up the phone.

"How much of that did you hear?"

Sayyid winced. "I listen to most of it."

"You still have a spot open on your crew?"

"One spot for you, yes."

"Plus you still owe me a favor?"

162

"One big favor. Shamaness says this is how I bond."

"Then I'm going to stay. And I know exactly what favor I want to ask you."

# Sixteen

When Daniel told Sayyid his one request, Sayyid was more than happy to oblige him.

"This the Sayyid can do. First, we drive down to Kismayo and ask the Emir where he buy you. Then it is easy as a trigger pull. We can make a sport of this, too, yes. You get wish and I train you to kill order." Sayyid couldn't contain his smile as he talked about it on the road to Kismayo. The two men rode south, with Daniel riding shotgun. Sayyid had taught him how to gnaw on the khat leaves, and Daniel chewed stem after stem, staring out in to the desolation, a loaded Ruger 9mm resting in the pocket of his expedition vest.

She married Burton Fucking Woods.

Journalism didn't matter.

Love didn't matter.

Money was all there was.

Money and the social status money could buy. It was a simple equation: If he had had more money than Burton Woods, Bally would have married him. Because he had less money than Burton Woods, he did not get to marry Bally. Now he was going to get money. Serious pirate money.

He chewed those khat leaves. Unconsciously, he had quickly developed a vast understanding of why the pastime was so popular. He felt so focused, like he never had in his life. He scoffed at the idea of the books and portfolios of pictures he toted around the city back home from apartment to apartment. The clutter he lived in, which at the time seemed normal, perhaps even essential to what he was doing. Books, to do lists, drafts of papers, zip drives.

All of that was meaningless.

Despite all his struggle and worry, all of it could be taken from him in a moment. Thieving maid. Thieving friend. Burglary. Fire. Misplaced at a coffee shop or a university carrel. Snatched by the wind from an unsecured zipper pocket. Then never even knowing it was lost. Worrying all his days over things he would never even know he had lost.

Fucking Bally. She knew she was going to do this all along. Burton Woods. Daniel searched his memories, her going to Burton's squash tournaments, his swim meets, and sneaking off to call Burton even though it was public knowledge he was stuffing a half dozen other girls. Burton never cared. Only now that he'd made it, that he was bona fide and settling down did he appreciate her. Daniel had appreciated her his entire life and now she was someone else's. And not just anyone else's. But Burton. Fucking. Woods.

They arrived in Kismayo, the city recently pummeled and subsequently evacuated by TFG and Ethiopian forces. Daniel hadn't even noticed the razed city. Or the absence of troops or remembered what had happened when they fled some weeks ago. Perhaps it wasn't recognizable to anyone because it had changed shape. Assumed a new form. It was a different place entirely but what of it remained still resided in the location of the old.

Before he was even aware, Sayyid was leading him through the unguarded gate of the emptied Bantu Slave Market pavilion, down the amphitheater steps and through an open, unmarked metal door where Daniel had been marched out to be sold to the highest bidder. But he wasn't thinking about this as his Ruger weighted his vest and a khat stem

166

dangled from his mouth. He was thinking about all the shit everyone had always given him, how little money he'd made during his days on earth, how little appreciated his work had been, how many assholes he'd encountered, how badly Bally had hurt him and how badly he wanted to do something sinister to Burton Woods in public not just to even the score, but to send a stark message to all the other Burton Woodses of the world. He wanted retribution to redeem the name of justice.

Sayyid spoke with those two scrubbed attendants who had put Daniel at ease when he had arrived at the Emir's compound, made him feel safe, like he was going home. They led Sayyid down the hall to the Emir's familiar office, where the bespectacled Emir sat behind his desk reviewing one of his porno magazines with a serious intent cast across his face, as if he were studying a textbook.

Sayyid and the Emir had an exchange in Somali, which Daniel did not understand. He watched as the Emir looked at Daniel with uneasy eyes. Daniel ripped the last few khat leaves from the stem, chewing them in to a nice thick ball of cud. There was dust on the bookshelves, paint cracked around the ceiling, a dust ball in each of the two visible corners of the room, the stack of porno magazines on the shelf having ballooned since Daniel's last visit. There was a smudged magnifying glass lying on top of a Quran. A hollow in the wall, disguised to be unnoticed, was betrayed by an inconsistency in the painted brown lines that broke up the cream room, where the absence of dry wall was black.

Sayyid and the Emir's conversation came to a sputter.

"He says you were purchased west of Bilis Qooqaani."

Daniel raised the pistol from his expedition vest, aimed it at the Emir's head, and pulled the trigger at point blank range. The explosion in the small office was deafening. The Emir recoiled in his chair, red brain mush splattered all over his pornography collection.

167

"Daniel this not part of the deal," Sayyid said with some hesitancy. He didn't speak with the urgency of condemnation, but he rested his hand on his Uzi and began nervously glancing at the office's entrance.

Daniel walked over to the secret door and pulled it open. A draft breezed into the room, up from a set of stairs illuminated by a single light bulb revealing a stone cellar. Daniel descended the stairs. Although he hardly noticed, Sayyid was following close behind him. There was a thick, carpeted door at the bottom of the stairs. Daniel tried to force it open, but eventually blasted two bullet holes where there normally might have been hinges and kicked the thing in.

In the room were two young boys in small cages, bondage sexual devices hung from the ceilings, video equipment rested on tripods next to VHS tapes, DVDs, and dusty HP computers. A set of rusty keys hung on a nail by the carpeted door. Sayyid snatched the keys and unfastened the locks on both cages. Shouting and voices could be heard in the office above.

Daniel started to take the lead, but Sayyid yanked his shirt, pulling ahead. Sayyid walked deliberately up the stairs, not rushed but not hesitant either and when he approached the door he kicked it, with Uzi in hand, and, with a defeaning roar, popped everyone in the room. Daniel summitted in to the room just behind him, prepared to execute anything that moved. A half dozen freshly fashioned corpses decorated the room, and Daniel hurried down the hall behind Sayyid, with both the young boys clambering behind as well. One of the boys was crying, but the other wrapped a tender arm around his counterpart's shoulder and exhorted him to hurry along. When the party made daylight, the boys sprinted up the amphitheater stairs quick and without ceremony. They scrambled across the boulevard and disappeared in to the streets of Kismayo.

Sayyid glided up the amphitheater stairs backwards, watching that door until he peaked at the gate and they hurried over to the Land Cruiser.

"I did not see that happening that way."

Daniel said nothing in reply.

168

Sayyid laughed. "You are a killer Daniel! A pirate you already are, yes. To Bilis Qooqaani we go! I hate to see what you do to the next guys."

# *Seventeen*

There was less than nothing along the road to Bilis Qooqaani. It was an area forgotten, or perhaps never discovered, depending on one's perspective. They chewed through the original bag of khat, with Daniel doing most of the jawing, so that Sayyid stopped the Land Cruiser and found a slightly expired bag among the weapons, camping equipment, spare tire and other rubbish in his trunk. They continued driving and continued chewing.

I understand why people chew this.

I understand why.

I understand.

I.

I, Daniel.

The universe was no less than a thing created to stimulate his perception. It was failing now, beyond the purvey of the car window, all save for the khat, Sayyid's temerity, and the horrible folk music they'd been listening to ever since they left Mogadishu. Each motivated by his own sensibility. Likes and dislikes. How they ever got to be that way was a scientist's puzzle. If he only knew how he'd developed his own, well, possession of that piece of knowledge would be miraculous.

Daniel wouldn't have recognized the goat farmer's place because he'd only seen the outside once, and then he'd been distracted by the other men and the act of maiming the skinny one.

"This is it," Sayyid said. "This is the place the Emir say it was. Look familiar?"

"Yes."

It didn't.

There was a small sad hut, hardly large enough for a couple roughing it for an evening, much less for a multigenerational homestead, but there it was. There were goats and scrub brush and not much more. Daniel discarded the magazine he had used in Kismayo and took a new one from his expedition vest. He had a few of them, magazines, in there. Then he pulled on the barrel, until the first bullet popped in to the breech. The hammer hung out there, ready to go to work. His finger dangled recklessly taut on the hair trigger.

Sayyid pointed to a horseback rider on the distance. Daniel nodded. While watching the horseback rider gradually trot his way back to the encampment, Daniel stared out towards the slaughtering shed, the place where he'd been kept, abused, maligned for all that time. There were a couple of reserve jugs of gasoline resting next to the shed. Daniel looked in SUV's cup holder and saw a lighter.

He put his thumb on the hammer, pulled the trigger and let the hammer to rest gently on the pin. Then he stuck the pistol in his waistband, snatched the lighter and marched over to the shed. He lifted the first jug of gasoline, its weight testifing to its fill. He unscrewed the cap and whiffed the diesel destruction. He doused the wall first, then the door, then splashed what he could on the roof. When he was satisfied, he kicked the door open, tossing inside the jug along with what diesel fuel remained. There was a goat in there awaiting the slaughter, along with some chickens. He took a step back, flicked the lighter aflame, leaned in and held it to the closest place he'd soaked real good.

It caught fire.

At first, there was just a patch, but once it spread it was a proper conflagration. The beasts inside whined for pity. The horseback rider across the plain started galloping towards his ignited property. Daniel took the pistol from his trousers, held it behind his back in his right hand and pulled back the hammer. He started walking towards the horseback rider.

At seventy yards he could tell it was the skinny one. At thirty yards, he raised the pistol and started firing off shots, one two three four five. It took six for the rider to fall off the horse. Daniel ran towards him, pistol trained on prey, and as he stood over him, he saw he'd struck the skinny man in the stomach. The man writhed on the ground, stomach acid already eating its way through his kidneys and liver. Maybe a half hour to live. Aw, Daniel thought, there's his bit off ear. Daniel traced the man on the ground with the pistol, but he wasn't worth a bullet. The man had earned his suffering.

There was a gunshot in the distance, shifting his attention immediately. Daniel turned to see the fat one holding his hands over his head, while Sayyid approached him with his raised Uzi. Daniel started walking over there, before bursting into a run.

"Down," Daniel ordered, pointing to the ground. He snatched a knife off the man's belt, cutting him in the stomach, opening his belly like a Ziploc bag and letting its contents pour out onto the desert floor, cutting the man on his face and on his arms and the man screamed and begged but his words did not slow Daniel in his work. Finally, Sayyid shot the man through the head.

"Why did you do that?"

"One day you will thank me, yes."

"I asked why did you do that," Daniel asked, with an insatiable fierceness in his voice, swinging that bloody knife through the air.

"Put the knife down, Daniel. You scare me. I know not what these men do to you, but whatever they do, do not let you do worse by them to yourself."

"You cannot speak English like a normal fucking person?"

Sayyid ripped the knife from Daniel's hand like an adult strips something from the hand of a child. Daniel hadn't even had time to react before Sayyid had pitched the knife off in to the distance, lost.

"I have grant you your wish. Revenge is yours, brother. Now let us go home, yes."

Sayyid turned and walked towards the Land Cruiser. Daniel, his chest heaving in and out, and after some grumbling, eventually submitted to the ride home.

**Sayyid gave Daniel some Ambien** on the ride back to Mogadishu. Daniel slept, but when he woke they were both asleep in their car seats in the middle of the desert, surrounded by earthly blackness decorated with starry sequins. Not home yet. Sayyid's stamina had given out before they made it back.

Realizing for the first time the full implication of what he had done yesterday, Daniel opened his car door and vomited on the clean desert ground until there was nothing left in his stomach. He lied on the ground for a while, dry heaving, thinking his stomach wasn't the only thing that was empty. His surroundings, his heart, his life were all empty. Sayyid and the Land Cruiser were his only connections to the world. Then he felt the plastic and metal of the Ruger in his waistband and considered severing those last connections. He had a firm grip on the pistol, an instant ticket to oblivion.

"I won't stop you."

Daniel turned to look at Sayyid standing over him.

"Why."

"A man who is no good to himself is no good to anyone."

"Yes yes yes yes yes. Why do you not say the word you always *fucking* say?"

"I say yes because it is a positive word. I no say it now because I no want to influence your very important decision. Do you live with your crime, swallow that action or do you choke on it? Every little notch in this life either make us stronger or kill us. Look at you on your hands and knees in this desert. Pathetic. But under my wing, you can get rich. You can have girls. Forget the one. You can have all the girls. You can get a car.

174

You can have the people say 'Daniel, Daniel,' because I Sayyid will teach you how. This is your chance now. But if you cannot live with yesterday, then I promise you cannot live with tomorrow."

Trembling, Daniel stood. He clasped his hands on Sayyid's shoulders, and with weak, tear stained eyes said, "Good." A moment later they got back in the Land Cruiser and Sayyid followed the vehicle's high beams through the undemarcated terrain back to Mogadishu.

**He had become estranged from freedom,** so that he didn't have much of an imagination when it came to its application. But after a day of psychological turmoil, loneliness, and perpetual thoughts of suicide he decided to visit the WHO facility and Doctor Caitlin Cordon. The mere thought made him feel better. He didn't know whether he would tell her everything or nothing. He guessed somewhere on the spectrum of in between.

**Caitlin had thought back to her time** at Stadium Mogadishu and the Orient Pearl often. She wondered how the man, Daniel was doing. Whether he was alive and well or tossed alongside other refuse in some mass grave. It saddened her that she may never know.

She hadn't ventured alone in to Mogadishu since the Stadium incident. Life had been more predictable around the clinic, but not quite boring. She was still living vicariously through the memory of that one episode, having had enough thrill on that day to last her up into the present. She treated burn victims, gunshot wounds, malnutrition, and food poisoning. Then there were the undiagnosable malaises, which were unnamable because they simply didn't exist in the civilized world. She wondered whether she would return to England when her two-year contract expired, or whether she would renew it for another term. Wouldn't England be even more boring than this place? At least there she could wonder the streets with impunity. Here, well.

She was treating a young woman for a botched circumcision. Folk custom dictated that a woman in Somalia should have her genitalia cut in youth, otherwise the thought was she would be ineligible for marriage. There was little knowledge about rusty knives, tetanus, and antiseptic among the populace. The Doctor finished the girl's medical treatment, and was cheering her up before she moved on to her next patient. The girl was sitting on the examination table in a hospital gown, and Caitlin opened the drawn shades to let in light.

Caitlin shuddered when she saw Daniel inexplicably standing there in the hallway. What is he doing here? He seems, different.

"Excuse me," Caitlin asked her patient. The girl nodded, and Caitlin approached Daniel in the hallway.

Her pulse quickened. He had escaped, and she wondered what was required of him in this country to secure his release. She felt guilty for having not done more.

"May I help you? Usual protocol is you sign-in, then an attending nurse shows you to an. . ."

"I came here to see you."

"But usually. . ."

"There's nothing wrong with me," he said.

Maybe physically, but something, some unforgettable image, memory or feeling was clouding his inner light. He tried to smile, but instead this creepy visage, with some fraction of a smile, spread across his face.

"The situation I was in when we met, that's not my situation anymore. I'm not beholden to those guys."

"Then you're leaving Somalia?"

"No. I've got a job. In the private industry."

"Doing what?" She asked, looking around to see if any of the other staff were walking the halls. They weren't. She didn't know what to do with her hands. They'd been in and out of her pockets, on her face, and then she crossed them. Why hadn't she bathed this morning? She would look so much better if she had just rinsed off.

"You seem like a nice woman. Someone I could talk to."

"I am nice. But I'm also busy."

"I can understand that. Especially here, in your profession. Or in your profession anywhere, I suppose. Every place needs a doctor."

"Seems so."

"Maybe we could get together sometime?"

"Like a date?" She asked, tightening her arms, seriously scanning the area for some assistance. There was a security station in the next corridor over. Two large native-born Somalis. Big guys.

He shook his head slightly to the negative.

"Doesn't have to be. I'd just like to have someone to talk to, you know, someone who could get it."

"Get what?"

"Whatever it is we have to say to one another. Look, I see you looking around all nervous, so I'll say I'll leave soon and I will, if it will put you at ease. I didn't come here to be threatening or forward, you're just the only person I've met in this country I felt like I could relate to. Now I'm going to be living here, so I thought I'd ask if you'd like to hang out sometime, but if you don't, it's fine to say so."

She uncrossed her arms. Her white coat was unbuttoned and it cracked open, revealing her gray mass-produced t-shirt and the tight knot that held up her green medical scrub pants. She became self-conscious of how tight they fit. Not because she had put on weight since she came to Somalia, but because they projected a sexier look than she intended. She burrowed both her fists in the pockets of her white coat, casting her gaze on the ground.

"I think I could say yes to the right invitation," she said. She heard her voice squeak. She wished she hadn't taken all those psych classes in college. She was always analyzing herself, which made her even more self-conscious, creating this negative feedback loop that shattered her confidence.

Dr. Mehfoud turned in to the hall, studying a clipboard. He was the co-chair, the second in command of the doctors. Shift supervisor. Kind, but all business.

"That's my boss," she said.

"Get back to work then, but first could I get a good number so I don't have to come all the way across town? Phones are a lot safer around here than streets."

She blushed.

"I know," she said. She slid back in to examination room, where the young Somali girl was still sitting patiently on the examination table, scrawled her name and number on the back of a blank diagnostic form, folded it, returned to Daniel in the hallway and handed him the folded slip.

"Daniel Barnes," he said, back peddling towards the exit. Mr. Mehfoud was standing between them now with a *what's going on expression* painted on his face.

"I remember," Caitlin said.

# *Eighteen*

On the eve of his inaugural pirate raid, Daniel was captivated by thoughts of how much money he stood to make. Sayyid told him the fourth hand could make anywhere between twenty and fifty thousand dollars a raid. It was an unfathomable amount, where he was making just under fifty a year when he lived in Washington, DC. He did the math, and if they did one raid a week then on the low end he stood to profit as much as a million dollars a year. He medicated himself with dreams of the toys such wealth could buy him: the yachts, cars, clothes, dinners, leisure, and airfare anywhere anytime in the world. He could be as ubiquitous or nonexistent as he pleased. What would Bally or Burton or any of it matter soon? He was to become a pirate, the raw material from which great stories were mined. His world was about to expand beyond and envelop the horizon. Forget even spatial references, he would draw up the blueprints for the sun's bedchambers to suit his own predilection. Then poets could wax about his act of creation and speculate about the emotion of what it was like to have assembled those atoms that combined to form the very experience that shaped their perception into the artist who would react to the forces imposed on them. Without a person to experience there was no act.

He understood why Sayyid had wanted him to write the article in the first place. The problem was the inescapability of understanding.

Looking out the window of his room at the Orient Pearl, loaded pistol lying in his lap, it was hard for him not to think about lodging a bullet through the skull of the man he now knew was a psychopath; but he so loved the world created by his own perception that he dared not end the experience for the sake of the people whose existence was perpetuated by his acquiescence.

A loud conversation in the next room evolved into an argument. Though it was conducted in Somali, Daniel didn't need to exercise much inference to acknowledge that Yousef was disappointed his older brother hadn't fed the infidel to the desert predators. Yousef no doubt would like to see Daniel sausaged into carrion and consider the problem solved. Without exercising logic, Daniel stood and walked into the room, pistol gripped in his hand. The two brothers quieted. Daniel scratched his neck and his chin and there was a singleness of mind that might have led one to question whether he was sentient or some reduced being.

"What time are we heading out?" Daniel asked.

Yousef's face turned sheepish, unable to turn his gaze from the pistol Daniel pointed benignly towards the ground but with the effect of brandishing. Sayyid glanced over at his brother.

"Yes, what time did you say we are leaving Yousef?"

Yousef studied his brother as if to discern whether or not he had forgotten everything they had just argued about, about whether or not Daniel was fit to live and work amongst them, but Sayyid displayed a deft poker face and when Yousef really glared hard on Sayyid, the older brother merely examined his finger nails as he awaited his reply. Only once the silence had been underscored did Sayyid turn and face his brother.

"What time?"

The little brother was without an ally and perhaps some logic stirred inside him that without Daniel they were short-handed and that perhaps working with a familiar infidel was better than dying at the hands of a strange one.

"I think we should leave in an hour. Macalin has gone to retrieve the coordinates of a special ship. I believe he is also bringing back bullets. We can leave as soon as he return."

"You hear this Daniel? It is not so very long until we depart for your first pirate mission. Are you ready to a kill again? To shoot the gun? Pow pow," Sayyid said, cocking his fingers in to a faux pistol. He laughed. "Look at you. Of course you are."

Daniel would kill someone if they were trying to kill him. He would return fire with fire. But what if someone only posed the threat of shooting him, but hadn't actually shot at him? He would kill them, too. What if he was mistakenly threatened? Well, it would be a mistake to threaten him. A big mistake to threaten him.

**Off the coast of Eyl**, they were supplied with intelligence and schooners from the field general, Quimbly, at the flotilla. Their mark was a cruise ship occupied by a 150 wealthy clientele and a staff of equal ratio. They were navigating 1200 miles off the coast of Somalia, 1000 miles being a presumptively safe distance. The flotilla turned that seafarer's advantage on its head. Way out there, they were far removed from the security corridor provided by international naval forces, Combined Task Force-151. Unlike last time, where they were able to use deception to ease the seizure, there was no way a cruise ship carrying civilians was going to respond to a distressed life raft in hostile waters. The cruise ship would call in the sighting to CTF-151, nothing more. Today, the plan was a straightforward strategy: a full-frontal attack.

Macalin had brought RPGs back from Bakara Market, and Sayyid dusted off a second Uzi for the occasion. Yousef shouldered a sniper rifle purportedly accurate at the distance of a mile. They fully expected the ship's crew to attempt to murder them dead in their speedy schooners rather than take the smallest risk of the pirates damaging the ship or disturbing any of its affluent passengers.

Macalin piloted the boat as they skipped across the rippleless plane, their wake the only disturbance in sight, as they followed Sayyid and Yousef in the lead boat. There was so little of anything out there that it was startling when the cruise ship appeared as a misfigured rectangle on the edge of the ocean. The ship grew larger, resembling a flightless duck staring into the muzzle of a gun.

Death was on the horizon.

"Pick up the RPG and get ready to fire it at the bow of the ship," Macalin yelled over the repetitive collapsing of the boat on the broken plane of the sea. Daniel hefted the cylinder on to his shoulder, pointing the projectile towards the front-end of the boat, as he had been told. "Just wait to fire it when I tell you. Timing is everything." Daniel relaxed back in to his seat with the boomstick levered over his shoulder. Strange that he felt relaxed there in that seat, with that instrument of mass death in his hands, sea spray striking his face like shotgun pellets, death in the eaves waiting to be dealt. The only unknown was who would to be the dealer.

Dozens of flashes of light could be seen from the cruise ship that was just a thousand feet ahead. Then phantom splashes, instantly followed by a singeing of the air. Squinting, he could see tiny human dots assaulting them from the ship's deck.

"Ok now. Show them what we brought," Macalin said.

Daniel stood, looked through the sights and with a firm grip on the tube, pulled off the safety latch and pressed the fire button. The tube shuddered and ignited an explosion and for a moment Daniel thought he was going to be carried away but then the projectile whizzed out in front of him, streaking across the sky with a red tracer and spiraled just past the bow of the ship. The flak from the cruise ship ceased for a moment but then returned with a desperate intensity. The bullets were kissing the water closer to them now, the pirate schooners spreading out into a wider formation but still hurtling towards the cruise ship.

"What do we do if they don't stop shooting?"

"We shoot them."

"What if we can't kill them all?"

"Then we sink the ship and kill them all."

Daniel imagined this giant cruise ship burning, plummeting into the ocean floor. It would be a tragedy of titanic proportions. Media outlets across the world would carry the story. If anyone lived to tell of the assault, they would be hunted men throughout the world. No state of anarchy would be desperate enough to provide them quarter. Daniel examined the ship, the flags flying above the masts, the multiple leisure decks, balconies craning off staterooms, the magnificent condition of the entire vessel. Without doubt, until moments ago it had been a floating paradise.

"That waterslide on top looks fun."

"We'll be riding it in half an hour," Macalin said.

**It was actually forty-five minutes later** before they had picked off each of the cruise ship's marksmen. Once the sentinel had felled in a burst of red, Macalin hooked a ladder on the low freeboard deck and shimmied up. Daniel was close behind. They immediately ran across the deck with M-16 muzzles pointed forward, vigilant for hidden assassins with a designs on their lives. It was eerily quiet, not a passenger or live crewmember within sight. Daniel and Macalin ended up doing much of the initial killing while Sayyid and Yousef were presumably circling around the other side of the cruise ship, beyond sight, distracted with some task Daniel had not the leisure to speculate.

They met no one until they secured the bridge. There the Captain stood pokerfaced with his frightened officers. Macalin had all but one of them ziptied on the ground, the last one allowed free to continue piloting the ship.

"Go see where Yousef and Sayyid are. They are probably taking the spoils without us," Macalin said.

Daniel exited the bridge and ran along the decks, looking over the sides of the boat in the increasingly choppy water for the pirates' boat. There it was, floating unmanned several hundred meters out. Their ladder was hooked on the side of the ship as well. All good signs. But where were they? Daniel continued around the decks of the ship, passed lounge chairs, passed the open-air poolside café. The common areas were devoid of passengers and crew alike. Hotdogs burned on a grill, frozen margaritas melted in the heat of the sun. The emptiness of the fun ship was disconcerting. They must be all huddled somewhere, or trembling in their rooms.

Finally, Daniel heard a familiar pair arguing. He nudged the door into the main dining room, finding Sayyid and Yousef in a screaming match, where the majority of the ship's huddling civilian passengers watched in terror. A grand chandelier hung from the ceiling, like a dwarf star. Daniel could smell the fineness of the linen tablecloths. The panoramic floor-to-ceiling windows were no less than spectacular.

Sayyid took Yousef by the shirt collar just as Daniel entered, but Sayyid turned to shoot the intruder before acknowledging that it was only Daniel.

"Announce yourself so you no killed, yes?" Sayyid said.

"Sorry. I just was looking for you guys. Macalin and I were worried. We have the bridge. What are you guys doing?"

"Baby brother here think it a good idea to lead the hostages in Muslim prayer as soon as we take the ship. I tell him we not seize the ship to convert it to a mosque."

"It is our duty to convert to Islam! Those not with us are against!"

"Yousef you must temper yourself, yes. These people just want to live. We are the ones attacking them, yes?"

"No it is our duty to hear them sing to Allah!"

"We are pirate and we come here to pirate ship. You confuse these two missions and risk the safety of all, yes."

"We do this pirate for Allah."

"No, *you* do this pirate for Allah. I do this pirate for Sayyid."

184

"You give the money to the hospital. You give the money to the shura. You give give give. Why you not see why we do this? Why not show these people the way while they are given to listen to us? So they can take Islam back to their infidel brothers?"

"Because you confuse our mission. Today is not about religion. It is about taxing the wealthy."

"It is about religion! Everything is about religion, otherwise we no do this! Otherwise we herd goat in the desert. Who do you think you work for? You work for the Sheikh!"

Several of the passengers whispered among themselves. There was a room full of them, cowered in various positions, some hunkered under tablecloths, behind the buffets, near exits, screaming in the distant bathroom. It was impossible to discern whether or not some of them might have concealed weapons on their persons. This sort of dissension in the ranks is exactly the break the hidden wolves would seek before surprising the pirates with a counterattack.

"Can't we debate the philosophy of this work later?" Daniel asked. Both brothers turned to face Daniel, spite bulging in the curvature of their eyes. "I thought we came here to seize a boat?"

"We do, but I cannot finish until Yousef get a head about himself."

"Why no you go on and loot your pleasure and let me stand guard of these passengers. Then everyone win?"

"That sounds reasonable," Daniel said, but Sayyid was clearly uncomfortable leaving a room full of sheep alone with a shepherd with a mind to shear.

"No we need to go together, for the safety, yes," Sayyid said. Sayyid's gaze was stone. "There is nothing left to be done here. We need to finish our work."

Yousef exhaled.

"What do you want me to do?"

"Go to the bridge and help Macalin, yes," Sayyid said.

185

Yousef trudged away, through the dining room doors and disappeared.

"That brother of mine is going to get me killed one of these days, yes! He think he so religious, but what is pious about endangering your brother's life?"

"Come on," Daniel said.

Sayyid and Daniel chained all of the exits to the dining room and secured them with masterlocks. Once the last lock was fastened, Sayyid's mood improved markedly. He was grinning and his teeth shone radiant white.

"This is a very nice boat," Sayyid said as the two walked along the luxuried corridors. "Did you see the casino?"

"You think they keep cash?"

"I think so, yes."

Sayyid took off running towards the area adorned with flashing lights, soft beeps, and the sound of coins clinking against one another. Images of dollar signs, sports cars, mansions, gold bricks, pots of gold, rubies, diamonds, emeralds, sapphires. At a range of ten yards, Sayyid fired a single round in to the first slot machine they encountered. Coins spilled from the belly of the machine and Sayyid caught a gaggle of them and dropped all of them but one and held it up for examination. They were ship-specific coins, bearing the vessel's likeness, worthless everywhere but here on the *Sensation*. They left the machine while its faux fortune clinked away to the ground. Sayyid headed straight towards the Cashier's Stand. The counter was secured with steel bars painted gold and the location of the doorway leading into the money counter's box was not obvious. Sayyid beckoned Daniel to stand back. He took a small rectangle of plastic explosive from his backpack, stuck it on the lower portion of the granite counter, armed it with a thirty second fuse and led Daniel to a safe distance.

The explosion was catastrophic. Every alarm and sensor on the ship seemed to have been triggered at once, so that the deafening roar of the explosion that tortured their eardrums was aggravated by the subsequent emergency alarms. Sayyid stepped heavily through the smoke and noise into the decimated casino area where broken glass and unidentifiable metal lie scattered everywhere. Sayyid's plastic explosive had blown a sufficient hole in the base of the cashier's window to permit him to enter the secure area. There was a second locked door beyond the cage, but Sayyid dislodged it with a few machine gun blasts. He nudged the ruined door open with the muzzle of his Uzi, immediately jumping back as a couple of hostile bullets ricocheted off the door. He took two deep breaths and charged the threshold, lighting the smoke-filled perimeter with both Uzis until nothing moved. Then he jumped back in to the cashier's cage with Daniel where he crouched down against the floor, reloaded his Uzis and waited for the smoke to clear in the other room.

"Do you like surprises?" Sayyid asked.

"No."

"Me neither." He snapped a grenade off his belt, pulled the pin and tossed it in to the room. Seconds later the air deafened and the walls shook. Then there was silence.

"Do you hear that?" Sayyid asked.

"No, what?"

"Nothing. I make sure you hear the same as me."

"Which is?"

"Nothing, yes?"

Then Sayyid stood and walked into the room with the confident assuredness of a king wandering the halls of his castle. Daniel followed him into the money room, more alert, but with his M-16 shouldered and ready to fire. It wasn't a large room, and in the back corner were two men huddled together riddled with bullets and shrapnel. They were very dead, and their blood spilled into a puddle on the floor. Stacks of money lined the shelves. Sayyid set to raking the piles in to a duffle bag. As soon as Sayyid gathered all the larger bills, they left that ruined place.

They strolled out along the deck, passed the water slide Daniel had seen from the schooner during the initial attack.

"It's magnificent."

"Yes, there are none like it in Somalia. You would like to ride?"

"I mean, not now. We're in the middle of an attack."

"The attack is over, yes. The passengers are hoarded in the room, their sentries are dead or surrendered. Go on, I watch you from here. Who know when you have the next chance to have such the fun ride."

Daniel nodded and hurried up the stairs, passing lounge chairs, discarded liquor drinks, bottles of Coppertone, all qualities of beach bags, white cotton robes with the *Sensation* logo. All of it abandoned. A ghost ship filled with amusements. At the top of the slide, Daniel scanned the panorama three-hundred sixty degrees.

Ocean stretched out in every direction.

No sense to be made of it. There were fish in the water, sure, but what place did Daniel have in its vastness?

The cruise ship was like an apparition, plowing through nothing towards nothing. Its entire purpose was self-contained, but commandeered. Daniel shuddered at the thought of all those frightened people rounded up in the ballroom like domesticated animals, their vacation ruined by this occurrence. A cigar fumed in the near distance. Just that long ago these people were having a perfect time, some excitement, even. They'd probably kidded about pirates over the preceding days when they entered Somali waters, stoking a sense of adventure in their souls, but none believing there was ever an actual threat. Now they were cornered in a ballroom with the continuation of their lives contingent on the whim of wild-eyed pirates. Daniel tried to sharpen his focus on the horizon, how although the surrounding waters were growing choppier, the horizon was stagnant. A straight line. The origin of the concept that had so aided man in all his endeavors. The lubricating water was burbling out of the spout, and Daniel sat down in the slide's wet lead, flung his M-16 over his shoulder, scooted himself to the edge, sliding down the curving, twisting tube, filled with adrenaline.

# *Nineteen*

Daniel told the story of the raid on the cruise ship *Sensation* while he had a white table-clothed moment with Caitlin at the Orient Pearl's rooftop restaurant, the Oyster Bed. She seemed relaxed enough. He thought she might have been terrified by his story, but even though she responded to his story with amusement, he was glad he censured numerous parts to make it sound more officious, more Robin Hood than it really was. Once they had finished eating raw oysters, but before their main course arrived, he presented her with a small velvet box. She readily accepted the box at first, but then its appearance with the cruise ship emblem on the box gave the story an air of reality. The box popped open to reveal a thin diamond tennis bracelet. As she glared down at the small treasure, he realized his error: she might be repulsed by this ill-begotten gift, but instead of mortification she quickly snapped the little sparkling thing on her wrist. She squealed a little bit, like she was excited. He was excited now, too.

"You really did all that?"

He thought her mouth trembled. He realized he tended to over analyze, and he affirmed with a nod.

"That's so exciting. I don't see how you have the courage. I mean, I don't see how anyone has the courage. Like people in England today get rich by being cunning, but you take it the old-fashioned way, like in mobster stories. You take it by being meaner and all those slights of hand the bankers and lawyers in London do to get rich mean nothing. It's like you're a character from history," she said. She had more to say, but stopped herself. Perhaps she had revealed too much too quickly. Or perhaps her emotions towards Daniel weren't as unresolved as her words indicated. She looked down at that bracelet on her wrist, and it sparkled like the stars above them in the pale luminosity of the sky and the flickering candlelight.

"When will you go again?"

"We got back here yesterday. We're headed to Eyl tomorrow for work later in the week. It's a whirlwind," he said.

"I bet," she said. Her eyes were locked in his now, her irises indecipherable from those stars orbiting overhead. Then all there was were her eyes.

"I'd like to take you out again, when we get back."

"I think I'd like that a lot."

**The bracelet glistened on her wrist the next day** at the clinic, but he didn't message her. She checked her phone between every exam, once even excusing herself from a routine procedure only to see there were no new messages. She wondered what he might be doing while she disinfected. He didn't call the next day or the day after that. She began to surmise he was either dead or had moved on. He was a pirate. Didn't they have harems of girls? Why had she even considered him? He was probably diseased. Violence no doubt stalked him on land and sea. But hadn't he been such a nice guy when they'd first met? She must be crazy. When they first met he had just killed a man. But he was gentle. Why hadn't he called?

She started leaving her phone in the residential quarters when she went to work so she wouldn't be distracted while making her rounds, but when her shift ended she still found herself hurrying back to her room, filled with curiosity and hope that he had texted, that somewhere he was seeking her out, on his lips a new tale of adventure recently harvested from experience. Because she longed for him, she was disappointed night after night.

Eight days after their first date, her phone lying on the dresser, began vibrating. She had finished her latest round two hours earlier and was sitting on her modern-looking, uncomfortable IKEA sofa reading a compilation of poems by Charles Wright. One minute she had been enthralled by Wright's lingual elegance, the next moment she had tossed the slender volume to the floor and almost dove across the room for the phone. It was his number illuminating the screen. She put it to her side, counted "One, two, three," inhaled a deep, calming breath, and flipped open the phone. He asked her to dinner again at the Orient Pearl. His words were sharp, to the point. He didn't give her the opportunity to be coy, proud or gaming. He basically only gave her the option to make one decision, and it was a predetermined one at that.

She hurried to the bathroom, no time to shower, washed her face and applied some base makeup. Straightened her hair. Traced some lip liner, a little makeup, fumigated the important parts with her expensive perfume. Dressed in her most becoming casual clothes, examined herself in the mirror.

She looked good.

Her hair was too put together, so she jostled it about, just right, to give it a weathered look. But not too weathered. Her time was running scarce. She packed a small clutch and hurried along the residential corridor. She gritted her teeth when Dr. Mehfoud turned into the hallway. She wanted to hide, but it was too late.

"You look like you're going out. Did I overlook a social?"

No point in lying.

"I'm going to town."

Dr. Mehfoud raised a curious eyebrow.

"I'm meeting someone. A contractor from the states, just a friend. He's picking me up."

His eyebrows lifted further.

She stood there like a dummy.

"I'm not going to lecture you about safety out there. You're a smart, grown woman. You know," he said. Then he added with a noticeable absence of enthusiasm, "have fun."

She nodded and skittered along, her thoughts juxtaposed between what the boss thought and what Daniel thought and where she was going to be taken tonight and what would be said about her while she was gone and what would be required of her to defend her honor around the clinic tomorrow for venturing out tonight.

Her thoughts quieted when she saw him sitting in the driver's seat of a white Land Cruiser, just beyond the outer gate of the WHO clinic, staring out into the voided distance. When the guards opened the gate, the disturbance caught his attention and he turned to face her. He was clean shaven, unlike last time. She slid across the passenger seat in to the SUV beside him. He smelled like cologne and adrenaline.

"You look nice," he said with a conjured smile.

"Thanks, so do you," she said. She caught herself wringing her hands and forced her palms on her knees. She felt like she looked so boorish, but she didn't know what else to do.

"Where are you taking me?"

"I thought we'd go back to that place at the Orient Pearl. I hate to be so redundant, but I feel. . . comfortable there."

She felt like he was about to say something else, but dismissed the thought from her mind. She liked the Orient Pearl, too. Unlike so much of the rest of Somalia, the Orient Pearl maintained the veneer of civilization. Plus it was romantic and the food was much better than anything else she had eaten in the Horn.

They hadn't been seated at their table long, fumbling through small talk, when the man she recognized as the pirate, Sayyid, entered the restaurant.

"Daniel!" Sayyid said. "Do I catch you in the end of an exam?" The native pirate leered down at her. She saw a chipped incisor in his mouth of otherwise untarnished teeth and she wondered how it got that way.

"No, we were just having dinner. Two westerners talking western things."

"Well, Macalin has finally succumb to the sleep, yes? Yousef has gone to consult his imam. He is of little use after work, yes?" Sayyid laughed. "Would you care if I join you two?"

She had hoped to have the evening alone with Daniel, but she was both too terrified and intrigued to deny his request. She didn't understand either of these men, and didn't wish to inadvertently trigger any of their murderous PTSD responses. Sayyid shifted his gaze back and forth between the quieted pair several times.

"Have a seat," Daniel said, eventually.

"Thank you I think I will, yes. They have very good food here. Nice place, too, yes." He stared at her like he expected a response.

"It's a very nice place."

"Daniel, this place is much calmer than the *Maran Centarus,* yes?"

"What's that*?*" she asked.

"It is a ship we hijack," Sayyid said. He studied Daniel. "Have you not told her of our work?"

"We just sat down."

"He told me about the *Sensation*," Caitlin said.

"The *Sensation* is nothing. I must tell you of our last job, yes!"

Daniel looked uncertain, as though he was afraid Sayyid would reveal some detail he would have rather her not known. Or maybe he had a reason for not telling her. But she was excited. She felt as though she had lived the last week in anticipation of this story, and she felt confident she wouldn't be disappointed.

"We tracked a Greek oil ship, the supertanker *Maran Centarus*. The report was it had a hundred-million plus in oil headed for U.S.A., yes. Daniel fired an RPG at the bow, and I circled around in front of the ship until they cut the engine, yes. But when I go to board they strike me with water hose! We back our boat out of range, and my brother Yousef shoot the hoses with his rifle, bang, bang, bang. Like shooting ducks at the carnival, yes. By the time we get on the boat, the whole crew, captain and all have locked themselves in a safe room deep in the ship's helm. So ok. We have the ship and start it back towards Somali coast, yes? To not make sound too easy, without hostage we vulnerable to CTF-151, or the world navies. They can land on the ship and fight us without worrying about sailor death. So our friend Macalin set to pilot ship back to shore as quick as is possible, while Daniel, Yousef and I try to break door to safe room to make the sailor hostage. You agree with all this, Daniel?"

Daniel didn't deny it.

"It was not the CTF-151 that give us the trouble, though, but it was other Somali pirate! They hear we capture the big oil ship and because we not so very far from the coast of Somalia, they race out to try and steal our spoil from us! So now the skinnies who I never even see before are yelling at us to stop with a bullhorn and shooting the machine gun at us. First they're two skiff, then there are five! We have to leave the passengers at be for the moment to fend off the attack. These are not regular pirates, not former seaman or nomad with honor but city thug who steal boat and come out looking for money. They not even swim, they know so little what they doing. There is many of them though, and just because they no seamen not mean they cannot shoot. Bang bang, bullets bounce off boat everywhere we go. Their boats circling us. Macalin yelling from the bridge what we doing? We worried even more boats would come to attack us before soon. Then Daniel here," Sayyid said and grabbed him by the shoulder, "took an RPG, steady his feet even though bullets whiz passed him everywhere and shoot at the lead boat. He hit the gas tank with the grenade and the little boat go kaboom! Everyone, our friends, the other pirates' friends, everyone stop like, 'Oh shit did he just do that?' One of the boats roll over but there no survivors. They all in shock and in the mean time we all take out our rifles and bang bang bang. We kill one or two of their pirates, so they eventually turn back. They leave us alone. How is that story for the Daniel?"

It was really hot.

She felt really safe sitting next to Daniel. She unconsciously leaned closer to him and their calves mated under the table. Part of her was obviously terrified by these men, by what they were capable of doing. But her terror of the whole country was what had allured her here in the first place, and if she had to make friends, it might as well be with the most dangerous men in the city.

Daniel was scrutinizing her, perhaps trying to gauge her reaction. Sayyid's phone rang, and he leaned away and began a conversation from which he attempted to exclude them.

"That's not exactly how it all happened," Daniel said. "I mean, there was more to it than that. Those other guys, the one's that attacked us in the little boats, they weren't pirates like us. They were militants, jihadists. Deranged men."

She didn't care. He didn't have to explain. They were trying to kill him and he killed them first. Weren't those the stakes of the game?

Sayyid's conversation ended, he folded the phone and slammed it on the table. Then he barked in laughter. "Daniel, I just get off the phone with the Sheikh. He already negotiate the ransom for the boat today!"

"How much?"

Caitlin leaned in.

"Guess."

"A million."

"No, guess."

"Two million."

"Higher, yes."

"Five million."

"Five point five million dollars, yes! The Sheikh is to give us a bonus for this one! You make sixty thousand for one job. The work is dangerous, but the money is not bad, yes!"

"It's not bad at all," Daniel said.

"The Americans need their oil and we Somalis need our money!" Sayyid said.

Daniel and Caitlin's food arrived. Sayyid stood from the table.

"Where are you going?" Daniel asked him.

"I need more khat to celebrate this. I feel myself unable to think."

"I thought you were going to eat with us."

"You already order. You on a date. I only wanted someone to talk to for a minute, so I not spoil your time."

"Don't be silly," Caitlin said, words exiting her mouth with a stammering lisp.

Sayyid winked at her and bowed to Daniel, then he strolled across the deck of the rooftop pool, twirling his Uzi around his trigger finger and whistling, and exited through the two clear glass doors in to the air-conditioned dome that housed the elevator and staircase down to the hotel.

With Sayyid's storytelling now absent, Caitlin was able to reflect more on her own feelings and internal emotional state. She was breathing hard. Daniel started eating, so she ate, too. But her heart continued to flutter. She couldn't keep her eyes off his forearms, couldn't prevent her mind from speculating about his biceps. The muscles that supported his neck held her enraptured. His stone green eyes were as dangerous as a lit firecracker with a short fuse in the hand of a child.

"Tell me something, Dr. Cordon?"

"Yes?"

"Why Somalia? Why is an intelligent, beautiful woman like you here?"

She exhaled before she began to speak. "I guess there's two answers to your question: why I originally came and why I stay."

"I'd like to hear them both."

"Well, when I finished med school in London, I got this amazing offer to work for a renowned orthopedic surgeon, Dr. Walker. My Dad really wanted me to do it. But I was so tired of London, you know?"

"Not really."

"I mean, life there was so mechanical, predictable. It's like everyone watched so much TV and spent so much time trying to be like everyone else that there wasn't any originality. I was bored. I knew if I worked for Dr. Walker, I would end up getting a great job in London, and then before I knew it I would be too old to adventure, roots in the ground and life would be over."

"You wanted adventure."

"So I got an offer from WHO to work at the hospital in Somalia, and I took it. I could come here, knock out part of my residency, see a different part of the world, enrich myself along the way. Get some perspective."

"Living here charges a big price for some culture."

"Which brings me to why I stayed."

Daniel nodded and crossed his arms, go ahead.

"Being cooped up at the hospital all the time was boring, so I started disguising myself as a man and wandering out into Mogadishu for kicks."

"That's retarded."

"I'm going to overlook your political incorrectness and agree with you, but it was still better than the alternative. Boredom is one of the most dangerous diseases, you know? It kills more than cancer, and anyway, I felt better taking chances than laying around the WHO compound reading books and watching movies. That's synthetic life. I came here to live, to experience, not watch cinematic portrayals of what's going on elsewhere in the world."

"Anyway."

"Anyway, I started wandering out disguised as a man, and eventually happened on this friendly little khat café. I never chewed the stuff, I would just go and drink a sprite or something. Pray alongside the Muslims at the call of the adhan. I had a nice thing going, a fun little escape of the routine around WHO. One day though," she said, exhaled heavily. She saw a light breeze of concern blow across Daniel's face. "One day, I was walking to the khat café when these jihadis stopped these kids on the street, they couldn't have been older than ten."

She started misting up.

"They had little school books in their little hands. One of the men started admonishing the children. I guess they were accusing the little ones of stealing from a local warlord. I kind of gathered the one doing the talking had been accused of stealing himself, and he was looking to pass the blame. Because his own life was at risk if the perpetrator wasn't found, he was reluctant to release the children due to mere considerations of their youth. The leader seemed to weigh his options, then he had the children lined up with their faces turned towards a crumbling wall. I yelled to stop. I was crying and snot was running down my nose, and I tried to run to stop them. But no one even looked at me. Those men executed those innocent little children. Then they just walked off, one of them was fucking whistling, *whistling*, like they just finished some fucking errand. Like they'd just dropped off their drycleaning."

"That's terrible. I'm sorry that happened. I'm so sorry you had to see that."

"So that's why I stayed. I mean, I'd thought about going home before, when I was bored, and I actually did go home after that incident, but for a different reason."

"Why?"

"I basically knocked on every door I could to get the British government to intervene down here, to end the depravity."

"You tried to get Britain to invade Somalia?"

"They need peace keeping forces."

"I can attest to that."

"Only no one would do anything. Finally, I got in to speak to this undersecretary, the Deputy Secretary of State of Defense. He told me to go back and send information to Britain, to find the stuff that would pull on people's heartstrings. So, I bought a GoPro, came back to Somalia, and started trying to film the violence."

"That's why you were at Stadium Mogadishu."

"Someone sold me a ticket at my regular khat café, and it seemed like a logical place to go, the headquarters of Al-Shabaab. I never dreamed of getting messed up in the action."

"I'm sure."

He had something on his mind, and it was clear he was leaning towards keeping it to himself.

"What are you thinking?" she asked.

"Just, why me then? If you're on this crusade to rid Somalia of the bad people, why have dinner with me? Why open up to me?"

"You aren't like those men killing children."

"I'm a pirate. I pillage for a living."

"You're a good man. You're helping these Somalians make the best of a bad situation. You're not evil like the others."

"We're not so different."

"I know you're different because I like you."

"Why do you feel that way?"

"I don't know why I feel the way I feel."

He nodded affirmatively. Fair enough.

They shifted in to small talk, and she struggled to reply with subdued comments. She had never felt this way about a man before.

Once he paid the bill, he offered to take her home. She had hoped he would offer her a drink in his room. He could have been even more forward than that. He could have said or done to her whatever he wanted, but the flimsy state of her confidence prevented her from making the first move, precluded her from taking any course of action other than acquiescing to his wishes.

Whatever those wishes were.

# *Twenty*

Three days later the four pirates left the pirate flotilla to attack their next mark, a purported merchant ship alleged to be hauling light arms to Uganda. The pirates' luxury yacht and deep sea fishing boat gradually miniaturized on the horizon as the sea began rising and falling in hills, making Daniel uncomfortable. When he expressed these concerns to Macalin, his colleague dismissed the anxiety as mere unfamiliarity.

"We work in much worse," he said. "Besides it's just a gale moving through."

"What's a gale?"

"Weather."

What was a mere choppiness when they left the pirate flotilla became an incessant rise and fall in the sea level of eight to ten feet. Daniel became sick. He had never experienced motion sickness; he must be ill with worry.

Finally, prey appeared on the distant horizon. Sayyid sped forward at such an accelerated pace that Macalin was unable to have his customary look through the binoculars, due to having to exercise all his skill just to keep up with Sayyid. Although he wasn't reckless, Sayyid seemed indifferent to the ship's defenses as they jetted towards their mark. Daniel wished Sayyid occasionally stopped to consider that not everyone was as capable as him. He wished Sayyid would realize there was less danger when they were patient and equipped with as much information as possible. At least if they were prepared, they could do everything in their power to compensate for the risks they were soon to encounter.

Once they realized their error, it was too late to disengage the attack without repercussion.

Without warning, Sayyid circled his boat in a full 180-degree reverse.

"What the deuce is he doing? I've never seen him lose his nerve, not once," Macalin muttered, as much to himself as he did for Daniel's information.

Soon Sayyid was on the two-way radio.

"Reverse full speed. This is not a merchant ship. It is a U.S. Navy warship!" Yousef yelled through the radio static.

The blunder had been recognized at only a thousand yards. While Macalin steered the boat back towards the pirate flotilla, Daniel watched in horror through his M-16 scope as the U.S. Navy warship gained on them, steaming ahead through the swells as if it were maneuvering a calm sea. The schooner zipped over the tops of the swells, collapsing on the plane of the sea with calamitous thuds, sending the unsecured gear rattling around the boat. Daniel feared if they weren't struck by a rocket, that the boat might disintegrate under the stress of the beating it was receiving. In this chaotic water, he would drown.

The warship gained to 750 yards, charging forward with a host of black skies in tow. The pirates were steaming towards blue sky; however, the false promise of a successful escape lay before them. The warship had already closed a quarter of the distance between the parties and the pirates still lacked approximately fifteen miles to the flotilla. Daniel wondered what they hoped to achieve if they did reconnect with the mothership. Surely the struggle would end in every boat being sank and all the pirates killed.

A helicopter lifted off the warship behind them.

"Macalin," Daniel cried out.

Macalin turned to look. He didn't seem moved by the spectacle, but Daniel determined his partner's panic was already at a maximum condition.

"When you can take a good shot, shoot it with the RPG," Macalin said.

Daniel enlisted to levy tax on merchant marines who were reluctant to put up a violent resistance, not pick a fight with the U.S. Navy. Who knew what weapons they had aboard that warship, how many helicopters, how many other battleships in the vicinity? It seemed they were doomed men, regardless of how many improbable acts of attrition they were able to commit against this aggressor. He had been so foolish. Of course there was going to be a reaction to these pirates sticking up the world's economy for millions of dollars per sting. He wondered how he had ever permitted himself to be talked into this malignant business in the first instance. What could he look forward to if he was caught? Maybe they'd take pity on his whiteness, discover his American origins and offer him life in prison. Delightful. At least he had some experience behind bars; at least there would be experience, unlike death, where, if after all of his crimes, he would be lucky if there was just nothing.

The helicopter was within three hundred yards when he showed his hand, lifted the RPG, and took his first shot at the Blackhawk. The helicopter simply turned to one side, like a picture supported by two nails when one comes undone and the picture drops, hanging there crooked. Only the helicopter righted itself horizontal immediately once the hazard was past.

Where before it had merely been hovering up there, closing in on them and observing, now it was pissed off. Bullets traced through the water from those heavy-mounted–machine guns. Macalin let the wheel go as both he and Daniel hit the deck to cover their heads and kiss their ass. Lying in the fetal position, Daniel counted every breath a blessing. Each one a bonus. Their boat skittered wildly, taking a wave not so artfully under its natural course, and tossed them out in to the jostling sea.

His orientation was lost to the dizziness. When his cognizance came to, Daniel immediately pulled off his pants, knotted the waist and a leg, and began blowing air in to the open leg. He prayed they would hold some air, and he was lucky they did. He floated there alone in that immense sea, being lifted up and down by the rattled ocean, occasionally catching a glimpse of the warship, hearing nothing but the constant reconfiguration of the unfathomably powerful ocean and having no idea where Macalin or Sayyid or Yousef might be.

Every so often he opened one of those pant legs and blew. For the time being they retained their floatation, but he realized he was on borrowed time. Whether it was his pants or his lungs or his energy or his consciousness, eventually he would succumb.

This was it.

He wished he'd been more forward with Caitlin the last time they'd visited.

He wished they'd attacked that damn warship rather than flee and die like cowards.

He wished. . .

**He awoke to his back being scraped** across some rough surface. He opened his eyes to see Yousef dragging him into the schooner. Daniel looked down to see his pant legs tied around his waist, his parts naked below the midsection. He coughed up water and cupped his hands around his genitals.

"What the hell happened? Why aren't you dead?" He felt dizzy, and dry heaved.

Sayyid was puttering the schooner across a much calmer sea. The blood vessels in his eyes were cracked red, his muscles tensed. He breathed like an animal.

"We meet deception with deception. The boys at the flotilla call in a false pirate attack. It work. The warship considered saving Americans more important than hunting us to death. I guess they figured you and Macalin dead already," Sayyid said.

"Macalin?" Daniel asked, but saw him lying wrapped in mess of wool blankets and equipment bags.

"So that's it?" Daniel asked.

An evil leer spread across Sayyid's face, but he didn't speak a word.

"How much further?"

"Thirty minutes or less to the flotilla," Yousef said, matter of factly. Daniel couldn't help but notice that Yousef didn't bother to fetch Daniel anything warm from around the little boat, left to recover on his own from the shock of being adrift at sea for some time unknown. Long enough for him to lose consciousness. Long enough for him to think himself dead. Daniel flattened his saltwater soaked pants and pulled them over his hairy, naked legs.

What they saw next on the horizon wasn't just their friend's boats, but explosions. Daniel sat up to see what was going on. He took an M-16 lying near and looked through the scope. Sayyid radioed in.

"Once the Americans left the Dutch came to mop up. They found us," said Quimbly, the flotilla field general.

Daniel saw it through the scope, a small warship. More of a coastguard boat really. Daniel's initial alarm at the second attack diminished rapidly, as he watched the .50 caliber rip up the defenses of the smaller Dutch job. It had been armed with only two machine gun turrets. The pirate ship, with its powerful arms, quickly chewed up the smaller, less equipped Dutch ship. Daniel watched as the firing stopped, and the pirates called for the Dutch sailors to surrender on the deck. No one appeared at first, so the pirate ship opened fire once again, making its superior position known. The sailors were told they wouldn't be harmed if they surrendered immediately. They didn't have a choice, and they must have calculated this because a row of them finally appeared on the deck with their splayed fingers stretched towards the heavens.

Daniel, Youself, Sayyid and Macalin all climbed abroad the main yacht during this final transaction. True to their honor, the pirates didn't further molest the Dutch sailors, but outfitted them with three rubber life rafts, some water and set them afloat. Then the pirates commandeered the small naval ship for application to their own ends.

Quimbly greeted the battle-wearied pirates, but left them to take immediate action to evacuate the area. Certainly the Dutch radioed their friends in CTF-151 and there would be reinforcements in the area promptly. Things quieted down a bit as the fishing trawler and the commandeered Dutch naval ship split up, each making for a separate horizon.

Daniel and Macalin had been given blankets and soup, and they were slurping it up when Sayyid came looking for his brother.

"Have you seen Yousef?"

"No, we haven't," Macalin said.

Sayyid had a nervous look about him, as if he had just heard a tear in the universal fabric. He marched out of the stateroom where the two were being cared for. Daniel trailed the master pirate out of the room. A rifle report wailed in the air. Then another and another.

Sayyid began screaming.

Daniel ran to the top deck to see what was happening. He peeked over the top of the stairs just in time to see Sayyid form tackle Yousef on to the ship's deck, wail back a mighty fist and strike his brother until he toppled over limp, unconscious. He saw the rifle laying untended near the brothers, and followed this clue in to the water. There, in one of the rubber life rafts lie two dead Dutch sailors. Their brothers in arms cried out for the loss.

"What happened?" Daniel asked one of the deckhands.

"I don't know. He was yelling something about Allah and those men not being Muslim, then he started shooting."

**The remainder of the return to shore** was tense, and Daniel was overwhelmingly relieved when they arrived in Port Mogadishu. He called Caitlin as a matter of routine, even though he wasn't certain he was emotionally prepared to see her given the mental trauma of the day's events, but he called her anyway and she consented to see him.

He noticed something different about her as they drove between the WHO and the Orient Pearl. She seemed prettier than normal, fresher. Her conversation was wittier than he remembered. She wasn't expecting much from him. She was giving him a pass to just pick her up and be in her company. He felt on some deeper level, she understood that he wasn't in the mood to entertain. They both knew he needed distraction. He needed her company, and he was charmed she was eager to provide it.

They parked the car and entered the elevator. He pressed the button for the pool deck, the Oyster Bed, what had become their usual date spot.

"Could I use your bathroom before we go to dinner? The ladies room in the restaurant isn't exactly up to par," she said.

"Sure." Daniel pressed the button to the tenth floor. He'd gotten himself his own room for the down time. It was hard to get sleep with Macalin and Sayyid chewing khat and blowing cocaine all hours of the night. Then there was Yousef's pontificating. He just wanted sleep. Before he got his own room, he thought he would have a breakdown if he had to spend another night in those circumstances.

He slid his room key in the door and eased it open.

"The bathroom is just there," he said, with a slight head nod.

She turned to face him. She took two steps and wrapped her delicate arms around him. She pressed her breasts and stomach against his torso. She touched him on the face, caressed his nose. He wrapped his arms around her, first both around the small of her back, then one on her neck. His movements were coordinated as if there was a magnet at work.

They kissed. And kissed.

She dropped her hand to his chest and clawed her nails through the opening between the interspersed buttons of his shirt. He picked her up with a hand underneath one of her thighs and threw her on the bed without letting an inch of space gain between them. Neither obstructed the other with the least degree of resistance.

# Twenty-One

Daniel had been holed up in his hotel room for four days. Dirty dishes from room service were strewn about, intermixed between a few bowls of lavender. He left his room to drive Caitlin back to the WHO compound for work. When a twenty-four hour shift ended, she would call him to retrieve her. And he would.

He was lying on the bed, considering her, where she stood in front of the mirror applying makeup to her face, her body only covered from the waist down by a wet towel. Her hair rested on her shoulders somewhat damp, where she must have taken precaution to prevent it from being fully immersed in the shower. He examined the contour of her toned back, skin pulled tight against her ribs, a testament to her fitness. She wasn't too skinny, very well-conditioned.

"Why are you putting on makeup? Are we going somewhere?"

"I can't just lie in bed with you all day and do nothing."

"I wouldn't call what we've been doing nothing," he said.

"Well, you know what I mean," she said, her voice laced with a palpable gaiety.

She stood with her back to him. They locked eyes through their reflections in the mirror.

"I can pretend that I do, if that's what you want," he said.

She smiled, placed her compact on the dresser, turned and crawled across the bed until she laid on top of him, belly to belly. Her damp hair wetted and tickled his cheek. He was overwhelmed by a confluence of fragrances, her shampoo and conditioner, toothpaste, deodorant, eau de toilette, and the lavender. Despite all the food waste and lack of maid service, her presence, unlike the rest of this desecrated land, was clean. He had pioneered the unmarked trail of his life to her, and their being together was what he had unwittingly sought all along. And now he had all this money and willpower and freedom.

The phone rang.

She rolled off of him so he could answer, and once he began the conversation he lingered far enough away so that she wouldn't be able to overhear the subject. He made his responses intentionally vague. Her brow furrowed in curiosity at first, then gradually paled into a scowl.

She crossed her arms so that her breasts were covered.

"Where are you going?" she asked.

"Just down the hall. We've got a meeting."

She stood and walked away. He was afraid she was leaving, but she returned in an instant, clad in a hotel robe. She resumed applying her makeup.

"I hope you aren't mad. It's just work. It's the only reason I would go. Surely you know that, after the time we've spent together."

She continued applying her makeup.

"I don't get upset when you go to work," he said, pulling on a pair of trousers. He slid on a t-shirt and stood behind her and wrapped his arms around her. "I'll be right back."

"I know, I just," she started. She craned her head to hold his gaze over her shoulder then turned away from him. She forced a giggle. "I'm just being silly. I know you'll be back. Just go on. Just hurry back."

"I will," he said. He kissed her on the cheek, stepped into his shoes and exited the room.

This is getting serious, he thought as he walked down the hallway. He ran into Macalin.

"What's up?" Daniel asked.

"We got a big new job!" Macalin said.

"What is it?"

"Just let the Sheikh tell it."

The two entered the Sheikh's suite, where Yousef was already sitting cozily beside the lord of jihad. Sayyid stood across from them, leaning against a wall. The Sheikh and Yousef were bantering in Somali, but Sayyid stood on the opposite side of the room in solitude, dipping his hand into an onyx bowl of marbles.

The Sheikh beckoned the two remaining pirates to enter the room. Then he had one of his anonymous servants dim the lights and operate a projector from a laptop computer. The Sheikh narrated the presentation.

"This is the Boeing 787 model 8 jet airplane. It seats approximately 210 passengers, is propelled by two jet engines and has a range of up to 8,200 nautical miles. In a week's time, one will be departing from Nairobi, Kenya in route to Dubai, United Arab Emirates. One of the pilots is my nephew, Jama Fadumo. You will all be on board this flight. Once it is in the air, you will pirate it and bring it home to Somalia."

"We aren't terrorists," Sayyid insisted.

"No, no you get me all wrong," the Sheikh said. "I have no intention to commit terrorism. This is about pirating on the next level. Just think for a moment. When we attack a ship, we ransom it for a few percentage points of what it is worth, basically nothing. We capture a train, where can we take it? Nowhere. We can only loot it and leave it behind. But a plane does not need to have treasure. The plane *is the treasure*. Do you know how much a new one of these planes cost?"

No one answered.

"Two-hundred twenty million dollars! Two-hundred twenty! There is no strings attached to this. No CTF-151 threat. No one can board a jetliner in the air! Once we take it, it is ours."

"This is the great job," Yousef said. "Think of all the money we will make now. One plane two-hundred million. Five planes, one billion dollars!"

"I don't know," Sayyid said. "Stealing planes is much close to 9/11 attack. I not want the world to think I associate with terrorism."

"Brother, you are paranoid."

"In a dangerous business, my worry keep me alive. Now I steal one of these planes, and the world thinks I a terrorist, then the world will come looking for me. Maybe pirating on the seas not pay as much, but we understand the risks. Yes? We make a good living from this? Yes. Do you no remember what happen the last time we do a new type of job and rob train? Cameron die. Cameron is dead because we didn't stick to what we know, yes."

"I have a ready and willing buyer," the Sheikh said. "Even after the discount, he still agrees to pay $190 million. Now I have other costs involved with this because it is a new endeavor, but I am still prepared to pay each of you 3% of the take. If you do the math, that's $5.7 million a person."

Five point seven million was enough for him to live the rest of his life. One last job, then he could just abscond with Caitlin to anywhere in the world. Live in luxury until old age. It wasn't like they would have medical bills, after all, and he bubbled a little at the thought.

"What do the rest of you think?" the Sheikh asked. "Macalin?"

"These jobs do present many new dangers, but you have found a way for us to make much more money than what we do at present. What's more dangerous? To steal this one jet or pirate ships for five more years? How long can a pirate live on the seas before he's captured by his fate?"

Sayyid nodded, seeming to consider Macalin's perspective more objective than the religiously motivated actors.

"Daniel?" the Sheikh asked.

Daniel thought stealing a jet seemed like an act of sheer lunacy. Yet the payday was quite an incentive. Sayyid was studying him hard. He decided to hedge his bets.

"I follow Sayyid."

The Sheikh sat stoic for a moment without betraying his emotion, then nodded his head affirmatively.

"That is fair. I would prefer to be led into battle by Sayyid myself," the Sheikh said. "So what is it Sayyid? Do you feel game to the big leagues?"

Sayyid examined each man in the room before he spoke. He must have felt the peer pressure veering down on him. Perhaps the great pirate felt he was being paranoid, since the rest of his crew were decidedly in favor of attempting the raid.

"Ok, let's try it," Sayyid finally said. "But I want to talk to you about it, in private Sheikh. I want you to give me all the details I ask for."

"That's fair. I had planned on briefing you all once you accepted the job anyway."

"I would like them now, yes," Sayyid said.

The Sheikh asked his associate whether or not he was free to discuss the matter with Sayyid that instant, and the associate responded affirmatively. The remainder of the pirates filed out of the room to let the officers discuss the battle strategy. Daniel was glad to leave, to return to Caitlin. He felt no shame in hurrying down the hall in front of both Macalin and Yousef, their laughter barking in the distance. Let them make fun of him. He didn't give a damn.

He slid back in to his room to find Caitlin dressed in thin black robes, her burqa veil lying on the bed. Apparently entertaining the notion of going out on the town. Perhaps she thought he would take her to Bakara Market.

The reignition of their conversation was a bit tortured, even idle. Not worth commenting on. So he finally just divulged what he thought was on her mind.

"Yes, I would like to get out. I would like to go to Bakara. Isn't it where the action is in this city?"

When cross-examined about his meeting, he told her the truth about the plan for his next raid and immediately regretted having done so when he could have just told her anything and she would have believed it.

"You've been operating in a gray area, but you're drifting from a gangster to a terrorist. This skyjacking crosses the line," she said. She threatened to leave the hotel, leave Somalia. He brushed off her threats. He was too close to the real money now. Besides, he was invincible in Sayyid's wing. He patently didn't want her to leave, but he determined to call her bluff. She couldn't return home in less than 24 hours even if she wanted to. He'd quiet her fears when he returned. They'd take the money from this final job and abandon the place. Go anywhere, somewhere they could live together, happily.

# Twenty-Two

The car ride across western Somalia was mundane, but there was nothing ordinary about catching up with a contact in Nairobi before a skyjack. Listening to downloaded music with his headphones, Daniel tried to imagine what it would be like to seize control of that giant airplane and bring it back to Somalia. The shouting, the passengers they would subdue, the stewards who would fight back. He winced at the notion of killing someone for protecting corporate property. There was a certain sadness to that sort of business.

He imagined what could go wrong, to prepare himself. After raiding those boats he could fathom a multitude of possibilities. He was convinced he and these pirates were meaner, better experienced than anyone. And they had the element of surprise. Sure, they would sustain casualties in a four on four fight if both sides were adequately prepared, briefed on the rules, armed, and preconditioned with equal strengths and vulnerabilities; but the skyjack was a chess match and the opposition wouldn't be starting with attack pieces. It would be like seizing a king protected by a thin veneer of pawns. So what if the pilots locked the door? They would tear it down. What if the pilots tried to land the plane before it could be seized? The pirates would wait for the right moment, time the seizure to maximize their chances of success. What if they had 100-to-1 bad luck and there was a sky marshal on the plane? What would *a* sky marshal do to them? Not much. He wouldn't put up anymore resistance than he had encountered on the high seas.

Macalin slowed as they approached another Al-Shabaab checkpoint. The others hardly gave the occurrence an eye shift's worth of attention. It was probably the fifteenth road check they'd passed that day.

Sometimes these militants just raised the gate, either recognizing some insignia of Al-Shabaab affiliation or being too lazy to risk a conflict. But this time the gate remained lowered, and six men shouldering AK-47's surrounded the vehicle.

Macalin opened the sun visor and took the letters they carried for these purposes, signed by both the Sheikh and the shura.

"Good afternoon," Macalin said and handed him the permission slips.

The militant briefly reviewed the letters, then ripped them up in Macalin's face, the disfigured pieces flurrying through the humid air like flakes of snow. Before Macalin could launch a protest, the militant had opened his door and jerked him out of the Land Cruiser.

Sayyid lunged out of the back seat, Uzi in hand, knocked one of the men to the ground and took another man from behind and squeezed his bicep around the man's neck. Sayyid trained his Uzi on the militant lying on the ground.

The militants responded by pointing guns at Macalin, Sayyid, and the Land Cruiser. Daniel tossed his M-16 out the window, but quickly drew his 9mm pistol as he stepped out of the car, training it on the only militant positioned on his side of the vehicle.

Yousef slid out of the vehicle, hands up. He began lamenting *walaalo, walaalo,* which Daniel recognized as "brothers, brothers!"

Sayyid trained his Uzi on the militant who lie on the ground, and spoke to him. The man tossed his machinegun, out of arms reach.

Yousef walked around the side of the Land Cruiser, pleading. Of the six, one of the hostiles trained his rifle on Sayyid, while the pirate had two of them subdued. A fourth trained his gun on Macalin, the fifth on Yousef and the sixth on Daniel.

"Waxaan nahay walaalo halgan oo isku mid ah, fadlan na si nabad ah u gudbin," Yousef said, but despite his lamentations the situation had deteriorated beyond the point of friendly words.

Daniel examined the man on whom he trained his pistol. There was a naïve unfamiliarity in the man's eyes that left Daniel to wonder whether the man thoroughly understood the ramifications of the business in which he was engaged. The serious nature of the stakes.

A comprehension of the stakes as Daniel knew them.

Daniel looked at the man's weather worn but unabused face and determined that if he was acquainted with fighting then he must be damn good at it because he bared none of its badges. The other men working the Al-Shabaab checkpoints had maintained an air of discipline about them. These particular men were trying to extract their honey from a beehive and they weren't properly trained for the job. If they had been, if this was their trade, then they would have done a better job of it. Surely this wasn't the first time a group of renegades passed through Somalia. The more he considered it the more he was certain they were amateurs. Still, he wasn't quick to underestimate their threat. The novice's danger is sourced from his unpredictability. Untrained, his reaction to any situation is uncertain. Daniel almost tuned out Yousef's pleading because he spoke only Somali and Daniel understood none of it. Still, he kept his wits about him.

"End this," Sayyid said in two final words. Daniel was still trying to interpret what Sayyid meant when gunshots wailed.

The familiar action of Sayyid's Uzi roared on the opposite side of the Land Cruiser. Daniel dropped and rolled as he put two bullets in to the militant's chest. Yousef dove behind the engine of the Land Cruiser. Sayyid's Uzi continued to pop, each blast accompanied by lamentations from unfamiliar tongues.

Then there was silence.

"Everyone okay?" Sayyid called out. Daniel peered through the Land Cruiser windows, watching as Sayyid distributed another bullet to each of the militants, the bodies of the fallen convulsing as they received the gratuitous lead. The guy Daniel shot had taken two to the heart. The guy was dead. Daniel walked around to inspect the rest of the carnage. Sayyid was covered in blood, none of it his own.

With a small assist, Sayyid had managed to kill all of these faux-militants himself. When Yousef finally stood, he was in tears.

"Why did you do this brother? I was about to talk reason to them? Now they are dead, warriors for the cause."

"They who would kill us, I kill," Sayyid said. "It is this simple. I die for no idea."

Yousef cracked into tears. Sayyid wrapped a comforting arm around him, assuring that in misunderstandings, Allah offers forgiveness. Yousef ranted about the pigs of the West, the godlessness of their women, their churches, the corruption of their government, the risk the Muslim world accepted by not waging all-out war against them.

"I know, I know," Sayyid whispered. "But we have to stay focused on what it is we do. There is no tact in running at them straightforward; we must attack them as part of a larger strategy. That is what we do. We pirate to fund the noble fight."

This seemed to make Yousef feel somewhat better, but he still sat in the front seat of the Land Cruiser and sobbed for the remainder of the drive to the Kenyan border.

# *Twenty-Three*

Ingress through the Kenyan-Somali border was controlled by a Kenyan military installation that became visible on the desolate, semi-desert periphery. A cement fort dated to antiquity constituted the nucleus of the position, which was flanked by a liberal sprawl of barb-wired, electrified fence. Patrolling sentries dotted the roof of the two-story structure. Desert camouflaged military trucks were parked on the opposite side of fence, some idle and others occupied and prepared for immediate deployment. A siren cried in the distance and soon an entire company supplemented the original squad of soldiers. The tire-track forged road they had followed for miles and miles fainted until it was imperceptible. After the path ceased, there was a gulf where there was very little human activity; then close to the citadel, there were a row of acacias that led to the gate, a hat tip to landscaping that served as the only possible indication of friendliness in the place.

A bullet dinged off the hood of the Land Cruiser. Sayyid continued driving, but stopped when the second bullet took off a rear-view mirror with such deft precision that Sayyid conceded the weakness of their position. A Kenyan got on a loud speaker and addressed them in Somali. Sayyid stopped the car, opened the door and exited the vehicle with his hands on his head. He was covered in other men's blood. All of them were splattered crimson except Daniel, who had managed to remain untarnished in the reckoning. All of the pirates stood outside the Land Cruiser with their hands on their heads, unarmed. Three large Kenyan military trucks exited through the portal, passing by the row of acacia trees. When the trucks came to a halt it was in a circular fashion around the Land Cruiser. Dozens of Kenyan soldiers jumped from the beds of these trucks with their machine guns pointed at the pirates and a look of *I dare you* intensity pinching their eyes.

Each pirate was patted down, their weapons confiscated, and led to a separate truck unbound, save for Yousef and Macalin who were taken together. The Kenyan soldiers kept their guns lowered to the bed of the truck, but shouldered and ready for action. Not one soldier diverted his attention from the captives until the four pirates were reunited in a locked cement room inside the citadel.

They weren't permitted to talk, and Daniel wasn't certain what was going to happen. Kenyan and Somali relations could be tense, and Kenya was generally the host country to pirate trials. If their identity were uncovered, they could be jailed until tribunal. They could be imprisoned indefinitely in Kenya at the expense of international tax dollars. Daniel was unprepared to concoct a story to explain how they had arrived at this place in such sodden condition. Certainly they looked sinister in blood, heavily armed and unusually well-heeled in the Land Cruiser. The fact that they were actually up to something sinister only doubled the jeopardy of the situation. Daniel doubted these soldiers would accept the explanation they were sightseers or journalists. Daniel was unacquainted with journalists who traveled with automatic weapons and bathed in blood.

Following an interlude of being observed from behind a two-way mirror, an officer of ambiguous rank entered the room. He wore a patch on his arm with a symbol that could only indicate a fence, and his uniform was neatly pressed but bore no other insignia. He dropped a pack of cigarettes on the table where the pirates were seated. The officer was flanked by half a dozen men with machine guns, which they held pointed towards the ground, but otherwise ready to fire.

Daniel fidgeted. Despite all the violence of the past weeks and months, he still found it disconcerting to have six strangers pointing rifles at his back in a sound proof room. He really hoped the upcoming conversation went well. He was all attention, though at a loss for how to argue their way out of the situation.

"Please don't let my men offend you. My commanding officer thought it wise to have extra security given the rather suspicious condition in which you arrived. Would you mind to tell me what you're doing here?"

"We are refugees," Sayyid said.

"Refugees? Yet you give the impression of mass murderers. Tell me how do you explain the heavy arms you carry? The blood caked all over you? Why is there this white man in this region of the country? Surely he knows the color of his skin makes him a target in western Somalia."

"We lived in the village of Wajid," Sayyid said. "We were nomads and public servants, the white man a visiting journalist. When Al-Shabaab began expanding through the country, first we negotiate our peace with them through payment. Things were normal for a while. But Al-Shabaab grow and grow. They have many new soldiers who need income, food, shelter, supplies. Eventually the tax they required became too expensive, and we no longer had to pay them with. So they finally attack our town, only we were prepared and fight back. There was only so much a few nomads could do, there were so many Al-Shabaab, so when it was clear all was lost, we stole their car and fled for Dadaab in hopes of finding shelter and protection from our Kenyan brothers."

The officer had given Sayyid his attention, but it wasn't clear whether or not he had bought the story, the officer excusing himself to consider the veracity of the account. Other guards remained. When Daniel started to speak, a soldier ordered him to keep quiet.

Several minutes later the Kenyan Officer returned with a younger soldier carrying a notepad and pencil. The younger one wore glasses, was slender, and didn't fit the usual profile of a soldier. The younger one appeared to be a clerk of some kind.

"How many strong was Al-Shabaab?" The Officer asked.

"Two-thousand," Sayyid said.

"Were they heavily armed?"

"They each had machine guns. They had cars, cell phones, radios. It was a coordinated attack. They approached the city from three different angles. We weren't able to fight on three fronts. Our defenses folded quickly. My friends and I thought it better to flee and fight another day rather than stay and be executed."

The younger soldier was scribbling across his notepad furiously.

"Did you get all that?" The Officer asked once the young soldier quit writing.

"Yes sir."

"Go on then."

The young soldier gathered his writing materials and exited the room.

Sayyid and the Officer reengaged small talk, discussing the route by which they had come, daily life in Wajid, and how familiar he was with the Dadaab camp. Daniel felt confident the Officer was looking for a hole in Sayyid's story, and Daniel was incompetent to evaluate whether Sayyid had betrayed himself by his own testimony.

Eventually the young soldier returned, whispered something in the Officer's ear, gave the pirates an uncertain look and departed.

"I am sorry for the loss of your home," the Officer said. "I apologize for your detention. You must understand that these are perilous times, and such precautions must be taken. There is a transportation passing through here in route to the Dadaab camp this evening. You will be welcome to continue to your destination then."

"What about our weapons?" Sayyid asked.

"Yes. I am afraid your arms cannot be returned. We have a strict policy in Kenya about prohibiting firearms from passing between Somalia and Kenyan. It is a measure to protect the peace with which we now provide you."

Sayyid pondered this in silence for a moment. "So be it. Thank you for your assistance, yes. It is nice to know we have such good friends as neighbors."

**The pirates were escorted to a makeshift building** where twenty or so refugees were awaiting transportation to Dadaab. The pirates spoke to one another sparsely while they waited, mostly holding their silence or napping intermittently on benches while one of their number remained vigilant.

Their transportation arrived at eight o'clock in the evening. They were helped in to the back of the cargo bed surrounded by a wooden enclosure to prevent them from falling out along the bumpy road. It was a physically uncomfortable journey made that much more unpleasant by the apparent sufferings of the other passengers who joined them for the ride. Unlike the pirates, these true refugees had performed no malice to merit their destitution. They were victims of circumstance. Their futures were uncertain. They were traveling to the last place on earth that would receive them.

At 10:30 that evening they arrived at the gates of the Dadaab Refugee Camp, where they registered, were processed, each given a blanket, two helpings of plumpy'sup and escorted to the temporary housing section where they were to lodge until reassigned a permanent home. The UNHCR worker gave directions to the nearest help desk, then left them for the evening. The four pirates were alone for the first time since they had been detained at the Kenyan border.

"Well, we made it to Kenya, yes?" Sayyid asked.

"Great work, Sayyid," Yousef said as he stood and applauded. "You've got us jailed in this refugee camp without guns, without a means of escape and the plane we come for leaves Nairobi in 36 hours. I doubt whether we shall ever see Somalia again, much less take the jet as planned."

"You have so little faith in me, my brother, but it was the Sheikh himself who supplied me with this backup plan, yes."

Yousef had been defiantly staring down his brother with his arms crossed, but he let his arms fall to his sides and dropped in a chair. "Continue," Yousef said.

"The Sheikh tell me if anything go wrong we pretend to be refugees, just like we have done. He tell me the name of an Amniyat agent, Khaled Shire. If only we can find him, he maintains a tunnel and network to transport us to Eastleigh."

"You don't know where to find him?" Yousef asked.

"Well no, but this is the task before us, yes?"

"There are over a hundred thousand people in the camp. How do you expect us to find him in time to transport us to Nairobi and stay on schedule?"

"We will have to use our intelligence, yes."

"This impossible. The mission is lost. The Sheikh will be furious with us."

"It is with that attitude," Sayyid said. "Daniel, would you like to come with me? We will find Khaled together."

Daniel rose and followed Sayyid away from the tent. They walked among seemingly infinite aisles of makeshift tents, covered with miscellaneous linens, plastics and other shading and insulating materials. They trod across red sand, on the flat terrain that seemed to stretch flat forever, as if there were no geographic diversity in the world. Some tiny fires smoldered near the center of a tent neighborhood. They passed by anonymous black faces in the black night as they walked hither and thither. Sayyid eventually approached a middle-aged man reclining in a chair hewn from a log. They maintained a brief conversation in Somali before Sayyid continued on and Daniel followed.

"What did he say?" Daniel asked, when they were beyond earshot of the man.

"I tell him we new to the camp. I ask him where the place is things go on at night. He say there is a market a quarter mile this way, the Dagahaley market. This is the name of the particular camp we in, yes."

"I wonder where he got the log to carve that chair," Daniel commented. "This place is a fucking wasteland."

"People can be resourceful when they need to be," Sayyid replied.

They walked on through the darkness, passed those similar but unique tents, the haunting whispers of Horn languages incomprehensible to Daniel. He shivered once when he heard laughter come from a circle of men, emanating from some unrevealed place. People stood around with gallon jugs of water clenched in hand, as if the jug's contents contained life itself. Everywhere it smelled like shit because people shat everywhere hoping to fertilize anything. Shitting prayers in hopes of a miracle, because it would take no less than a miracle to fertilize this impotent desert soil. Daniel bumped into Sayyid several times as they walked. Eventually he became conscious he was doing this and tried to prevent it, but he continued to tumble against his friend all the same.

They arrived at a market which wasn't influenced by European considerations. Tents were pitched closer together, a few blankets laid on the sand and occupied by goods of a various nature: pithy food stuffs, cruddy mobile phones, tissue paper, water, recycled plastic water jugs, and other refugee camp trinkets fashioned from rubbish into useful objects. Nothing for sale enticed Daniel's consumer side, with the exception of the cell phones which he lamented for not having the currency to purchase. He had only $60 U.S.D. and two pre-paid debit cards, but credit card scanners were unheard of in this place. Daniel was pleading with the entrepreneur to knock his price down from the $70 requested to the $60 he had, showing the man everything in his wallet, but Daniel had made the error of opening his bid at $60, thus giving the merchant no space to declare a negotiation win for himself, ensuring Daniel would not purchase a phone. At least not from this particular vendor.

Sayyid grabbed Daniel by the arm and dragged him along.

"Where are you taking me?"

"Shh, I find something, yes."

"What."

Sayyid led Daniel around the corner to the first aisle of tents off the market, and pointed to a flag with a crescent moon on its right side, a cavity filled with with three stars.

"So what? It's the flag of Islam."

"No, look at the detail. The moon is on the opposite side of the flag. There are three stars instead of one. This is the sign of Amniyat, yes, yes and yes."

The two approached the tent, and Sayyid spoke a gentle greeting in Somali through the fabric door. A moment later a man crawled out of the makeshift abode sleepy eyed, and examined the two callers.

"Are you Khaled?" Sayyid asked.

"Yes," the man responded.

"Khaled Shire?"

"Yes," he responded. He squeezed his eyelids tight, and when reopened they were more alert than before.

"I am Sayyid," Sayyid said. Then he leaned in and whispered, "I understand you are with the cause."

The man looked furtively around the surroundings, but there was no one within sight. He beckoned the two strangers into his home at once. Inside, the man asked Sayyid to explain himself. Sayyid stated his affiliations and made his requests. Khaled said that he understood Sayyid's dilemma and would be able to help them exit the camp without detection and arrange for transportation in to the Eastleigh neighborhood of Nairobi, where they could rendezvous with the network there. Khaled instructed them to retrieve the other two in their party. They could leave immediately.

Sayyid and Daniel left Khaled's tent without further ceremony. They hurried along the aisles of tents, each wishing they had given heightened attention to the direction from which they had came. Once they took a wrong turn, but Sayyid stopped to request directions back to the temporary housing area and soon they recognized the vicinity from

226

whence they had originally departed. When they returned to the tent, Macalin and Yousef were gone.

"They must have gone out looking for Khaled themselves," Sayyid said.

Of course they had, but when would they be back? Having little else to do but wait, Sayyid and Daniel got comfortable on the ground, wrapped in their blankets and munched on some Plumpy'sup. They mused idly on what life would be like if they were to spend a great deal of time in the refugee camp. Sayyid speculated it would normalize and become like life anywhere else, but Daniel wasn't so certain. Daniel didn't believe he could make the adjustment. From the people he had seen during their brief tour, he wasn't sure many of them had made the adjustment either.

A cacophony birthed in the distance. Neither of the pirates paid it any mind, at first. But then it grew in magnitude to insurrection proportions, and Sayyid and Daniel burst out of the tent to witness what risk had bred the commotion.

Not a hundred yards from their own tent, their worst fears were confirmed. Yousef and Macalin fist fought with countless men. Their aggressors were made invincible by the fact that they would emerge from a crowd of spectators, deal a few blows, then disappear, without responsibility, into the crowd. It was a limitless crowd the two had chosen to fight, and their chances of escape did not appear promising. Daniel stood there watching as two of their own fended off as best they could the tentacles of the crowd, and was surprised that for once Sayyid seemed reluctant to intervene. Daniel estimated how long they could last given the undefeatable character of the opposition. Not that long.

Suddenly, Sayyid was gone from Daniel's side. Then what little light illuminated the mob grew suddenly darker. Daniel saw three torchbearers. Then there were two. Suddenly everything was in darkness. "Sayyid," Daniel whispered, then he screamed.

A hand grabbed Daniel by the arm, and Daniel took a swing.

"No time for that!" Macalin said. Daniel saw Macalin's eyes and the abstract form of Yousef and Sayyid sprinting out in to the distance. Daniel hesitated long enough to glance over his shoulder, to see the vanguard of the angry crowd chasing after them. Daniel's wits returned to him as he sprinted along after his comrades.

They ran through the night, chasing Sayyid. Daniel prayed the super pirate remembered the route back to Khaled, prayed they could escape the mad house before they succumbed to it.

The sight of the familiar market brought a degree of relief. Then Yousef tripped, wailing out in pain.

"It's a cramp!" Yousef yelled.

"Then man up why don't you!" Macalin replied.

Sayyid doubled back, hefting his brother over his shoulder, while Macalin and Daniel hurried ahead with their own safety in mind. The clamor of the mob was ever present on the distance. The surrounding campers were watching these men rush by with great curiosity. They might not be safe anywhere in this camp, not safe anywhere until Nairobi. Then he saw Macalin stop, for he knew not where they were going. Daniel surged ahead, saw the tent with the indicative flag and dove through the linen entrance. Macalin was close behind, and Sayyid came in last with his brother over his shoulder, and flung him inside the tent and let out a great exhale as his chest beat like a native's drums at a mating ceremony.

"Let us go!" a wild-eyed Sayyid told a frightened Khaled. Khaled led the men out the back of his tent, through a back alley of a row of tents, quietly like mice, until they entered through the backside of another tent. All inside, Khaled removed several blankets and heaved a heavy rug aside, revealing a trap door. He thudded the trap with a prearranged knock, and executed a colloquy with someone beneath the ground. Only then did the trap door surge open. All of the men, except Khaled descended in to the earth. Then the door closed, the pirates led by a flashlight-bearing stranger through the narrowest of poorly reinforced mud tunnels, perfecting their escape.

**The next morning the pirates motored in a passenger van** in to the peaceful neighborhood of Eastleigh in Nairobi, Kenya. Daniel felt relieved to arrive in the home of

228

the Sheikh's affiliate. The housekeeper beckoned them inside the large two-story apartment sitting atop a five-story building. She had been expecting them. She ushered them in to a comfortable sitting room and offered the men some black tea. Once they were settled she left them alone.

"She said our host will be with us shortly," Sayyid told Daniel. Sayyid was the only one still on his feet, pacing all over the room, until he turned, facing Yousef. "What the hell is wrong with you? Why you cause trouble?"

"Me? Seriously? I wouldn't have had to go looking for Khaled if you hadn't gotten us sent to Dadaab in the first place."

"We had nowhere else to go."

"We wouldn't have had trouble at the border if you hadn't killed our friends."

"They weren't our friends."

"We are allegiant to Al-Shabaab.

"You are, yes. I am not. I work within the system, but I am not on board with those crazies like you."

"Allah is not crazy! This is apostasy!"

"That you judge yourself equal with Allah is the craziest I ever hear. You are the most full of himself I know."

"I full, I full of myself?" Yousef was on his feet now too. "You the super pirate tell me I full of myself?

Macalin jumped, filling the gulf between the two brothers. "Why don't we just calm down boys, put these differences aside. Our host will arrive momentarily, and we have a job to do. Let us no show disrespect or lose focus less we misplace the opportunity."

The brothers fumed for a moment, but both eventually reclined in a chair, each facing away from the other. In his youth, Daniel had wished for a brother. Now he laughed at what a challenge they could be. A long history can lead to a list of insoluble conflicts.

A half hour later a knock came at the door. Before anyone could react, an elderly man entered the room. Macalin jumped to his feet, but the rest were too comfortable to move as quickly.

"Please, don't get up. I am Abasi. This is my home and I am at your assistance," Abasi said.

Abasi held everyone's attention, when a prepubescent boy entered the room carrying a large marred leather suitcase nearly too heavy for him to carry. The boy deposited it beside Abasi's feet, and then took a step back behind the host.

"I hear you had some difficulties along your journey," Abasi said. Spindling veins popped on the Abasi's knuckles as he grasped the arms of his chair. "I hope despite these troubles you still feel able to work tomorrow."

"We are always ready," Sayyid said.

"Excellent. Then I have some tools for you," Abasi said. He lifted the large suitcase with greater ease than his young assistant, despite the frail state of his appendages. He dropped it heavily on a coffee table and popped it open.

Inside was a bulging manila envelope, three pairs of shoes, a plaster cast, and three combs.

"Hoby, go get the cane please," Abasi directed the little boy. "Here is your gear for the job."

The pirates looked perplexed. No doubt confused how a few pairs of tennis shoes would give them the advantage needed to seize a commercial aircraft. Hoby returned with the cane, and Abasi twirled it through the air with delight. Then he presented it to Sayyid.

"So I wear the cast so they let me have the cane, but is the cane scary enough to take the plane?" Sayyid asked.

"Not just a cane," Abasi said. "Lift the handle."

Sayyid lifted, and underneath the brass handle were the familiar prongs of a crowbar.

"See? You take this so you can access the cockpit, if necessary." Abasi said. He tossed one of the shoes to Macalin.

"You think we can footrace the flight crew into turning the plane over to us?" Macalin said.

"No. Push on the circular dimple on the heel."

Macalin did, and a blade the shape of the sole slid out. Abasi slid the blade out of another shoe himself, took a comb and demonstrated how the blade could be locked in the handle of the comb to assemble a knife. The ah-ha moment circulated the room.

"Gentlemen, these are the tools you'll have: weapons and travel documents," Abasi said, patting the manila envelope inside the suitcase. "The flight leaves tomorrow at 1:18 P.M. You'll leave here two hours before the flight. Until then, make yourselves comfortable. If you need anything, don't hesitate to call for my housekeeper, Ashanti. Food, drink, anything to make your stay more comfortable."

**The plan was simple enough**. They would board the plane, assemble their weapons in the bathroom, and at the right moment, spring a coordinated attack. If they pulled it off deftly, the threat alone would be enough to coerce the pilots to subdue the flight crew and land the plane in Somalia. Daniel played these thoughts on repeat through his head as they were chauffeured to Jomo Kenyatta International. Nothing would go wrong. They would beat their chests, the flight crew and passengers would instinctively surrender, and the plane would be theirs. Simple as that.

Their taxi van parked in front of the departures terminal, the men all unloaded and gathered their faux bags from the trunk. Sayyid paid the driver and the men continued on to the ticket counter. There was a long line, and each was required to check-in individually. 75 minutes remained until their flight departed. They entered the security checkpoint line. Daniel had imagined passengers sort of just gliding through security in Kenya without as much as a second glance. But his expectations didn't echo into reality.

There were metal detectors; x-ray machines for the luggage, and every third passenger was being pulled aside for additional screening, including full-body pat-downs. As they advanced through the line, Daniel watched the passengers remove their shoes to be run through the metal detectors. Daniel's palms moistened. There were at least two guards reviewing the X-ray monitor, a bomb-sniffing dog at the head of the line, and a whole platoon of Kenyan security forces occupied the room. If they were discovered, flight would be futile. Not to mention the meager weapons they possessed were useless in a concealed state. Daniel's hair prickled on the nape of his neck. It was a sensation he hadn't experienced since riding roller coasters as a child. He hadn't expected to know it again here today, at least not after everything else that had happened.

Twenty passengers stood between the pirates and the security checkpoint. Daniel watched as every third or fifth passenger was arbitrarily pulled aside for additional screening. A little boy not older than five or six years old tried to walk through the metal detector without removing his shoes, but was ordered back to the X-ray conveyor for their screening. Daniel gulped in horror. He had no desire to spend the remainder of his days in a Kenyan prison, not for the chance at a fortune, not for the chance at anything. Sure, if one of the pirates was found armed then security wouldn't necessarily suspect the rest of them to be his accomplices.

Or would they?

Would it take only one of them doing something stupid to put the whole airport under lockdown and get everyone searched, assuring his arrest?

Daniel was the last of the pirates to place his baggage on the X-ray conveyor. Macalin walked through the metal detector first. He made it through with no problem. Daniel watched anxiously to see if they wouldn't have his shoes recalled to the X-ray for further inspection, but they didn't. Daniel watched with subdued relief as Macalin retrieved his shoes from the security bin.

Sayyid went through the metal detector next. He tried to bring his cane along with him, but he was directed to place it on the X-ray conveyor. He did as he was told, then hobbled back towards the metal detecting portal, selling his role, until he was waved to walk through and ordered to stop until the results of his scan were complete.

A round plastic clock ticked nearby. A child cried out, was scolded by his parent, then held in arms until quieted.

The guard motioned for Sayyid's attention, nodded, and Sayyid hobbled over to gather his belongings. Surely enough, they allowed him his cane.

Yousef breezed through the security checkpoint as well.

Only Daniel was yet to pass.

He watched as his shoes rode the conveyor into the blackhole of the X-ray machine. A guard beckoned him to walk through the metal detector, which he did. He stopped just on the other side, and saw a red light flash in the guard's eyeglasses.

"Step back and walk through again, please," the guard said.

Daniel nervously trod backwards, waiting until the guard waved him forwards. Daniel saw the same red reflection in the man's glasses again.

"Sir, do you have any metallic objects on your person?"

Daniel touched his pockets and felt a small cylinder in there. He dug his hand in his pocket and retrieved a U.S. penny. Daniel walked back to the X-ray conveyor, where a guard tongue-in-cheek placed the one-cent piece in a plastic bucket and ran it through the X-ray machine. Daniel was waved through the metal detector for a third time, and this time he saw a green light reflected in the guard's glasses.

"You can go," the guard said. Daniel contained his physical symptoms of relief as he started towards the X-ray conveyor. "Oh and sir."

Daniel froze rigid. What? *What?*

"Next time remember to empty your pockets before trying to pass through security," the guard said.

"Yes sir," Daniel replied.

Daniel grabbed his bag, shoes and penny, sat on a bench and laced his weaponized sneakers. Then he started through the terminal towards his gate. When he arrived the rest of the pirates were already there, standing in line to board. They were interspersed throughout the crowd as if they weren't together. Soon Daniel was at the head of yet another line, only this time handing the stewardess his boarding pass.

"Enjoy your flight," she said, tore his ticket and returned him the seating stub.

# *Twenty-Four*

Daniel felt meaningless. There wasn't a good reason to do anything. He slept often, ate when it was necessary. He had been alone in his hotel room at the Orient Pearl for five days. The skyjacking was completed, but no one called it a success. He assumed they would be paid sometime, but that didn't really matter. His sole motivation was to forget the whole nasty business. Yet it was impossible. He sent out for alcohol, cocaine, and khat, but they didn't ease the pain.

No matter how quiet he lie in bed, he couldn't escape the horror of their screams.

Rather than face anyone, he stayed in the dark with the shades drawn. He knew the light might help his mood, but an instinct, call it guilt, convinced him he wasn't worthy of solace.

How had he ever decided to come to Somalia? Why had he ever taken such an uncalculated risk? Even worse, once he was free to leave, why had he stayed? He could have left. None of this was necessary. Now who was he?

He was a murderer.

Not only did he know what it was like to kill, but he mourned the loss of the inhibition which previously prohibited him from committing the transgression. What scared him most was the uncertainty whether he would ever be able to control the urge again. Over how trivial an offense would he kill? Perhaps if given the slightest provocation. Oh hell, he really didn't know what he was capable of.

He thought about killing himself.

He was capable of that.

Images of just pulling the trigger and ridding the world of Daniel Barnes consumed his mind. But somehow this was too easy an end for such human waste.

He was too cowardly to live and too cowardly to die.

So he lied in his hotel in the dark, having drugs and alcohol delivered. He ordered food in but rarely ate. He hadn't a stomach for it. No appetite to speak of. His gaze fell on that piece of perfectly grilled salmon topped with a lemon slice, carefully laid on a bed of quinoa. Intellectually he knew it was a good-looking plate of food. He just had no desire to eat it.

He got the idea to Google drug combinations that have lethal effect. In the meantime, he tried to get fucked up enough to garner the courage to pull the trigger.

**An uninvited knock came at his door.**

He had been lying on his bed, beer wetted sheets twisted around him. But maybe he was finally being kind to himself; he'd likely pissed himself. What did it really matter why he was wet? He struggled just to sit up, then groggily hoisted to his feet and sauntered across the darkened room and unbolted the door.

"Rise and sunshine. *Oh my Allah*," Sayyid said. The super pirate stood at the door in a freshly cut suit looking regal as a pirate ascending the throne of a deposed emperor. "What the fuck has happened to you, man? You look terrible, yes." A big grin spread across Sayyid's face. "Let me guess, wait, you already borrow against all your five million? Daniel you fool! You waste a lifetime's money in just a week!"

"I've hardly spent any money," Daniel strained. He sauntered back to the bed and collapsed, the wet sheets dampening his shirt.

"Then why are you living like a, well, what are you living so unhappy for?"

Suddenly the radiance of the sun exploded in to the room as Sayyid tied the blackout drapes against the window frame.

"Can you just leave me alone?"

Daniel watched out of the corner of his left eye, where he lie face down on the bed as Sayyid picked up a tray of cocaine. He dusted his finger across the tray and rubbed a little on his upper lip. "Mmh," he said. Then he placed the tray on the bureau and slammed his nose down to rail the line. "Oh yeah man! That's the shit! You had some girls in here or what Daniel?"

Daniel didn't respond.

"Well, we going to get some girls then, yes!"

"I'm not going anywhere."

"Actually, I come to get you so we go to the Sheikh's."

"That's the last place I want to go."

"But we must go to get our money from the last job."

"I don't want the money."

"Daniel," Sayyid said and laughed. "What do you mean? The work is done. Now you and I get paid, yes."

Daniel whimpered, and buried his face in to the blanket.

"Daniel, listen. I understand. You upset how it went down on the plane?" Sayyid said. Sayyid's tone uncharacteristically softened. "Listen. No one like that business that happened on the plane, but the job is over. *It is over*. Now let us reap the spoils yes! Five million dollars! That should make you happy, yes. If not more, think of the happiness you can bring others!"

"Ok. Bring me my cut."

"But no Daniel you don't understand. The Sheikh, our employer, he wants to see us. He wants to give us this pay personally. You understand don't you? It is bad, how do you say, form, to not show up personally."

"If that's how it is, then I'm staying here."

"Daniel. The job is done. The oryx is slain. Wouldn't it be a waste to let the meat rot? Let us at least honor this job by making use of the spoils."

For some reason, through all his haze, Daniel accepted Sayyid's position. He wasn't certain whether he actually agreed with the logic or if talking to Sayyid just made him feel better. But he didn't care anymore. He didn't anticipate any more danger on the streets of Mogadishu than he did alone in his hotel room. He wasn't afraid of offending someone. If the Sheikh had him put to death for saying or doing something inappropriate, then let him. Daniel was in the market for an executioner.

**Daniel had every intention** of keeping his visit at the Sheikh's villa as brief as possible. He would accept his payment with a feigned graciousness, explain he had another appointment, and leave.

Daniel, Sayyid and Macalin arrived together outside the gate to the Sheikh's villa. Yousef, as Daniel understood, had been staying with the Sheikh since the skyjack. A ten-foot cement block wall with protruding iron bars at the top guarded the perimeter of the Sheikh's villa. Two guards stood sentry to the gate's exterior. Sayyid idled the Land Cruiser just long enough for one of them to glimpse his face, then they unshackled the gate and the pirates were free to enter.

The grounds were incredible. Orange trees lined the winding drive. In split-second glimpses, through the trees, he saw horses, llamas, and the movement of other creatures whose identity he was unable to confirm. The drive eventually paralleled the beach some thirty-odd feet below the road's edge, where another cement wall was erected to restrict access. When he turned his attention from the ocean to the road, he saw the Sheikh's villa. It was a sprawling modernistic complex of glass and steel-cantilevered cement. When they arrived at what was presumably the front door, they parked near enough elegant cars to make an NBA player jealous.

The pirates were ushered through a long corridor to a living room constructed to house an orchestra that overlooked the sea, gliding to and away from the beach. There were at least four separate sitting areas in the room, and the pirates chose the one closest to the windows.

"Here they are," the Sheikh said as he and Yousef entered the room together. The Sheikh hugged each of the newly arrived guests, kissing each of them on the cheek. Daniel conceded to the hug but tried to evade the kiss, but the Sheikh was unrelenting until his slimy lips pressed against Daniel's cheek. His breath smelled of some unholy rottenness.

"Please, let us all sit. Can I get you anything?"

No one replied affirmatively.

"Well then, what a take, ay?" The Sheikh said and rattled in laughter. Yousef, who had been sitting rather quietly at the Sheikh's side, operated his lips into a fake smile parallel to his lord. "One-hundred ninety million. Five million apiece for you all. I can't believe how – no, I can believe how successful we are. But believing in oneself and achieving the gains are two very different feelings, ay?"

Everyone nodded.

"Yousef has told me the job was no easy task," the Sheikh said. Then he turned his attention square on Daniel. This is the last thing Daniel had hoped to happen. "I understand you were the Most Valuable Player?"

Daniel didn't respond.

The Sheikh's brow furrowed in curiosity.

"Have I been misinformed?"

"No it is all true that I say," Yousef quickly interjected.

"Why don't you speak up then, son? Take credit for your actions?"

"I came here to be paid. Not swap stories," Daniel said, the fury he harbored subdued behind gritted teeth.

"You aren't one for people skills are you, son?"

"I'm not your fucking son."

The Sheikh leaned back and stroked his silky mustache, as if considering how to respond. As if he wasn't used to being talked to like this.

Yousef leapt to his feet. "You don't talk to the Sheikh like a dog, infidel!"

Daniel stood, clenching his fists. Yousef froze. The two stood glaring at one another in the eyes, poised to strike.

"I see what Yousef has told me is true. Is it haunting your conscience? I forget, you are but new to the profession, are you not? You aren't used to the Somali way. Look at the dark circles under your eyes, your gaunt cheeks. I'd wager you haven't been sleeping. I bet you have nightmares about it. If you've been reliving it, then you must remember it well. Why not share the story with me?"

Daniel started towards the door.

"Where are you going?" the Sheikh asked.

"I've had enough of this."

"But you haven't been paid."

"Then pay me."

"I asked you all here so that I might invite you to a party tonight I am hosting in your honor," the Sheikh said. He turned to face Daniel. "If you must leave now, then expect to be picked up downstairs at the Orient Pearl at 6:30pm."

"I'm not coming to your party," Daniel said.

"Then don't expect to be paid," the Sheikh retorted, turned away from Daniel, reengaging the other pirates.

Daniel exited the Sheikh's villa. Outside, a guard asked if he was lost. Daniel explained he was merely leaving earlier than his friends. The guard asked him if he had a ride. Daniel replied he didn't. The guard told him there were a few men going downtown in just a few minutes if he would like a lift. Daniel accepted the offer. While he waited on the front porch, a large truck arrived that read *Xisbiga Mogadishu*. Men labored to carry tables, stages, folding chairs, portable generators, five-foot tall silver candle sticks, amplifiers, extension cords, fondue fountains, bales of khat. The caterers hadn't unloaded a quarter of the equipment they'd brought along when Daniel's ride arrived.

**Instead of going back to the Orient Pearl**, Daniel decided to see Caitlin at the WHO facility. She was the only one who could make him feel better, or feel good. He hadn't given much thought to it in the fog of his depression, but he dreamt of leaving Somalia for good in the company of Caitlin. Only she could give him the spark he needed to get out. He knew he liked her. Maybe even loved her. At the very least, he could make himself love her. He wanted to throw himself into something, or someone's arms. Caitlin would make a great travel companion. They could leave Somalia and start a new life together. In time, Daniel would forget everything about the place. It was nice to believe, anyway.

He was familiar enough to be permitted easy access through the heavily-secured outer membrane, and allowed to pass the nurse's station straight back to the patient examination rooms. He saw her in the hall, talking to a circle of her colleagues. He approached them, and when she saw him she stepped away from the conversation to head him off midway.

"You shouldn't be here."

"I need to talk to you."

"I don't think we have anything to say."

"Why?"

"I asked you not to do something and you did it. It's pretty simple, really," she said, dropping her voice to the faintest whisper. "I'm not interested in dating a terrorist."

"It's not like that," he said. "We did it for money."

"Money, religion, political agenda, what's it matter? It's terrible."

"I agree. That's why I want to leave."

An uncontrollably warm expression flashed across her face, but cooled just as quickly as it appeared.

"Look, I'm really busy now. TFG and Al-Shabaab have been exchanging mortar rounds in the northern section of the city. We've got wounded coming in by the truckload. Can we talk tonight?"

He scratched his head.

"You've got plans," she inferred. She started to walk away.

"It's not what you think. There's this party I really don't want to go to, but you could come."

"With your friends? No way. Not a chance."

She started away again, but he grabbed her wrist. A concerned look crossed her face. He wasn't certain he knew what he was doing anymore, but he didn't let doubt deter him.

"Look, I don't want to go to this stupid party. But I have to go if I want to leave Somalia," he said. She looked unconvinced. "I'm getting paid a large sum of money at the party," he whispered. "Once I have it, I can leave. I want you to come with me. We can leave here and go anywhere in the world. Anywhere you want. I just want to be anywhere with you that isn't here."

He let go of her wrist. She probed his eyes. He knew she was wondering how she could be sure about him, and he had no argument to make. He was a risk, a liability. She knew that. An attempt to present another persona would make himself a liar on top of a pirate. His reputation couldn't suffer any additional negative attributes. In this moment, he was just going to have to let her decide for herself.

"Let me think about it," she said, and walked away, rejoining the conversation circle, which had shifted its attention to trying their damnedest to infer what the hell it was Caitlin and the pirate were talking about. Then she walked through the swinging doors in to the adjacent corridor, disappearing from his sight.

# Twenty-Five

With uncertain feelings, Daniel arrived at the Sheikh's party on an Orient Pearl shuttle well after the event had commenced. On arrival, a lanky Somali staggered from the villa, sprayed a slur at the cadre of guards, dropped and smashed his glass against the ground, then fell into his own pile of broken glass and spilt liquor. Noticeably apparent was the explicit suspension of Shariah law, partying and lewd behavior combining to create the atmosphere of the party. When he passed through security, a guard mentioned he had missed the shura's presentation. He pretended to be disappointed by the information, but was secretly glad. He had timed his arrival to skip the pageantry.

The spectacle on arrival was startling. It was like he'd stepped into an African tribal-themed bohemian party: scantily clad women rhythmically swaying and bending all throughout the place, multicolored lasers piercing the air, full bar, buffet with traditional food complemented by what he estimated was a six-foot tall mountain of khat, a rock band performing popular western songs remixed with Somali folk lyrics and traditional poems, people dancing, wildly dancing and writhing with suggestions provocative enough to make Lucifer blush. There were eye whites and pearl teeth piercing the darkness in the distance in accompaniment to those lights, which were a show in and of themselves. In a prominent corner stood the four men Daniel recognized as the Amniyat. In front of them were stacked large, impressive titanium steel luggage suitcases.

His money.

All the Amniyat were heavily armed. That they were disappointed with the display of debauchery was apparent, but they stood stolid like the professional gunmen they were.

Daniel felt a set of flabby arms wrap around his torso. He flexed his muscles and burst free of the subjugation, turned to face his aggressor. The Sheikh swayed before him, dawning a shemagh like he was some sort of Saudi Arabian prince or something. Daniel caught a whiff of his breath, noted the blood shot eyes and realized the Sheikh was incredibly drunk.

"Daniel my son. We have been waiting on you!"

"I bet you have!"

"You missed the shura!"

"I know. I hate that."

"Boring shit anyway. It pays to respect one's elders though."

Daniel said nothing.

"You haven't learned that lesson yet though, have you boy?" The Sheikh patted Daniel on the cheek, just a degree of intensity below being slapped.

Given the Sheikh's edgy state, Daniel quickly processed that he had little to gain by pushing back against the Sheikh's gibe.

"It's usually wise to submit to natural authority," Daniel said.

The Sheikh bellowed, clasping Daniel on the shoulder. He pointed with a crooked middle finger towards the table with suitcases that Daniel had just been eyeballing. The Amniyat men stood a little straighter with the Sheikh's attention on them.

"There it is. Five million dollars," the Sheikh said. The Sheikh passed Daniel what appeared to look like a valet stub. "Give them this before you leave, and they'll give you your money." The Sheikh grinned and started in like he was going to give Daniel another

244

one of those slobbery kisses, but he stopped short, apparently satisfied to forgo further public display of affection. The Sheikh quickly found more admiring company nearby and disappeared back in to the sea of anonymity.

Daniel looked around the room at all the strange faces, at the stacked cases full of money, the ticket in his hand. To the right person, this would be a party to remember. To Daniel, a celebration in this wretched city was little more than an obscenity.

He wondered around the residence for a while, looking for the gang, but he couldn't find anyone. Not even a familiar face.

He wandered around two levels of pools, one feeding a continuous stream into the other, through a three-story library, through the kitchen, hallways upon hallways of bedrooms, a private mosque, a map room, and finally back to the main living room where the force of the party was focused. He saw the suitcases of money stacked at a distance, and for a moment he thought he might claim his and leave.

He saw Caitlin.

She was wearing a blue-wrap dress with indigenous tribal designs. Her skin was tan and her hair bleached by daily exposure to the equatorial sun. She had already spotted him. He felt a flash of heat, as if he'd had a stroke or just walked by the exhaust of a large furnace. They magnetically began to approach one another. They met on the steps between the upper landing and the lower living room turned dance floor.

"You came," he said.

"I thought about what you said."

"About leaving?"

She bobbled her head.

"You'd consider it? You'd leave your job?"

"I," she started. "I started thinking after you left. My first impression was that leaving with you would totally defeat all my reasons for coming here. But then I tried to think why I'd come here and the reasons weren't as clear as I'd thought."

245

"Why did you come here?"

She smiled mischievously. "To piss off my father," she said, and yelled with abandon, "*I don't know!* I don't know. I wanted adventure. I thought Somalia was a way to get that and keep my career."

"You'd give up the adventure?"

"*You are* the adventure," she said, and took a long step closer. "Besides a few times sneaking out of WHO to go to a khat café, my memorable times are with you. Believe it or not, life around WHO isn't exactly thrilling. I mean, maybe in an ER sense, but seeing all these poor mangled people come in day after day, it's disheartening. It's depressing. Even the vets around the clinic admit it. I guess there's the type that becomes numb to it, and the type that never does. I've been here 13 months, but I'm never going to get used to seeing this amount of carnage and human suffering. Tragedy isn't adventure. It's just sad."

"I agree with you. Tragedy *isn't* adventure. I came over here to sample this lifestyle, and I've ended up becoming it. I never meant for things to happen the way they have. I need to get out of here, rediscover who I can become. I want to rediscover myself with you."

She appeared to be assembling her next sequence of thoughts when Macalin interrupted them, walking between them and wrapping his arms around each of them.

"Daniel and the pretty lady. Good party ay, guys?"

"We were kind of in the middle of something," Daniel said.

"Oh, ok sure sure. Listen Daniel, I wasn't meaning to interrupt you, but I was hoping to talk to you about something important for just a moment in private."

No way.

"Just for a moment please, Daniel. It's very, very important or I would never interrupt the two of you."

Daniel crossed his arms. Macalin needs to go away.

"Give me ten minutes and I'll leave you alone for the rest of the night. Ten minutes, and I'll even personally make certain no one else bothers you the rest of the night."

"Well go on," Caitlin said with a sigh. "I'll still be here when you get back."

Daniel examined Caitlin's eyes. She wasn't going to stop this.

So Daniel let Macalin lead him away from her. Daniel followed Macalin out passed the pools, down a winding set of steps cut in to the cliffs that led to the wall fortifying the villa from the beach. Macalin spoke briefly to the guards controlling the wrought iron gate, which was the only egress point to the beach. The beach was deserted with stars twinkling overhead and milky cosmic cream of creation sprayed across the sky. They both pulled off their shoes and walked alongside one another, shoes in hand. Nearby, the waves crashed with a thunderous clap. It would have been a good place to surf, were it not for the sharks.

Only when they were more than one-hundred yards away from the Sheikh's guards did they begin their conversation.

"This had better be good, Macalin."

"Listen Daniel, I have not always been honest with you. Actually, I haven't been honest with anyone."

"What are you talking about?"

"What I'm about to tell you could get me killed. So take no offense, it's not just that I don't trust you. I don't trust anyone. I'm only telling you now because it's absolutely necessary. Can I trust you to protect me?"

"Macalin," Daniel said. "How many raids have we been partners on? We kill for one another. What greater level of protection is there?"

"There's none."

"No trust at all?"

"In a land of anarchy, deceit *is* the standard."

"Why pick me to share your secret then, if you trust no one?"

"Because it's a risk I have to take."

Macalin almost seemed noble in this moment, a remarkable piety about his demeanor. How could Daniel deny a man relief from his burden?

"Ok, I'll keep your secret. What's up?"

Macalin stopped walking and gazed contemplatively out to sea. "I will tell you then."

Both men took a seat on the sand, staring out into ocean, out over the horizon of their hunting grounds, a million stars twinkling in the sky above crying out for a wish.

"When I come to Somalia, everyone thought I was a high school kid who was selected by an imam at a mosque in Minneapolis, Minnesota. That's what it's supposed to look like, but it's not the truth. I was actually in the U.S. military, a Marine. I fought in Iraq in 2005, then went through Airborne and Army Ranger School. At the end of Army Ranger School, I was tasked with a special assignment."

"Infiltrate Somali pirate circles?" Daniel heard the incredulous pitch in his voice.

"Not exactly. They wanted me to spy on Al-Shabaab, only the Sheikh recognized my skills early on and he had me transferred to work with Sayyid. The Sheikh is heavily networked with the shura of Al-Shabaab, the elders who gave the presentation tonight before you arrived. In some ways this is perfect, because I can keep tabs on both the pirates and the militants, even though they'd originally intended me to only monitor the jihadists."

"So you're an American spy. But why tell me this now?"

"That's what I'm getting at. When we got pegged to hijack the airplane, clearly I set all my local assets to work to double and triple check what was really going on. The financial motive for the skyjacking came back clean enough, but there was other information uncovered that really terrified us."

"What?"

"The Sheikh's other pirate gang, I think you remember them from when we brought the gold back from the train, when Sayyid had that tense moment with the Sheikh outside the hotel?"

"Yeah. The guys here tonight guarding the money."

"Exactly. Well, they're also Al-Shabaab secret police, an assassin squad, a Somali Gestapo. They raided a Russian ship headed for Venezuela while we were off on the Kenyan job. They had intel about the merchant ship which was covertly carrying some tanks, anti-aircraft guns, a thousand machine guns—all stuff the Sheikh and Al-Shabaab would be very interested in. Well, they took the boat, but they found something much more interesting, or devastating depending on how you look at it. They found two nuclear bombs. And now the Sheikh has them."

"What's he going to do with them?"

"I think it's pretty clear he wants to detonate them in western cities. All we know is that he's tapped Sayyid to carry out his orders. You missed the announcements earlier, but tomorrow the Sheikh is planning a big Orca hunt as a celebration for skyjacking that plane. The Sheikh's giving Sayyid the mission between now and then. We don't know exactly when the Sheikh will dispatch Sayyid to carry out the mission, but we feel the Okra hunt tomorrow will be our last clear shot at stopping Sayyid. That's why we have to eliminate him tomorrow."

Daniel leapt to his feet. He wasn't killing Sayyid. Getting on board with that task was as good as laying down in front of a moving train.

"Why would I risk my life to kill Sayyid? If I double-cross him, I'll have nowhere to go. You'll have me hunted by the U.S., and I'll be hunted here by the Sheikh."

"We have to kill Sayyid tomorrow, otherwise he'll kill *millions* of people. Plus, if you kill Sayyid, or help me kill Sayyid, I'll see to it you get full immunity. You can go back to the U.S. Hell, they'll even let you keep your money."

Daniel picked up a seashell, and tossed it out in to the dark, thundering ocean.

"I want out of this business. Totally out. I can't stomach it anymore. I haven't been able to escape these suicidal thoughts since the last job. It's not just that I want out, I need out." Tears misted Daniel's vision, commingled with the salty air, stinging his eyes.

"No one is proud of what we did in Kenya," Macalin said. "This is your chance, our chance to atone. It's a chance for redemption."

Those words *atone* and *redemption* were soothing. Just before this walk, he had been focused on picking up that heavy suitcase full of money and disappearing from the Somalian scene forever. Caitlin had shown up at the party, and he thought he was close to convincing her to join him.

But he was haunted by thoughts of the Kenyan job. He was haunted by everything he had done. Could he live the rest of his life looking over his shoulder? Just waiting for INTERPOL or the CIA to snatch him up, only to be convicted to spend twenty years to life in prison? If they could find the money, they would take it away from him, too. If they were able to gather evidence of all the other crimes he'd committed, which Macalin no doubt had a detailed record of, he could be executed. Although he had options, there was only one clear choice.

Macalin watched, letting Daniel mull the job. Daniel felt the spy's eyes watching him while he deliberated. They pushed on him. Nagged him. No doubt Macalin was just waiting to launch his backup argument, if necessary.

It wasn't.

"I'll do it," Daniel said.

Daniel had expected Macalin to smile or betray some physical display of gratitude, but he didn't. Macalin didn't find this business any less disconcerting than Daniel. Macalin respected Sayyid, too. But this mission wasn't about liking. It was about protecting a major city from mass causalities. It was about protecting freedom. It was about acknowledging that right and wrong existed, and choosing between self-interest and innocent lives.

The men stood, dusted their shirttails, and walked up to the beach towards the gate. Macalin spoke a few simple words to the guards, and they were permitted entry. When they reached the edge of the party by the lower pool, they paused for a moment.

"I'll find a way to fill you in on any other specifics before the hunt tomorrow. It's in the morning, so look out for something before then."

"Ok," Daniel said.

He went in search of Caitlin.

She wasn't difficult to find. She had hardly moved since he left her a half hour earlier. She looked less radiant than she had before, like she had had too much exposure to the sun.

"Sorry about that," Daniel said on approach.

"I told you it was fine. So I've thought about your offer. I say we leave. Leave tonight. Tomorrow morning. Just as soon as we can," she said, her voice squeaking with unrestrained excitement. Then she whispered, "I can't stand to be here another moment than necessary. Just take whatever money you've got then let's get out of here."

Daniel gazed out the window, where a young Somali man poured liquor on his chest, lit himself on fire, and jumped in the pool. A crowd of gawkers applauded, yelled, and laughed so hard they spilled their drinks.

"What is it?" She asked.

"I've got one more thing to do before I can leave," Daniel said.

She looked away from him, staring at a place on the ceiling that held no particular significance. He had upset her, but there wasn't another option. An empty feeling settled into his stomach.

"It's always going to be one more, isn't it?" the hostility clothing her words acutely obvious.

"No Caitlin, it's just the nature of what it is."

"What is it then? Tell me what's so important?"

"I shouldn't tell you."

"That's convenient," she said and crossed her arms.

"Just trust me on this one?"

"You can trust me when I say I *don't* want to see you again," she said. She turned and started marching up the stairs, towards the front door. He hurried behind her, grabbed her around the bicep, but he felt her muscle bulge. She turned and looked at him with this look, this painful look of resolve that told him to give up explaining. He released her, and when he did, she flew away like he had let go a taut elastic band.

She disappeared just like that, melding into the abstract crowd, just another silhouette among a mass of partiers.

# Twenty-Six

The morning after the party at the Sheikh's villa, Daniel woke to Macalin pacing back and forth in front of his bed at the Orient Pearl. The scent of boiled coffee grounds dominated the air. The sheets were soft and clean, unlike everything beyond the walls of the gilded hotel. Daniel sat up in bed and rubbed his eyes. Macalin was dressed in a full wet suit, unzipped and pulled down to his waist, wearing a grey cotton v-neck t-shirt over his chest.

"Morning sailor," Daniel said. His dry, scratchy throat made it difficult to talk. He regretted having lingered at the Sheikh's party after Caitlin left him. He also regretted the vodka, cigarettes and khat. He felt like he'd woken up in an active construction zone, surrounded by building debris, such as nails and scrap wood, and the loud noise that whined in his head.

Pacing the room, Macalin launched into a diatribe, but Daniel heard none of it. Macalin's words were drowned by the noise of last night's party and the discomfort of blood rushing through millions of constricted passages in Daniel's brain. Daniel closed his dry eyes, hoping to moisten them.

"Do you understand what I'm saying?" Macalin asked repetitively.

"No," Daniel conceded.

"I'm saying it has to be *you*. The Sheikh assigned everyone to a boat. I'm not in Sayyid's boat, you are. When I woke up this morning, Sayyid was gone from the suite. I called downstairs and they said they'd given him a ride early this morning to the Sheikh's. Lucky I bugged him. The Sheikh gave him the activation key. Once the bomb is in place and activated, the Sheikh will be able to detonate it from anywhere in the world. What's worse, I can't get reinforcements here for another 48 hours. Getting that key is the only chance we have at foiling the attack."

"Couldn't we just steal it from him?"

"He'll be carrying it in the smuggler's compartment on his belt buckle. You'd have to hold him down and strip his belt off of him. Do you think he's going to let you do that?"

"No, I don't. But what if we just asked him to not go along with the Sheikh's plan?"

"Daniel, the man has killed every day since he hit puberty. Money and mayhem are what make him tick. Do you think you can reason with him? Sure, he's fun, but he's insane. You can't reason with a man like that."

"He's got beef with the Sheikh."

"Trust me, he's got a lot less beef with the Sheikh than he does with the Americans. The Americans are responsible for his parents' death. He's a man of havoc, Daniel. This is what everything's led up to for him, for all these guys, really. This opportunity to terrorize, this opportunity to even the score."

Daniel's thoughts were anchored in his plans to leave Somalia with his newfound wealth, starting the next phase of his life clean slated with the granule of hope that Caitlin would join him.

Macalin poured cold water on the fire of those dreams. He couldn't escape Somalia if this anarchic conflagration spread throughout the world.

"Ok. I'll do it."

**All the Sheikh's inner circle gathered** on the pirate flotilla's flagship, Quimbly's yacht, the one they had used to launch their pirate raids. Several small skiffs were roped to the lower deck below. With everyone gathered around, the Sheikh explained the rules. Five boats go out. No guns allowed. The only weapons permitted during the hunt were harpoons, lances, and bowie knives. Five men assigned to each boat. The first skiff to return with a dead Orca in tow would receive the a group prize of one million dollars.

The teams outfitted, climbed into the boats and readied themselves. Sayyid stood at the helm of his skiff, a great wooden lance with a glinting steel tip in his clutch.

"What do you think of today, Daniel? Not every day you get to hunt the killer whale, yes?"

"We're hunting Orcas."

"What do you think the Orca is? It is the killer whale, yes. You must read up on your marine biology."

As if the outing weren't already perilous enough. If he were tossed from the little boat, he would be left fending for himself in the open waters against a school of killer whales. While Sayyid faced him, Daniel looked at the pirate's belt buckle: a large scorpion was well preserved in a hard laminate. Not exactly inconspicuous. The tightened belt held his tattered black jeans, which were cut below his knees, halfway across his shins. A black tank top tight over his torso. Black on black on black. Daniel snickered.

They should replace the Jolly Roger emblem with a picture of Sayyid as he was in that moment. The muscle-rippled, battle experienced young man as the archetype pirate. His agenda today was on level sacrilegious, as if Sayyid's death would diminish the very idea of adventure. The Sheikh counted down, "Shan, afar, saddex, laba ka mid ah," raised a platinum Colt .45 long barrel revolver in the air and fired. The tiny skiff engines motored away from the safety of the flotilla, out into the hunting grounds. Daniel hadn't noticed it before because he had been so distracted by his private mission, but the aberration in the water was just yards ahead of them. Gigantic apostrophe shaped fish leapt from unfathomable depths, sailed momentarily through the air, and crashed back through the plane of the sea, disappearing beneath the water's subterranean boundary. A tremendous wake caused the boat to tremor as the pirates continued to steadily approach the hunted herd.

Whale hunting was a sport for which Daniel had no prior experience. He wasn't aware of whether or not any of these other men had aptitude with the endeavor. Certainly no one had asked him if he'd ever played this game.

The speediest boat in the contest chanced ahead of the rest, just beyond the last surfacing of the family of whales. The lead hunting party idled their engine and everyone in their boat stood ready with harpoons and lances. The remainder of the teams, including Sayyid and Daniel's boat, idled their engines and sat back a distance to let the most eager team try their hand at whaling.

The lead boat had guessed with lethal accuracy where the whales would next surface. The boat idled while all hands stood ready to strike with their instruments of death. Tension mounted in the air. Then, the whales breeched the surface, causing the little boat to rock and reel. The men hurled lances and harpoons in every direction. Their attack was wholly uncoordinated. Daniel watched as one of the whalers hit an Orca directly in its back with his harpoon. He jumped in celebration, only to be tossed from the boat into the tumultuous waters.

Not a single person in the regalia wore a life jacket. A foreseeable error, as many of the Somalis lacked the ability to swim. The witnesses began yelling and cheering like spectators at a soccer match, some offering coaching advice while others simply expressed their emotion. Blood leaked all around that troubled boat from an unverifiable source, likely the stricken whale, but one of the harpooners had fallen overboard and was missing in action.

A whale leapt through the air with stunning vertical agility, crashing through the splintering hull of the lead skiff. The harpooners flew every direction. The Orcas splashed and flipped about, the surrounding waters discolored with a crimson tint. Pure bedlam on the Black Sea.

Sayyid faced the other men in his boat. He held the rapt attention of everyone in that tiny, unseaworthy aggregation of wooden boards, antiquated weapons, and little motor.

"I think we should back up a few hundred yards to give the Orca some time to cool off," Sayyid said. The team was all nods. The pilot quickly fired the engine and steered them away from the carnage.

Daniel felt pity for the men thrown overboard. Images of them being mutilated in the water cut his mood like a mother mourning the loss of a child.

"This is good," Sayyid said when they were a safe distance from the likely location of the Orcas' next surfacing.

Sayyid laughed. He laughed a wicked uncontrollable laugh. Snot rolled out of his nose. He held his sides. He gasped as though he were in pain, as if his lungs were filled to overcapacity and were pushing on his rib cage and other vital organs.

"What?" Daniel said.

When Sayyid's laughter finally subsided, he looked at Daniel with tears in his eyes.

"Is it funny that we must kill to live? Kill to live. Eat the plant. Eat the camel. Eat the whale. We take energy to have energy. I find peculiar God make it this way."

Daniel found truth in Sayyid's observation. As if nature granted all beings in existence a license to murder. Yet the notion was subordinate to the thoughts that dominated Daniel's mind. He was aiming to kill big game, but had no design on an Orca. He was fixated on killing a pirate.

The men in Daniel's boat all sat there for long enough, doing nothing. Eventually they all fell to silence, waiting on some undetermined signal before returning to the hunt.

Another of the skiffs finally motored over to them from where they had been hovering at the site of lead boat's demise.

"They're all d-d-dead," the lance man said.

"I have study this idea myself," Sayyid said. "The last boat had no strategy. They jump right in to the litter of Orca, each fire their harpoon in separate directions, then get taken. We can be more tactful than this. The Sheikh wants an Orca capture, and he offer one million dollars to split. I cannot use two-hundred thousand dollars if I'm dead, but I could use one-hundred thousand if I'm alive. So how about we work together?"

The men in the other boat were quick to enter the agreement. Tales of Sayyid's reputation as the lord of violence were no doubt known throughout Mogadishu.

"Ok, so here is what I think. We not just jump in to the Orcas' jaws like the last fools, no, we motor over to the edge of the school. We stay together. We take turns with our harpoons, so we are all aiming for the same whale and not all different whales. This is how we will capture one. This is how we will stay alive."

Everyone agreed. Stick together, make a hundred thousand and stay alive.

For a moment, Daniel was so engaged in the group effort inspired by Sayyid's strategy that he almost forgot his original modus operandi. They were motoring in to that herd of killer whales with a strategy, a forged alliance, and a great pirate at point. Spirits were high among the skiffs as they jolted towards those killer whales, who were again surfacing for air, unwittingly chancing their lives.

"Cut the engines now," Sayyid said within twenty feet of the nearest whale, an adolescent calf not more than fifteen feet in length. They were drifting towards the fawn now, everyone with lance or harpoon in position. Sayyid clinched his fist in the air: hold steady. Daniel's heart accelerated. He looked around to see all the other men breathing heavily, careening forward in their little boats with unsteady balance, their faces red, eyes filled with terrified excitement. His legs felt so light he wasn't sure how they supported him. The increasing ocean breeze whirred past his ears, the mighty killer whales lolloped further and further away into the distance from their progeny.

Then, with a mighty thrust, Sayyid hurled the harpoon. Soon each man staggered for position, and one, two, three, four, five harpoons struck the killer whale as it thrashed about in the water. Daniel lost grip of his harpoon's rope, losing it to the sea. The other men had wrapped the rope around their bodies, and now they were tugging on the young Orca, reeling it closer to the boat. Sayyid called for his lance. He steadied the skewer above his head, waiting patiently for his opportunity to deal the deathblow.

Suddenly Daniel fell to his back. Their tiny boat rollicked in the water. Daniel watched as the three men who had wrapped harpoon rope around their waists were tugged overboard. The boat shook violently. Although he could not see the other craft, Daniel heard their shrieks with frightening clarity. Daniel saw a boot with what he thought was the stub of a severed foot fly overhead. He vomited a little in his mouth. The stomach bile tasted putrid. To make matters worse, Daniel's view was eclipsed by Sayyid's crotch in his face, the boat engine roaring and Daniel's back slapping against the hull each time the little skiff skipped over a wave. After a minute or so, Daniel nudged Sayyid out of his way, got out from under the pirate's crotch and sat up. Fresh air filled his lungs, clarity returned. Daniel looked at the sea behind them, where they hunted just moments ago, but there was no boat to be seen. He spun his vision around three-sixty, but he saw nothing. Wait, for a moment he thought he saw a disturbance in the water from where they had just fled, but then they passed beyond the point of visibility. He couldn't be certain of what he had seen.

Most of the hunters had been tossed overboard in the carnage.

Sayyid and Daniel were alone in the boat.

Alone in the ocean.

"You take," Sayyid said, delegating the piloting of the boat to Daniel. Sayyid carefully worked his way up to the bow of the boat.

"Should I continue in this direction?" Daniel asked. He didn't know where they were headed, only they were fleeing the vicious herd of killer whales.

Sayyid didn't respond.

"Which way are we going?"

"What do you think is more important?" Sayyid said, his attention fixed on the horizon before them. An odd serenity attached to his voice. "Where we are going or where we have been? Where we are going, it seems meaningless without reference to where we've been, yes? There's no reference. There is no movement if we do not know from where we come."

Daniel looked to the hull of the little boat where there lay a glinting cast-iron lance, singing out to Daniel to be launched through the mad man's back. He could cut Sayyid down, right through the middle.

"Everyone in the movies is always so concerned with this," Sayyid said. "Where are you going? What have you accomplish? Yet I don't like when success is measured by a point. It should be measured from a beginning to end, start to finish. Maybe some man is born with an Orca jaw hanging over his fireplace. Is he better than a man who die to claim one for himself? Is it not more worthy to take than to be given?"

Daniel glimpsed at the bowie knife double strapped at Sayyid's waist and thigh. Also in the hull of the boat was a rusty machete.

"Maybe I never know which is better," Sayyid continued. "One might even say that I was given strength, the ability to take what I want, while another man is given money or a car but he is never able to get one of these things without being given. Which of us was truly blessed? The man who receive gift of wealth or the man who receive gift of ability to take wealth? And is there difference?"

Daniel felt this was the moment. He let go of the motor. He leaned over, picked up the lance, and hurled it at Sayyid.

Just as he released the death instrument, the boat jostled unpredictably so that Daniel's pitch followed a wobbly trajectory. Death's hand sailed past Sayyid and disappeared in to the ocean, without as much as scratching the pirate. Sayyid saw the lance fly past his head, its intended target readily apparent. Sayyid immediately lunged across the boat at Daniel. As the men struggled, the unpiloted boat rocked and careened freely about the ocean.

Sayyid wrapped his fingers around Daniel's throat, but only for a few seconds. Then he reached down and unsheathed his knife. Daniel quickly head butted Sayyid, and Sayyid dropped the knife overboard during his daze. Daniel threw a kitten-strength punch, but luckily landed it right on Sayyid's nose. The petty blow was enough to stun Sayyid, who flailed back on uncertain legs, holdings his nose. For a moment, Daniel thought fortune had shifted to his favor. He was reaching for his own bowie knife when the boat skimmed over top the ocean in an unfamiliar fashion, such that it gave Daniel butterflies in his stomach, then, on an abrupt impact, came to an immediate halt.

Daniel leaned up from where he lie in the boat's hull. They'd run ashore. Sayyid had been tossed to the beach, but he seemed to be quickly regaining his senses. Daniel scanned the shore, and spotted steps leading up to a dilapidated villa. He ran towards the ruin for cover. When he reached the stairs, he turned over his shoulder to see Sayyid running after him. The sight was terrifying. Sayyid had murder clenched in his jaws, blood lust in his balled fists.

Daniel sprinted up the stairs, and leveled off in a field of long forgotten old-growth acacias blanketed in spider webs so thick that they looked like ghost trees. Daniel ran along the rows of ghost trees, glancing frantically for anything, a weapon, an avenue of escape, somewhere to hide, anything to perpetuate his existence. Then Daniel saw some sort of tree house, guard tower, or viewing platform accessible by a rickety old ladder. He sprinted for it. If he could climb it and raise the ladder, he thought.

An instant later the breath was knocked out of him. He was forcibly rolled over to see Sayyid's psychotic eyes working those sledgehammer fists that pummeled Daniel in the face, bursting his nose, cracking his eye socket, and bruising his jaws. Then Sayyid leaned over and picked up a large stone, lifted it high into the air and rested a moment to give his killer's smirk time to savor the conclusion of a successful hand-to-hand duel.

"Wait, wait!" Daniel pled, only seconds before Sayyid would smash his brains to formlessness. "Just let me tell you why, Sayyid, he gasped as he turned his head to spit out blood.

Sayyid's eyes widened, the stone in his hand eclipsing the sun overhead, and all Daniel could see was the pirate's silhouette and the whites of his eyes.

"Tell me why," Sayyid said, breathing like an animal. "Then I kill you."

Daniel no longer cared if he was alive or dead, but after everything the two men had gone through, he had to explain why to his brother.

"I know about the city you're going to destroy. I couldn't let you do it. I had to stop you. The pirating is one thing, but this destruction, the thought of mass murder is madness. Your next mission drove me to this."

Sayyid's heavy breathing began to slow, the intensity in his eyes slowly dissipated. He lowered the rock. The sun beamed down Daniel's face.

"How did you know about that?" Sayyid asked, as he lowered the stone. "I'm not destroying a city. I not even tell you about that mission because we have no plans to do it." Then tension returned to his voice. "Why would you try to kill me?"

"Because I wanted to save a city. Save a million lives. The Sheikh ordered you to do it. You must understand."

"You think I always do what the Sheikh says?" Sayyid said, rolling to his back and launching into a deep belly laugh.

"No," Daniel said. "I don't guess you do." When had he quit thinking? Why hadn't he even considered the possibility Sayyid would refuse the Sheikh's order?

Sayyid stared out across the orchard, apparently at nothing. Daniel watched Sayyid breathing heavily and mentally putting the pieces together: the bomb, his disdain for the Sheikh, and his crew steering into terrorist territory with their last mission. There was a long silence, which lingered until both men's breathing normalized.

Sayyid exhaled and turned to Daniel.

"We will not let this happen, Daniel. You have my word as a brother, yes," Sayyid said.

"That's great." Daniel felt his lungs expand at once; he realized he was holding his breath from the moment Sayyid let the stone roll out of his hands.

"There is a problem. I'm only to be given one bomb. The Sheikh is going to give the other to Amniyat, and I guess they will not just give it to us if we ask politely."

"We need to start tracking them immediately," Daniel said.

"This may not be necessary," Sayyid said. "The Sheikh is supposed to meet us at the airport with the bombs. Perhaps we collect them both there."

# *Twenty-Seven*

The makeshift airport was a flat, hard, dirt field nine miles beyond the suburbs of Mogadishu. Scrub brush grew wildly throughout the property. An orange windsock was the only formal demarcation of the site as an airport. Daniel, Sayyid, and Macalin were the first to arrive. Yousef had been out of communication, and they weren't certain he was with the Sheikh or whether he was involved in this mission at all.

The three had talked and extensively planned for the contingencies of the rendezvous. The fate of a million lives might be determined by how they performed in the next few moments. This point was not lost on them.

When 10 a.m. passed, their agreed upon meeting time, anxiety heightened. Five minutes late. Ten minutes late. Then a plane circled the field twice and landed. The pilot taxied over to the pirates, shut down the prop engine and made idle talk. Based on what he said, he thought he'd been chartered to ferry a few VIPs to Nairobi.

The pilot had no idea.

Daniel shifted his attention between the single dusty connector road and the few white clouds contrasted against the clear blue sky. Two Land Cruisers surrounding a semi-truck appeared conspicuously as the second plane was sighted in the sky.

Daniel breathed heavy, deliberate breaths. He switched off his M-16's safety.

He rehearsed the plan in his mind. First, secure the bomb they would be given; then, go after the second bomb. Secure the bomb they would be given, first; then go after the second bomb.

The second plane landed and taxied to the opposite side of the runway. Unlike the pilot, who now leaned against Sayyid's Land Cruiser with them, the second plane did not shut off its engine.

"Remember, wait until I'm loaded and gone before making a move," Macalin said. "We're supposed to load first."

The second convoy arrived at the airfield. The semi-truck and one of the Land Cruisers drove directly to the second airplane, while the second Land Cruiser approached Sayyid's group.

Daniel saw Quimbly, captain of the pirate mothership, driving the second Land Cruiser, the one approaching him. The Sheikh had pulled all his top men into this mission, though there was no sight of the principal.

Quimbly parked the Land Cruiser, and he and three other AK-47 toting men stepped out of the SUV. Daniel gave the men a once over. They bore all the hallmarks of Al-Shabaab. Besides the soviet-era machine guns, the men were armed to the hilt with hand grenades, one of them had an RPG tube on his back. A handgun hung from each man's hip. They wore matching keffiyehs around the head and neck. The only insignia of their allegiance was the flag of Islam patch sewn on the arms of their uniforms. They were serious, their attention not to be diverted. Their teeth didn't bare the ubiquitous khat stains. A hollowness in their manner suggested a cavity in their souls.

While Sayyid and Quimbly exchanged salutations, Quimbly's security detail loaded a heavy crate on a utility dolly and rolled it to the airplane. The pilot instructed them on stowing the cargo to satisfy the plane's weight and balance requirements. Macalin quietly trailed the men, keeping a good tactical angle on the group during the exchange.

Daniel looked beyond everything happening before him, watching what was happening with the other plane. The Amniyat were just getting out of the Land Cruiser. He saw Shongola, the presumptive leader, barking orders. Someone sitting in the back seat of the Land Cruiser with a black bag over his head. They'd brought a hostage. These guys played with a loaded deck.

Then Daniel caught a glimpse of Yousef, walking around the SUV, issuing orders to anyone willing to listen. Daniel knew the moment of betrayal was upon them. He, Macalin, and Sayyid had discussed it thoroughly at the Orient Pearl. Wait until all the cards were revealed, then move on Sayyid's signal.

A gunshot erupted and echoed through the distance. Daniel's attention whirled to see Quimbly knocked to the ground by the force of Sayyid's Uzi. Macalin cut down the two Al-Shabaab militants who had loaded the nuclear device on the airplane. The remaining guard took off running across the airstrip, towards the other plane. He popped off a single round that shoved the guard to the ground, where he fell splayed and lie motionless.

Everyone on the opposite end of the airfield began scrambling.

"Go get them! I'll take care of this bomb," Macalin yelled. Macalin intimidated the pilot into the plane, and soon the twin-turbines were rotating with a deafening roar.

"Get in," Sayyid said and jumped behind the wheel of the Land Cruiser. Daniel climbed in to the passenger seat. The two sped towards the opposite end of the airfield. "Don't shoot my brother unless he shoot at you," Sayyid said. Then he added, "please."

"I won't," Daniel said reflexively, but he wondered whether he really meant it. He'd really grown to dislike Yousef over time, but he would respect Sayyid's request until it endangered either the mission or his life.

Amniyat took cover and opened heavy fire. Bullets pinged and smashed all over Sayyid's Land Cruiser. Daniel ducked below the dash as bullets whizzed overhead and broken glass burst and tinkled. Unable to see to drive, Sayyid whipped the car perpendicular to the hailstorm of bullets striking the driver's side.

"Get out," Sayyid commanded. Daniel opened his door, toppled out, and rolled behind one of the wheels. A moment later Sayyid dove out of the front seat to the wheel opposite Daniel for cover. "This is what you call a sticky situation, yes."

Daniel might have laughed if there were anything funny about the situation. They had hit a bee's nest and unless they exercised tremendous skill, they were going to be stung. They were being shot at with a heavier caliber machine gun than the standard AK-47. They were being shot at with AK-47s, too. They were being shot at with handguns. They were being shot at from behind a car, from behind the plane, from the runway, from above, below, and straight on. The Land Cruiser was taking a beating, but it seemed the bullets were incapable of hitting their target.

When the barrage finally tapered, Daniel untangled himself out of the fetal position, hesitantly peeking from behind his cover. He saw the second plane's engines cranked. If Amniyat got airborne with that bomb, it was gone. Daniel and Sayyid were moments away from failing their objective.

"Shoot the plane engine," Daniel yelled to Sayyid. "We need to keep them on the ground."

Sayyid nodded.

Sayiyid pulled the pin on a smoke grenade and rolled it in front of his Land Cruiser. Once visibility between them and Amniyat was partially obscured, Daniel leaned out from behind the wheel basin and opened fire on the plane's right propeller. At first, bullets just pinged off the propeller blades, but then smoke began oozing out of the engine and the propeller powered down.

"I got it," Daniel yelled. He looked to see Sayyid leer up at him. "What now?"

"Let's waste their SUV," Sayyid said.

Sayyid counted down on his fingers, three, two, one, and popped up over the Land Cruiser's hood. Daniel started to edge around the rear end of the SUV, but there were too many bullets whizzing and dinging past for him to risk exposure. Daniel glanced up at Sayyid, who to his surprise wasn't firing. Had the pirate finally lost his nerve?

"Why aren't you firing?" Daniel yelled. Sayyid stared down at Daniel, then dropped back behind the safety of the wheel basin.

"I can't shoot."

"Why?"

"They have a hostage. Your girlfriend, Caitlin," Sayyid said.

Daniel's heart sunk. Everything turned black for a moment. He'd put her in this situation. Now they were using her as a human shield! This was so fucked up. There was no time to think, no time to calibrate his personal scales of justice. He deserted mercy.

He saw red and heard sirens.

Daniel watched as two of the Amniyat ran over to the plane, which was now totally powered down. They unloaded the bomb. Daniel fired off a shot at them, but was afraid to release terror in fear he might accidentally detonate the bomb. With the bomb loaded in the Amniyat's Land Cruiser, Yousef and his new comrades hopped in the SUV and started away from the airstrip, back down the dusty road towards Mogadishu.

"Fuck!" Daniel shouted. "What do we do now?"

Sayyid had already climbed in to the driver's seat of his Land Cruiser. It started, to Daniel's amazement, despite being riddled with bullets. Daniel hopped in and they sped off in pursuit of Yousef, the Amniyat, Caitlin, and the rogue nuclear bomb. When they drove past the plane, Daniel glimpsed over for a second, just in time to see that one of the Amniyat had stayed behind. The assailant opened fired on the Land Cruiser, and Daniel jerked his 9mm from its holster and returned fire. He didn't hit the man, but they didn't have time to double back for revenge.

The road back to Mogadishu was in very poor condition, nothing more than worn tire tracks along a dirt terrain, littered with potholes. Still, they couldn't catch up with Yousef, who was a solid half-mile ahead. Daniel unfastened the shoulder stock from his

M-16 so he could fire out the window if necessary. He wondered where they were going. Daniel feared if they lost sight of Yousef's SUV, they would lose track of the bomb and Caitlin forever. The thought of the prospect angered him, his compassion draining from his body.

The chase continued for what seemed an eternity. The Amniyat SUV would top over a hill and disappear. Then Daniel and Sayyid would peak over the same hill to see the Amniyat SUV speeding ahead, dragging an orange tail of dust across the barren desert. Then they began approaching some buildings on the outskirts of the city. Sayyid had managed to close the gap to few hundred yards, but his daring driving suggested they could be wrecked out of the chase at any moment.

The Amniyat SUV would turn a corner, and thirty seconds later, Sayyid would turn the same corner.

Finally, the chase entered inner city Mogadishu, where numerous multi-story buildings shaded the road, making it harder to see the dust trail. The streets wound in an illogical format, shirking traditional notions of the city grid. The avenues and alleys were a puzzle in and of themselves. Daniel trusted Sayyid knew them well, having lived in and around here most of his life. To Daniel it all looked the same, confused, dilapidated, crumbling buildings, loose electrical wires, people sleeping amongst piles of trash, all the hallmarks of a rotten city collapsing on top of itself.

Sayyid slammed on the brakes. A group of a dozen or so children kicked a soccer ball back and forth between themselves, directly in front the Land Cruiser's path. Daniel watched in horror as the Amniyat SUV sped around a corner, out of sight.

Sayyid blew the horn. "Ka wareeg!"

The kids ignored him. Sayyid unclipped his Uzi, and stuck it out the window. Daniel jumped to try to stop him, but Sayyid raised it towards the sky. The kids scattered, clearing the road. Sayyid immediately accelerated, veering through the open street and leaning around the last curve they'd seen the Amniyat SUV make.

Sayyid drove a few more blocks without sight of the SUV, until he slammed on the brakes, bringing the Land Cruiser to a skidding halt.

"Fuck!"

"What? Are you sure we've lost them? We've got to keep looking. They might be around the next corner!" Daniel said.

Sayyid rested his forehead in the palm of his left hand. He closed his eyes and metered his breathing. It nearly frightened Daniel, to see the great black warrior slumped in prostration.

"Sayyid. We can't just sit here. We have to do *something*."

"Ok," he said. He popped up, eyes wide, and heavy footed the accelerator.

"Where are we going?"

"I think where would they go if something went wrong and they wanted to feel safe."

"Yeah?"

"The Sheikh's villa. They have reinforcement there. I think if I were them, it is where I would go."

Daniel nodded agreement.

They sped through the city, until they left the multi-story facades for the outskirts of town, the road Daniel recognized as the one that led to the Sheikh's villa. Sayyid pushed the Land Cruiser to its limits. Daniel prayed Sayyid's intuition was right. He realized if they charged in to the Sheikh's villa, given all his security, it might be their last trespass. He and Sayyid might be mowed down before they even got passed the gate. The Sheikh might still win. But at least they would have done everything they could to thwart the monomaniac's scheme.

Then Daniel saw the beginning of that familiar whitewashed cement block wall with iron prongs protruding out and around and coming to a gashing tip.

A lonely militant stood sentry to the gate's exterior.

"Cut him down," Sayyid said.

Daniel leaned out the SUV window, while Sayyid held the Land Cruiser at a steady rate of speed. Daniel switched the gun to fully automatic, squeezed the trigger and held it. The gun caused him to shake rhythmically, as light flashed in the sky and spent bullet cartridges spouted from the breech. A tuft of red mist exploded, the guard fell, and a red splatter painted the white cement wall.

Sayyid semi-circled the SUV. Daniel sat back in his seat and fastened his seatbelt. Sayyid put his pedal foot to the ground, steering the SUV directly towards the center point of the gate. Daniel clenched both grab handles. At the point of collision, the gate snapped open without resistance, and they were on the grounds of the Sheikh's villa, speeding passed those rows of orange trees.

They were lucky to have not encountered more hostility at the main gate, but he kept his lucky feelings in check by reminding himself those missing guards must be stalking somewhere. He loaded a fresh magazine in to his M-16. While Sayyid's attention was focused on barreling towards the house, Daniel looked over the driver's shoulder, peering down at the beach, where he saw Quimbly's yacht anchored just off the shore. On the beach, Daniel saw Yousef and the Amniyat's Land Cruiser and two small motorboats.

"They're on the beach!" Daniel yelled. "How do we get down there?"

"There's an access road on the opposite side of the house."

Sayyid accelerated, zooming right past the main entrance to the Sheikh's villa. A guard who formerly lounged against a small Toyota pickup truck suddenly jumped to attention, but fumbled to ready his rifle, which hung from the shoulder strap across his back. When the guard stepped in the middle of the driveway, Sayyid ran him over. The multiple pops and definitive crunch made Daniel cringe, even given everything that had happened.

Where the drive appeared to expire, two lemon trees stood on either side of the asphalt. Sayyid slowed, rounded the corner and began down a hidden narrow strip that led towards the beach. A sharp cliff face rose on Sayyid's side, whereas Daniel had a view of the yacht and the beach rendezvous until old growth palms obscured his field of vision.

"What are we going to do?" Daniel asked.

Sayyid didn't respond.

There were a few remaining wrinkles on the access road before they emerged through an unlocked wrought iron gate comparable to the one they had just burst through on the main road. The vehicle wobbled as it nearly fishtailed when the tires lost their grip on the unfamiliar sand, but Sayyid managed to maintain control. Daniel saw surprise smear across Yousef's face, who apparently thought they'd made a clean escape from the ambush. Then Daniel saw Caitlin sitting on one of the two motorboats where an Amniyat gunman trained his muzzle directly at her precious neck.

Sayyid plowed the Land Cruiser through the sand and brought it to an abrupt halt between the Amniyat's SUV and the motorboat, where an Amniyat agent and Caitlin were separated from Yousef and all the other Amniyat.

Caitlin's captor started the boat and began motoring away, towards the pirate mothership.

"Go after her," Sayyid directed. "I'll hold Yousef and these others."

"What about the bomb?" Daniel asked.

"The bomb is on Caitlin's boat!"

Daniel examined the rapidly departing boat to see the familiar wooden crate, off the shelf death for a million. That snarling beast with one hand on the motor, the other pointing a gun at Caitlin.

Daniel dove out of the Land Cruiser, jumped into the remaining motorboat and sped off in pursuit. His boat was much lighter than the one he was chasing, so he gained promising ground. But once he'd cut half the distance between them, the divide between them became static as the captor pushed his boat to the limit. The yacht was not far off.

Daniel didn't know what hazards might overtake him if he waited until the yacht to stage his fight.

Daniel took his hand off the motor, set his M-16 to single shot mode, assumed a steady shooting position left foot in front of right. He looked through the sights of the rifle, gauging for the undulation of the ocean. Caitlin and her captor were speeding further and further away. Daniel feared once they were on the yacht, that the engine on his little motorboat would be no match for the superior speed of the luxury yacht.

Daniel focused on his mark. He internalized the rise and fall of the ocean. He traced his target across the green sea. They were fifty feet from the yacht now. Forty-five. Forty. Daniel held his breath, sighted the rifle ahead of his target. He pulled the trigger, the rifled recoiled. Daniel lifted the rifle stock as the man was punched into the open ocean and splashed out of sight.

Daniel jumped back to his motor and sped over to Caitlin's boat. When he caught up to her, he jumped in, briefly consoling her, before turning to examine what threats might be prepared to overtake them on the yacht.

There were only two sailors watching naively from the helm.

"How many others are on there with you?" Daniel yelled out.

They didn't respond. He fired a warning shot.

"I said, how many are on there with you?"

One of them men pointed at himself and then the second man.

"Come down here," Daniel said, motioning to the men to come help them board.

By the time Daniel brought the motorboat parallel to the yacht, the men had arrived on the lower deck, and helped Daniel and Caitlin up from the waterline. Daniel instructed the men to drag the crated nuclear device on to the deck. Meanwhile, Daniel kept the area secure by combing his surroundings with the M-16. On the yacht, Caitlin immediately collapsed on to a nearby sofa, curled up, and cried. He wanted to console her terribly, but he had to stay focused. He had to finish this job.

Once the men had the bomb on board, Daniel had to speak roughly to get Caitlin up, so he could lead the two sailors to the wheelhouse, so they could get the hell out there. He lacked the luxury of being able to search the whole boat for hidden gunmen, so he had to make do with the resources at his disposal. His biggest concern was leaving the crated nuke unguarded on the lower deck, but it was a risk he simply had to take. Piloting the boat was a more serious concern. If someone were to offload the device, he would see them fleeing and at least be able to mow them down. Otherwise, he needed to make sure this shorthanded crew was sailing them to friendly waters.

He glimpsed out to the beach once more, while it was still visible, to see Sayyid waging a gun battle on the shore. The odds didn't look promising for Sayyid, even considering how great a warrior he was. Daniel pondered Macalin's argument, that assisting with this mission would absolve him of his sins. Daniel wondered if this act alone were really enough. He wondered if he could ever be forgiven for the evil he'd committed in Africa.

Caitlin sat on the floor, looking absolutely ruined. She had clearly suffered acute emotional trauma.

"Caitlin," he said. But she wouldn't look at him. Her eyes had been misted over since they arrived on the yacht, though she wasn't quite crying. The area of her face all around her eyes was a severe red. She wasn't here, he realized sadly, as he examined the hollowness in those otherwise pristine eyes. She'd retreated somewhere inside herself, refusing to acknowledge what was happening to her.

"Where is we go?" one of the crewmates finally asked.

Daniel pointed on a map.

"No, no," the crewmate said. "CTF-one-five-one. World navy."

"I know," Daniel said. "That's who we're going to meet."

# *Twenty-Eight*

Aboard the U.S.S. Navajo battleship, Daniel was in the infirmary having four stitches put in above his right eye. He had asked the medics if it were really necessary to shave the eyebrow. They assured him it was. He sat on the examination table as patiently as possible, given there was a threaded needle passing through his skin only an inch from his eye.

A heavy knock came on the steel door. The medic beckoned the visitor to enter. Macalin strolled in to the room, with a slim file underneath his arm.

"Well look at you, still alive."

"Everything went well?" Daniel asked.

"Would you excuse us?" Macalin asked the medic. The medic clipped the thread over Daniel's eye and swabbed it with disinfectant gauze.

"He's all yours," the medic said. "I'll be back in ten to finish up. Don't touch your eye until then," he said and left the room.

"The mission was a success," Macalin said. "We recovered possession of both bogies. Unfortunately, we weren't able to capture the Sheikh, the shura, Yousef or anyone. There's also been no rumor of Sayyid."

Daniel nodded.

"What are you going to do now?" Macalin asked.

"Assuming that's my letter of immunity underneath your arm, I'm going to take it, find Caitlin and get the hell out of Africa. Take her somewhere civilized and live for a change."

Macalin gave Daniel the file, which was a letter of immunity signed and dated by both the Secretary of Defense and the Attorney General of the United States. Daniel closed the file, edging his way off the examination table with a pained grunt.

"Too bad about the money," Macalin said.

"What do you mean? You said I get to keep it," Daniel said.

"I have no problem with you keeping it. But I wouldn't think you'd risk going back to the Orient Pearl to get it, even assuming it's still there."

"I didn't leave it at the hotel."

"Then where is it?"

"I wired it through Dahabshiil this morning, before we left for the airport."

"Very clever," Macalin said. "Where did you wire it to?"

Daniel laughed, averting his gaze out the port hole to the green sea.

"Fair enough. Get some rest, and I'll get to work getting you on shore," Macalin said, as he turned to leave.

"Wait, where's Caitlin?"

Macalin froze by the door, but didn't face Daniel. "She's being seen by a physician, too."

"But where?"

"Daniel, I."

"Don't act like there's something wrong with her. I should know, I brought her here, after all. I know she's fine--"

"She doesn't want to see you."

"What do you mean?" Daniel asked.

"I'm sorry, mate. But she specifically asked not to see you. Given the ship protocol, I'm afraid you're going to have to respect her wishes."

Daniel leaned against the operating table, hurt by the revelation. "Ok," he whispered. "I'll talk to you soon."

Macalin left the room. Something was wrong, something greater than being spurned by Caitlin. He felt hungry, ill.

The medic returned shortly to finish dressing his wounds. Daniel was eventually led to a recovery room with a cot, chair, reading lamp and a Bible. The medic told him not to leave the room unaccompanied, otherwise he'd be in violation of the ship regulation, in which case he might find himself in severely less comfortable accommodations. Daniel assured the medic he had no intentions of wandering out of the room, but once the man was gone, Daniel determined to search out Caitlin. Given all this talk about regulations and protocol, he'd have to be stealthy and cunning to learn her whereabouts.

When he was certain the hallway was quiet, he eased out into the corridor that comprised the ship's infirmary, and spied on the nurse's station. He assumed there would be some records telling him where to look for Caitlin, if he could just get at that desk while it was unsupervised. He waited, but after what seemed like an eternity of metered breathing and standing still, he developed a more active plan. He edged to the opposite side of the corridor, where he remembered having seen a phone. He picked it up and dialed the medical number laminated on the wall above.

"Medical," the voice responded.

"We've just pulled a midshipman out of the sea. He's in quite a shock. Please hurry to the deck."

"Is he breathing?"

"Yes."

"In shock?"

"Yes."

"I'll be right there," the voice said. Then the connection ended.

Daniel eased the phone back on its receiver, listening as the medic shuffled equipment before skittering away.

Daniel hurried along the corridor with less caution now. At the desk, he picked up a logbook that was neatly laid out, scanned the short page to see Caitlin Cordon listed in Q-4. He had been in L-1. He walked down the hall until he found a small diagram labeling the rooms, then he walked into an adjacent corridor that housed Caitlin's quarters, the Quarantine Section. He hurried down the hall, but once he was at the door he edged his way in, careful not frighten her. She was lying on a cot, an IV in her arm, staring out a window with sunshine radiating through the thick glass draping her body.

When she turned and saw him, her mood immediately darkened.

"I told them I didn't want to see you."

"They mentioned that."

"Then why are you here?"

"Because I needed to convince you otherwise."

She started to speak, but he hushed her.

"Just let me finish. I don't have to go back to Somalia. I'm done with that place. Now when they let us off this ship in Djibouti City we can go wherever we want. Fly anywhere. Live there for as long as we like. We never have to talk about what happened in Somalia again."

She was shaking her head 'no.' "It doesn't matter if we never talk about it. Can't you see? This has been too much. It's not about what we say. It's not about what anyone says. It's about what I know. I know what you're capable of. I can't live my life with someone like that."

"Caitlin," he said longingly. He heard footsteps hurrying up the hall. He glimpsed to see the *call nurse* button buried in her hand.

"It can end happily."

"It already hasn't."

The medics, big cornhusking men, entered the room and dragged Daniel away. They carried Daniel out to the hall, to the next corridor and well away from Caitlin's room. A single tear glistened on his face.

"If we find you in there again, we'll put you in the brig until shore," one of them said in that desirable Midwestern accent. "Do you understand?"

"I understand," Daniel mumbled.

Then they released him.

**That night, Daniel stood on the deck,** chaperoned by Macalin. From a distance, Daniel watched as a female silhouette boarded a UN helicopter. The rotors deafened the air. He knew it was pointless to attempt to yell a goodbye. It was too dark to wave farewell. So he stood, feeling like crumpling to the ground, yet erect against the battleship's railing as the helicopter ascended and hovered away over the darkened horizon.

He watched his chances of happiness disappear in to the night over the Black Sea. He wanted to reach out and grab it, or think up an excuse to have it return, but such thinking was useless. She was gone. Life in Somalia was over. He needed the wretched time to be over, but the pain of leaving behind his most significant gains, the great love and mastery of the seas, were hard losses to accept. Standing there with Macalin, who was also about to leave him, Daniel stared out into the Black Sea. Even the thought of five million bucks to his name didn't lift his spirits.

**Thirty-six hours later they were in port at Djibouti City**. From the ship's deck, one could discern that the city wasn't exactly a hub of global trade like Hong Kong or New York City, but it was modern. Untainted by prolonged bouts of civil war. It had a post-colonial charm to it, much like the Bahamas.

At the port, Macalin followed Daniel down the gangplank.

"Should I arrange transportation for you?" Macalin asked.

"I made my own arrangements, actually."

"I wasn't aware you had communication privileges."

"I guess I've still got that Somalian penchant for taking what I need."

"I didn't know you knew anyone in Djibouti," Macalin said.

"I know one person," Daniel said. They walked through the dock, passed these giant stacks of steel shipping containers, cranes beeping and shifting through the air overhead. They arrived at a simple chain link fence barrier between the gate and public road. A Land Cruiser Defender idled in the taxi stand. Macalin trailed Daniel towards it.

"This is my ride."

"Well then," Macalin said. "I guess this is it for now. It was a hell of a time."

"Yeah, it was."

"What will you do now, you know, to stay busy?"

"I'm going to write that account of what happened, for Sayyid. After that, I'm not quite sure. I know I'll ponder that question as comfortably as possible. But I'll get word to you once I've got my situation figured out."

"Sounds good mate. Send me a copy of the manuscript. Otherwise, take care of yourself," Macalin said. He watched as Daniel walked along the side of the vehicle, and having no luggage, hopped into the front passenger seat. Macalin approached the window to tell him a final goodbye. When he peered in to the vehicle, he was surprised to see Sayyid in the driver's seat with a perfect specimen of khat in each hand, ruminating his decision.

Then Macalin laughed at himself, for having been surprised at all.


THE END